Eyes Like Stars

LISA MANTCHEV

SQUARE
FISH

Feiwel and Friends
NEW YORK

SQUARE
FISH

An Imprint of Macmillan

Library of Congress Cataloging-in-Publication Data
Mantchev, Lisa.
Eyes Like Stars: Théâtre Illuminata, Act 1 / by Lisa Mantchev.
p. cm.
Summary: Seventeen-year-old Bertie strives to find a useful role
for herself at the Théâtre Illuminata so that she won't be cast out of the
only home she has ever known, but is hindered by the Players,
who magically live on there, especially Ariel, who is willing to destroy The Book
at the center of the magic in order to escape into the outside world.

ISBN 978-0-312-60866-8

[1. Theater—Fiction.   2. Magic—Fiction.   3. Actors and actresses—Fiction.
4. Orphans—Fiction.   5. Books and reading—Fiction.   6. Identity—Fiction.
7. Theaters—Fiction.]   I. Title.
PZ7.M31827The 2009
[Fic]—dc22
2008015317

Originally published in the United States by Feiwel and Friends
Square Fish logo designed by Filomena Tuosto

Book design by April Ward

First Square Fish Edition: April 2010

10 9 8 7 6 5

macteenbooks.com

AR: 5.3 / F&P: Z / LEXILE: HL740L

CHAPTER ONE

Presenting Beatrice

The fairies flew suspended on wires despite their tendency to get tangled together. Beatrice Shakespeare Smith, busy assessing her reflection in the looking glass and thinking perhaps she shouldn't have dyed her hair blue on this particular morning, turned to glare at them when they rocketed past the end of her nose for the third time in as many minutes.

"If you make me spill this stuff on the stage," she said, "I'll squeeze you until your heads pop off."

Unperturbed by the threat, Mustardseed swung by her like a demented pendulum. "Going in there with fairy guts on your hands isn't going to make a good impression!"

"Nervous about your call to the Theater Manager's Office?" Moth asked, chasing Peaseblossom in circles.

"Not the best of timing," Cobweb singsonged, hanging upside down at the end of his line, "mucking up your head right before a ten o'clock summons."

"I'm not getting called on the carpet with my roots showing." Bertie coated another section with Cobalt Flame liquid concentrate, pilfered just an hour ago from the Wardrobe Department. "Do we like the blue?"

"Better than Crimson Pagoda," Peaseblossom said. "Your entire head looked like it was on fire that time."

"Maybe I should have taken Black Cherry." Bertie stuck her tongue out at the Beatrice-in-the-mirror. "Maybe Cobalt Flame will encourage the Theater Manager to get creative with his punishment."

"He'll probably just remove the desserts from the Green Room again," Peaseblossom said.

The others groaned at the prospect, then Moth perked up to suggest, "He could make you scrub out the toilets in the Ladies' Dressing Room instead."

"Or scrape the gum off the bottoms of the auditorium seats," said Cobweb.

"Ew." Bertie wrapped another strand of hair in aluminum foil and crimped it against her head. "An excessive punishment for whistling a scene change, don't you think?"

"'Whistling a scene change'?" Peaseblossom giggled.

"That's a euphemism and a half! You set off the cannon, blew holes through three set pieces, and set the fire curtain *on fire*."

"Quite the valuable lesson in emergency preparedness, I think," Bertie said.

Moth twitched his ears at her. "Pondering our recent criminal history, I must admit there have been more pyro-technic explosions than usual."

"Maybe the Theater Manager thinks you're doing it to impress Nate," Cobweb said.

Bertie felt the blood rush to her face until her cheeks were stained Shocking Pink. "Shut up."

"It *is* like you're acting a part for the dashing pirate lad's benefit," Mustardseed said.

Bertie snagged his wire, reeling him in until he reached eye level. "What's that supposed to mean?"

The fairy twitched. "You know. The hair dye, the black clothes—"

"The clove cigarettes!" Moth added from below.

"The drinking and cursing," said Cobweb.

"Is it method acting?" Mustardseed asked.

"This *is* a theater." Bertie, annoyed by the inquisition, dropped him onto the stage. Several feet of slack cable landed atop the fairy in a slithering heap.

"Oh!" Peaseblossom said. "You've buried him alive!"

"I told you it was silly to use the wires when you can fly perfectly well without them," Bertie said.

"But they're fun to swing on!" Moth protested as the fairies shed their harnesses and went to investigate the tomb of their fallen comrade.

Indefatigable, Mustardseed emerged from the pile, rubbing his bum. "If it's not for Nate, is it because of your abandonment issues?"

There was a very long silence before Bertie told her reflection, "The only reason I'm friends with any of you is because I outgrew the von Trapps, one annoying Austrian at a time."

"You could have joined the Lost Boys," Moth said.

"They did nothing but whiz on trees, and I'm not properly equipped for that."

"So you're stuck with us because of your innate inability to pee standing up?" Peaseblossom put her hands on her hips as she hovered nearby.

"That's right." Bertie used her brush to stir the dye.

"We can do lots of stuff besides pee standing up," Moth said.

"Like sword fighting!" Cobweb slashed and parried with great enthusiasm.

"Call the pirates and the shipwreck scene!" Mustardseed flailed his tiny yellow boots in an improvised hornpipe.

"I'm not supposed to make scene changes and thus I'm appalled by the very suggestion," Bertie said. "You're a bad influence, Mustardseed."

"The rules have never stopped you before." Peaseblossom looked knowing. "You just don't want Nate seeing you with your head all slimy."

Bertie put on her best Lady of the Manor air. "He needn't wait for an engraved invitation to pay a social call."

"But he prefers you pin a note to the Call Board," Peaseblossom reminded her.

The majority of the Players drifted in and out of existence according to the summonses pinned to the Call Board, but the more flamboyant, dashing, or mad the character, the more freedom they had to move about the Théâtre. The fairies dogged Bertie's every step, whereas Nate was one for protocol.

Probably all that rot about following the captain's orders.

Bertie's entire head tingled as the ammonia burned her scalp. She tried not to scratch at it, because that way lay madness . . . madness and funky-colored fingertips. "It has nothing to do with Nate. I need to finish my hair before the Stage Manager gets back."

"He should be thankful it's only dye on your head and not paint all over the stage," Peaseblossom said.

Bertie glanced at the walls of her room. The three connected scenic flats were part of the Théâtre Illuminata's enormous collection of backdrops, stored in the flies overhead and in the backstage scenic dock when not in use. "I haven't painted my set in years."

Lights up on BERTIE, AGE 7. She is painting over a dingy cream wall with something labeled "Violet Essence" as the STAGE MANAGER glowers at her.

BERTIE

It's my bedroom, and I'll do what I want with it.
(To prove her point, she splashes magenta and silver over the violet and smears it around with her hands.)

STAGE MANAGER

(grabbing for BERTIE'S ear and missing)
You can answer to the Theater Manager for this mess!

(The THEATER MANAGER arrives with MR. TIBBS, the Scenic Manager.)

(turning to the THEATER MANAGER)
Why you ever decided she needed to sleep here, on the stage, is beyond my powers of reckoning!

THEATER MANAGER

She needed a bedroom, and this is the best we could do.

STAGE MANAGER

(His face turns three shades of crimson and steam hisses out of his ears like a teakettle.)
But this isn't a bedroom! We can't stop the per-

formances for bedtime, which means she's under-foot until the stage is cleaned! And look at this mess!

MR. TIBBS
(chomping his cigar)
We do not change the colors of the flats. We touch them up, or faithfully reproduce them down to the last paint stroke and bit of gilt. But we do NOT change them!

BERTIE
Just because *you* don't change them doesn't mean I can't.

THEATER MANAGER
Bertie, this place isn't about change. It's about eons of tradition.

BERTIE
(crossing her arms)
It's my bedroom. I should be allowed to do what I like with my bedroom.

THEATER MANAGER
(studying BERTIE until she squirms a bit)
That's true enough. But I wonder what will come next. One day, it's your bedroom and the next—

STAGE MANAGER

Utter chaos and pandemonium!

BERTIE

(curious)

What color is pandemonium? It sounds yellow.

THEATER MANAGER

Beatrice, this is a matter of utmost importance, so I
want you to listen to me and answer very carefully.

BERTIE

Yes, sir.

THEATER MANAGER

You like living here, don't you?

BERTIE

(bewildered)

Yes.

THEATER MANAGER

Do you want to remain at the Théâtre?

BERTIE

Of course I do! (stammering) I mean, it's my home. . . .

THEATER MANAGER

Then you need to understand that while we will
tolerate a certain amount of . . .

(He pauses to search for the appropriate word.)

STAGE MANAGER

Wanton destruction?

THEATER MANAGER

No, I think perhaps the word I was searching for was "creativity." While we will tolerate, even encourage, your creativity, you must limit it to your personal space.

BERTIE

(frowning hard and trying to understand)
So I can paint my room?

THEATER MANAGER

Yes, you may. But you're forbidden to change *anything* else. In that regard, you will have to learn to exercise something called "self-restraint." Do you understand?

BERTIE

I think so. I mean, yes. Yes, sir. Now can I have paint the color of pandemonium, Mr. Tibbs?

MR. TIBBS

(scattering cigar ash about the stage)
No, you may not.

THEATER MANAGER

(another long moment of contemplation passes before he nods)

9

Gentlemen, let the young lady get on with her painting. Bertie, clean up after yourself.
(He begins to make his exit, pausing at the edge of the stage.)
Please do remember what I said about exercising self-restraint.

Bertie contemplated her reflection. "Perhaps I could have shown more self-restraint."

The girl in the mirror didn't blink, so Bertie averted her gaze and looked instead around her room. Viewed from any of the seats in the house, it would create the proper illusion of a teenager's abode. Mr. Hastings, the Properties Manager, permitted her to sign out bits and pieces to make it feel cozier, but most of her knickknacks and trinkets were glued or nailed down so they wouldn't scatter about the stage when the scenery was changed. The audience would never know it, but there wasn't anything in the dresser; all Bertie's clothing was kept backstage in Wardrobe, laundered and pressed by Mrs. Edith. The bed, an elaborate four-poster, resided on a circular lift that disappeared below-stage.

And then there was The Book.

THE COMPLETE WORKS OF THE STAGE

Sitting atop a pedestal in the far corner of Stage Left and just in front of the proscenium arch, it was the only thing that remained constantly onstage. Resting there, it emitted a soft, golden radiance usually lost under the thousands of watts of power that poured from the floodlights.

No one dared touch it. Even Bertie, who dared a lot of things that the others never dreamed, did not touch The Book.

"You have dye on the end of your nose," Peaseblossom said.

Bertie set down her brush and wiped her face with a handkerchief that came away smeared with Cobalt Flame. She peeked at herself in the mirror, confirming that quite a lot of her skin was now blue. Cobweb and Moth, who'd paused in the middle of attempting to draw-and-quarter each other to look at Bertie, fell to the dusty stage floor, laughing themselves silly. Mustardseed landed on her shoulder and smeared his hands around in the dye.

"Stop that!" Bertie swept him off with a practiced flick of her finger.

He somersaulted backward, then rushed to swing his tiny fist at her nose. Cobweb and Moth tackled him, leaving miniature explosions of glitter twinkling in the air. Flying fists and booted feet kicked over the bowl of hair dye, and Cobalt Flame flowed across the stage floor to surround Bertie's Mary Janes.

She made a mad grab for the fairies. "Come back here! You're making a huge mess—"

"I'll cut off his ears!" said Moth.

"I'll slice off his nose!" added Cobweb.

"And we'll cast the bits into the sea!" they howled together.

"Forsooth!" said Mustardseed. "You'll never take me alive!"

Bertie tried to get in between them, but it was tricky not to step on someone. "Stop it!"

Mustardseed grabbed the wet, sloppy brush and hurled it at his attackers, missing them only to hit the side of Bertie's head. Several wads of aluminum foil fell off, and dye-sticky strands of hair snaked over her shoulders. Bertie used a pithy curse common amongst the pirates, but Peaseblossom was the only one who noticed the air turning blue to match the spreading mess.

"Good thing you're wearing so much black," she said.

The boys rolled past them. Tufts of fairy hair, ripped out by the roots, drifted into the orchestra pit. Tiny scraps of clothing exited the brawling tumbleweed at sporadic intervals: a sleeve, a sock, a pointy-toed shoe.

"I'll beat you for a living!"

"You and what army?"

All at once the fairies froze, like butterflies pinned to a piece of felt-covered cork. They were only ever utterly still for one reason: Someone had placed a notice on the Call Board.

"What's it say?" Bertie asked.

The fairies shook free of the trance.

"All Players to the stage," Peaseblossom said. "Ten o'clock."

Bertie swore under her breath again. "Everyone to the stage, you say?" She waved her arm at the floor, which was covered in smear marks and miniature shoe prints. "The stage that's currently decorated with a crazed ballroom dancing pattern? 'Tarantella for Three Miscreants in Pandemonium Minor' perhaps?"

"Maybe we should clean up?" Moth suggested, sounding sheepish.

"You think?" Bertie ducked into the wings. Backstage, it was all black paint and dim lights covered in sheets of red gel. "We need to get rid of this mess before the Stage Manager sees it." She located his headset, lifted the mouthpiece to her lips, and whispered, "Cue scene change. *The Little Mermaid*, Act One, Scene One."

The fairies cheered the blackout. In the pale echo of light, vague outlines moved through Bertie's field of vision, but their details were lost to the dark. Her bedroom walls took flight in a soaring arc before disappearing into the rafters. The bed dropped below the stage while the armchair and dresser chased each other into the wings. Huge wooden waves slid in from Stage Left with the clank and wallop of mechanical water. Seaweed hit the stage with wet thumps, sand gathered in drifts, and saltwater misted the floor. Ground row lights painted the cyclorama in undulating shades of blue and green.

"Fabulous!" Moth shouted, and the words were bubbles. "Come on, losers!"

The others joined him, trailing froth and brine. Mustardseed climbed the pearl garland while Peaseblossom and Cobweb darted in and out of the coral reef in an elaborate game of tag. A chorus of starfish entered Stage Right and began to tap-dance, very softly, in the sand. Scrubbing the dye off herself and the floor with handfuls of kelp, Bertie watched the Sea Witch also make her entrance.

"Sad, isn't it?" said someone just behind Bertie.

She turned to find Ophelia trailing flowers and chiffon through the saltwater-and-dye puddles. Like the fairies, she came and went as she pleased, walking the ragged edge of her sanity and drawn to the ocean by some unwritten instinct.

"What's sad about it?" Little puffs of sand lifted and settled again as Bertie slogged from one dye splotch to the next.

"She loved once and lost." Hair drifting over her shoulders in unseen eddies, Ophelia looked at the Sea Witch's wavering image projected on the back wall. "You'd think she'd show more mercy."

"Whatever you say." Done with the stage, Bertie still had to deal with the dye on her head. "What are you doing here?"

"I heard the water running." Ophelia lifted her arms up and smiled into the ghostly, aquamarine lighting. "I thought I'd come and drown myself. I won't be in the way, will I?"

"Just watch out for the starfish." *Psycho*, Bertie mouthed

to the fairies, who made looping finger gestures at their temples behind Ophelia's back.

"Don't think I don't know what you're doing back there," Ophelia said before she drifted off to do what she did best.

The fairies, taken aback by the cheerful admonishment, were caught unawares by the smoke machine. Lights tinted the artificial fog the same dark blue as Bertie's hair, and the scene transitioned into Coming Storm, complete with rattling of the thunder sheet and flashes of brilliant lightning-white. The massive prow of the *Persephone* soared out of the mist, safeguarded against evil by the gold coin Nate had placed in the hull and the one of silver under the mast.

Jus' in case, he'd said when Bertie teased.

Despite the protective charms on the boat, the Sea Witch attacked with curses and errant waves, just as she did in every performance.

"Man overboard!" Nate's only line; he bellowed it with his usual gusto, the words underscored by the creak of the *Persephone*'s wooden planks and straining ropes. Bertie peered into the flies and caught sight of him leaning over the ship's railing, tendrils of hair torn free from his braid. Her heart gave a queer little flutter, which she instantly dismissed as both ridiculous and embarrassing.

Nate pointed at her and mouthed, *I'll be right down. Don't go anywhere.*

Bertie remembered what a mess she must look and

tried to figure out how much time she had to remedy it: One minute until the ship reached Stage Left, another two minutes to see to the rigging, and thirty seconds to disembark added up to hardly enough. With a muffled oath, she shoved her head into the bucket behind the wooden wave. *Splash!*

"That's going to be a lovely shade of blue," Peaseblossom said, pulling out the bits of foil.

"Shut up and help me get this stuff off!" Bertie scrubbed at her head with her eyes squeezed shut, wondering how much time she had left.

"Bertie!"

None, apparently. She came up streaming water; through the dripping cobalt, she caught a glimpse of clenched muscle under soiled linen and the glint of his earring before Nate wrapped her head in an enormous towel.

"Yer makin' a terrible mess," he observed.

Bertie flapped her arms, hardly able to hear him through the terry cloth cocoon. "Give me just a second to finish—"

"Best we get ye off th' stage as soon as possible, lass."

Bertie pulled the towel back so he would be sure to see her dismissive eye roll. "Don't give me that 'lass' stuff. You're not written that much older than I am."

"Years scripted an' years lived are two diff'rent things," Nate said. Greasepaint, false sunshine, and fan-machine winds had weathered his face, and though his hair and eyes were dark, lighter threads of copper wove through the plait that snaked down the back of his neck.

Bertie caught herself gazing up at him like a mooncalf and turned away, twisting the towel into a lopsided turban. "I'll be fine."

"All th' same, th' Stage Manager's in a rare, odd mood." Nate spat into the corner as a ward against evil. "Ye need t' mind yer step."

"If the spitting thing ever works, let me know. I'll be sure to spit on the Stage Manager every chance I get." Bertie thought about how Nate always stepped aboard his ship right foot first and would no sooner utter the word "drowned" than he would "Macbeth"; it was "The Scottish Play" or nothing at all. "You're such a practical and mercenary soul, but that superstitious streak of yours runs bone deep."

"I know ye don' take it seriously, but ye've no need t' tease," Nate said.

"Don't I?" Bertie pursed her lips.

"Bertie . . ." he warned.

"I feel like a little whistle," she said, retreating with her mouth still puckered up. "Just a small one."

Nate came after her. "No whistlin' onstage, or are ye forgettin' yesterday?"

He backed her against the heavy, velvet curtains and clapped a rope-scarred hand across her mouth just as she sucked in a loud breath. For a long moment, they looked at each other, and Bertie was acutely aware of the taste of his fingers: salt and sardines (as befitted a pirate) and chocolate icing (which didn't seem as appropriate).

A sudden, trumpeted fanfare sent them leaping apart, the blast of noise preceding the messenger from Act Four of *Richard the Third*. He entered Stage Right, unrolled a parchment scroll, and cleared his throat. In a strong, sonorous voice, honed to cut through the bedlam at court or merely backstage, he proclaimed, "And now, the bane of your existence, the killer of all joys, the Stage Manager—"

He was interrupted when the murderers from the same production leapt from the flies and stabbed him repeatedly with big rubber knives. The messenger pulled crimson scarves from holes in his tunic and did a lot of unnecessary groaning before his assassins dragged him offstage by the ankles.

"What was that all about?" Nate demanded.

"Early detection system," Bertie said. "I get advance warning that the Stage Manager is coming, and the messenger gets extra stage time."

"Clever," said Nate as the scene shifted around them.

"I thought so." Bertie bit her lip, watching the waves recede backstage, the watery lighting special click off, and the cyclorama fade from blue to white. The Sea Witch gathered her gauzy wraps and disappeared into the dim. Ophelia, drowned to her satisfaction, drifted out with the tide. The seaweed and pearls skittered offstage, and the Stage Manager arrived with a broom and a glare.

"YOU!" he exclaimed, striding onstage like a bantam rooster.

Bertie put on her most innocent expression. "Yes?"

"YOU!" he bellowed, as though that was the only word not sticking in his throat.

Bertie struggled not to laugh at the image of him squawking at the sunrise with his imaginary feathered crest ruffled up. "What did I do?"

"Who authorized that scene change? Who gave you permission to touch my headset? Why is it *blue*?" He wagged it at her until dye dripped off the earpiece. When Bertie started to answer, the Stage Manager yelled, "Never mind! Just go! The stage is for Players only! We're making an announcement!"

"I think you've used up all your exclamation points for today," Bertie said. "What's the announcement about?"

The Stage Manager smiled, a fearsome thing indeed. He looked mightily pleased about something, which didn't bode well. "Ah, yes, the announcement."

"You might as well tell me what's going on." Bertie glared at him. "I'll know soon enough."

"Ah, but you have an important appointment with the Theater Manager, and you shouldn't be late." He nodded to Nate. "See her to the stage door, please."

Nate took her by the arm. "You've been summoned to the Office again?"

"Yes, but I want to know what's going on!" Bertie dragged her feet. However, Nate could heave a wooden chest of pirate treasure without thinking twice, and she weighed significantly less than gold.

"I'll find ye afterward an' tell ye everythin', I promise," he said.

The fairies ducked into the hall with her just before Nate slammed the door shut.

CHAPTER TWO

All Players
to the Stage

Bertie turned and studied the gilt-framed Call
Board as the boys whined about wanting a snack.
Normally the cork would be peppered with schedules and
notices, appointments for costume fittings and personal
missives from one Player to another. All that had been
cleared off so that only a single piece of official Théâtre sta-
tionery was affixed in the center with a brass tack:

ALL PLAYERS TO THE STAGE. TEN O'CLOCK.

Thousands of costumes rustled as the Players answered
the summons. Bertie had once asked Nate where he was,
when she couldn't find him onstage or in any of the various
departments.

"Ye know," he'd answered, "I couldn't really say. 'Twould be like tryin' t' describe th' place ye go t' when ye sleep."

But no one slumbered now. Fools and martyrs, companions and consorts, the damsels, dilettantes, and Don Juans all crowded the hallway, queuing up to file through the door that led backstage. They whispered behind hands, masks, and feathered fans, trading speculations like an invisible currency.

"You're going to be late," Peaseblossom fretted, tugging Bertie's clothes into some semblance of tidiness.

"The Theater Manager's lecture can wait," Bertie said. "I want to know what the announcement is all about. Now where did the boys go?"

Peaseblossom jerked her thumb at the door adjacent to the Call Board. "To get something to eat."

Bertie often thought that if she had a grandmother, and that grandmother had a parlor, and that parlor perpetually awaited the vicar's arrival for tea, it would be just like the Green Room. Spikes of painted iris grew up the wallpaper, and the sofa's moss-velvet was rubbed so thin in places as to be nearly gray and kitten-soft. The mica window set into the petite cast-iron stove revealed the cheerful glow of burning coals. Tiny, unexpected posies bloomed in forgotten corners, while an enormous clock tick-tick-ticked away the seconds until showtime.

The refreshment selection varied wildly according to the Théâtre's whims, with cucumber sandwiches curling up their crustless edges in mortification one day while the next the table might boast flaming Christmas pudding and treacle roly-poly.

"Come on," Bertie hissed at the boys. "Your behavior can't possibly benefit from a massive intake of sugar, grease, or caffeine right now."

"Says you!" Cobweb protested. "Here! Have a doughnut!"

"Aren't you supposed to be upstairs?" Moth dove head-first into one of the cupcakes.

The horn speaker clicked on, its translucent bell trembling as it announced, "All Players to the stage, please. Repeat, all Players to the stage."

"I'm coming with you guys," Bertie said. "You can't ignore a call, so let's go."

"We shall resist until we have sated our appetites and slaked our thirst!" Mustardseed wriggled down the neck of a tall, glass bottle to guzzle fizzy orange drink.

"Stay here to stuff your faces, then!" Bertie ducked into the corridor, threaded her way through the Ladies' Chorus, turned a corner, and set off down the empty hallway at a half-run.

"Why are we going this way?" Moth licked the frosting off his arms as he caught up.

"I have to find another way in," Bertie said. "The Stage Manager's sure to be standing guard at the other door, but he won't think to check the catwalks."

"Hey, Mustardseed took a bag of jelly beans!" Cobweb whined, far less concerned about access to the stage than stolen snacks.

"You can have the black one."

"But I wanted the red one!"

A muffled noise, then, "Now it's up my nose. Still want it?" followed by a very sulky "No!"

"That's why I don't eat the green ones." Bertie turned another corner only to collide with Ariel.

"Beatrice." The word was molten magic poured from his mouth. Today, his voice was smoke in the breeze, banners caught by the wind. "Do mind where you're going, please."

Bertie flapped her hand at the butterfly familiars that followed him everywhere. "I'll do that if you take care of the bug infestation."

Ariel snapped his fingers, and the tiny creatures flocked to his hair. Their red and yellow wings winked at Bertie, opening and closing in time with the pulse at the hollow of his throat. When he swallowed, they disappeared under the white silken neckline of his shirt, summoned within.

Some of the Chorus Girls would love to follow those butterflies, Bertie knew. She'd heard them whispering in the dressing rooms, cooing over Ariel's fair complexion and the silver hair that tumbled over his shoulders. Never mind that he was also tall and lean, with high-cut cheekbones and not a superfluous ounce of flesh on him anywhere. . . .

Bertie was about to sigh like a lovelorn schoolgirl when she realized that he was using his powers of persuasion on her and stiffened. "Save it for the stage, Ariel."

He blinked, unaccustomed to such a reaction, but when Bertie went to sidestep him, he blocked her way with one arm. Although the fairies hissed a warning, he didn't relax his gaze upon her. "I was looking for you."

"And you found me. Now if you would be so kind as to get out of my way—"

"Why must you be difficult?" His sigh raised the hair on her arms.

Bertie rubbed at them and scowled. "Why are you even speaking to me, Ariel? Won't the Theater Manager be displeased if someone sees us together?"

Never mind Mrs. Edith.

The Wardrobe Mistress had made her thoughts about Ariel very clear years ago.

MRS. EDITH

(entering the Wardrobe Department with a swish of heavy skirts)

Bertie, dear. Put that tiara down this instant and come here.

BERTIE, AGE 10

I wasn't hurting it.

MRS. EDITH

I told you to polish it, not try it on and prance about the Wardrobe.

(She stands with uncharacteristic stillness, gathering the threads of Bertie's attention until her ward cannot look away.)

The Theater Manager just called me to his Office to tell me that you've been seen consorting with Ariel again. I thought we had an understanding.

BERTIE

(studying the pattern on the floor with great interest)

We only played on the panpipes together. (defiantly) He has a very nice singing voice.

MRS. EDITH

Yes, but what did we discuss? Do you remember?

(BERTIE sighs loudly and refuses to answer. MRS. EDITH lifts BERTIE's chin with her thin fingers and fixes her with a martinet's gaze.)

Ariel is difficult, dear, difficult to understand, difficult to control. And the more time he spends with you, the more headstrong and willful he becomes. The Theater Manager's orders were clear. You are to keep your distance from Ariel. Do you understand me?

> BERTIE
> (with tears in her eyes)
> Yes, ma'am.

Until Management intervened, Ariel had been her boon companion and the King of All Games. It was he who'd taught her to fly in a harness for the first time and bore the brunt of the Stage Manager's anger over letting a seven-year-old into the catwalks.

Bertie had pleaded with him not to yield to Management's decree.

> BERTIE, AGE 10
> (grasping his sleeve)
> No one ever needs to know. We'll have clandestine meetings, like robbers in a cave by the sea.

> ARIEL
> (His voice lowers to a soft breeze through her hair.)
> What did Mrs. Edith say, exactly?

> BERTIE
> (balling her hands into fists)
> Stupid stuff.

ARIEL

Don't fret, little one.

(He bends forward to place a gentle kiss on her cheek, no more than the brush of one of his butterflies' wings.)

I doubt you'll even miss me.

He'd been wrong about that. The desertion had cut deep, and Bertie still hated him for it seven years later. "Would you kindly get out of my way?"

"I suppose you're trying to find an alternate route into the auditorium?" When she didn't answer, Ariel bowed. "I can aid thee in thy efforts, Mademoiselle."

"I don't need your help." Bertie pulled a clove cigarette out of her pocket and lit it with the silver lighter she'd also lifted from the Properties Department.

One languid movement flicked the smoke out of his eyes. "The Stage Manager's blocked off access to the cat-walks and the balconies."

A curse slipped out before Bertie could stop it.

"Follow me. You can use my trapdoor. But first . . ." Ariel plucked the cigarette from Bertie's hand and closed his fingers around it. When his hand opened, only a plume of wildflower-scented smoke remained.

Bertie scowled. "What did you do that for?"

"It's a fire hazard and disgusting besides." He peered at her head. "What have you done to your hair?"

Heat crept across Bertie's cheeks. "Just colored it."

"Blue?" The word climbed an entire scale without visible effort.

Bertie bristled. "I like it."

"Not a surprise, considering your abominable taste. Hold still." When Ariel exhaled, gentle currents straightened her clothes and finished drying her hair.

Bertie closed her eyes, inhaling the scent of sunrise and spring. Something darkly tempting and longing-filled bloomed under the sun-warmed grass and damp earth. She opened her eyes, wanting to ask a question she didn't yet know, but before she could find the words, Ariel turned away.

"Are you coming?" he asked over his shoulder.

Bertie hesitated only a second before falling in step with him, chin up, head high, taking care to look unconcerned about the silence that hung between them like a curtain drawn over their past. Every other sound was amplified: the echo of her footsteps, the low whir of the fairies' wings, the soft sound of Ariel's breath passing over his lips, until they reached a tiny door, tucked in a corner like an afterthought. Ariel pointed his fingers at the iron pull, and a breeze tugged the door open. The fairies flew into the darkness with whistles and catcalls.

"Mind where you put your feet," Ariel said, steering Bertie into the dimly lit space under the stage.

Only his hand at the small of her back kept her from falling into the sea of black as her eyes struggled to adjust. She peered at the light that filtered through the cracks in the creaking boards; above them, the Company moved about, their murmurs no more than the rustle of oak boughs in the wind.

"Everyone's up there?"

Ariel stepped onto a platform. "Having second thoughts about sneaking in?"

Yes. "No."

Bertie ignored his outstretched hand and planted her feet. The trapdoor opened and the platform glided up, depositing them at the back of the amassed crowd. Bertie winced as the stage lights assaulted her eyes.

Ariel stepped into the brilliant pool without even blinking. "I shall leave you to your skulking, then."

Not wanting to call attention to herself, Bertie skipped making a rude gesture or telling him where he could stick his skulkery. Instead, she eased around the edge of the nervous chatter, doing her best to blend in while the fairies dogged her like four miniature, incandescent shadows. It was difficult to move at all, much less with stealth; Players filled the stage as well as the aisles, the orchestra pit, and every seat in the auditorium.

"How about over there?" Moth pointed at the revolutionaries from *Les Misérables*, who rubbed elbows with the buccaneers from *Peter Pan*. Jostling each other, they swapped tall tales and periodically brandished their weapons.

Peaseblossom wrinkled her nose. "The Stage Manager's going to have a fit. They're spitting tobacco juice on the floor."

"Then watch where you fly. You don't want to end up a target." Bertie stood on her tiptoes in time to catch a glimpse of Nate headed in her direction.

"I should have known ye'd sneak back in," he said.

"I don't take orders from that little Napoleon."

Nate didn't have time to interrogate her further, because the "little Napoleon" had entered Stage Left and climbed atop a box so he could be seen by one and all. Conversation died and movement stilled until silence settled over the auditorium.

The Stage Manager, aware that, for perhaps the first time in the history of the Théâtre Illuminata, he had the attention of the entire Company, held up his hands and cleared his throat. "The Management extends its thanks for your swift assembly."

"We hear there's to be an announcement." Bertie pitched her voice in the falsetto used by half the Chorus Girls.

The Stage Manager glared around the room, eyebrows bristling, but didn't spot her all the way in the back. The shadows did their job nicely.

"All in good time, all in good time," he said.

Bertie exhaled through her nose. If he took much longer, she'd never be able to explain away her tardiness to the Theater Manager. That long-suffering gentleman had heard all of her excuses before, so "I got lost" or "was that supposed to be *this* morning?" wasn't going to work. But Bertie was the self-appointed Queen of Improvisation; no doubt she'd think of something to mollify him. . . .

The Stage Manager puffed up with self-importance. "Some of you might have been present yesterday when the pyrotechnic cannon was discharged."

A few of the Players shuffled their feet, but none hastened to admit they were part of the crowd cheering Bertie on. Her stomach turned over, as though she'd gobbled down a dozen chocolate cupcakes and topped that off with a fizzy orange drink.

"The damages were considerable," the Stage Manager continued, "and this is only the most recent in a series of destructive and negligent acts committed by a single person."

"Bertie," the Players said with one voice.

Nate shivered. Bertie had never seen a pirate covered in gooseflesh and didn't take it as a good omen. Someone must have cued the orchestra; violins began to play with dark harmonics from the brass. The melody tickled at the back of Bertie's throat, and she shuddered as the music added layer upon layer of tension to the room. The surrounding lights dimmed until the only thing that existed in their universe was the Stage Manager.

"We have done all we could to raise her since she arrived here, a foundling child with neither family nor friends." The Stage Manager put a hand to his heart, as though it pained him to say this, though his mouth quirked with ill-concealed glee. "But the time has come for a change."

The air crackled with electricity. Overhead, in the flies, someone shook the thunder sheet.

The Stage Manager's voice crawled out of the storm, like a god's pronouncement from the heavens. "It is with deepest regret that I convey this news to you all: The Theater Manager is in his Office at this very moment, telling Beatrice Shakespeare Smith she must leave the theater."

CHAPTER THREE

What Will
Become of You?

Static crackled in Bertie's ears, like the time the technicians had roused her from sleep by running a sound check. She barely heard the fairies' wail of protest or Nate's reassuring words that it must be a misunderstanding as panic and disbelief hit her, twin punches to the gut.

"Say nothin' here, lass," Nate said. "We'll get ye upstairs an' ask for an explanation. . . ."

Stage whispers broke out all over the theater, echoing one another:

"He's asking her to leave?"

"Where will she—"

"What will she—"

"How can they *do* this?"

"It is my hope," the Stage Manager said, raising his voice

to be heard, "that she will be gone within the day, although it's not for me to say how long the Theater Manager will give her to gather her things and say good-bye—"

Bertie shoved her way to the front of the crowd. "You're lying."

The Stage Manager paled at the sight of her. "You're supposed to be in the Theater Manager's Office!"

"Surprise!" She sang the word like the last note in a musical number and waved jazz hands in his face. "I'm *here*!"

"I should have known!" he said, eyebrows bristling. "And I should have hog-tied you and delivered you upstairs myself—"

"What you should have done is not told lies about me!" Bertie countered. "Leaving the theater? What a load of rubbish!"

"Not rubbish this time, my girl," the Stage Manager said with toadlike satisfaction. "Your shenanigans yesterday finally exceeded the limits of even the Theater Manager's endurance!"

Bertie would have leapt at him, except Nate shoved his way between them and pointed a finger at the Stage Manager. "Keep yer hair on, featherleg, an' remember yer manners." The perpetual sandpaper stubble on Nate's chin contributed to an already menacing demeanor.

As the Stage Manager sputtered, the door in the back of the auditorium slammed open. Everyone jumped, startled by the echoing boom, and turned to see who'd entered.

The Theater Manager was the fun house mirror reflection of the Stage Manager; tall, where the other was short; cultured and refined, where the Stage Manager was rumpled and red. Today, however, something had disturbed his usually calm expression. "Beatrice Shakespeare Smith?"

The use of all three of her names sent Bertie running to meet him at the front of the stage. "Sir—"

The Theater Manager pulled a pocket watch out of his vest pocket and checked it as everything, even time, splintered around Bertie and crashed to the red-carpeted floor. "You were supposed to be in my Office fifteen minutes ago, Beatrice."

"I know that, sir, and I'm very sorry—"

He held up his hand for silence. "This is not something I wished to discuss before the entire Company, but missing our meeting and sneaking in here only confirms your lack of respect for the theater's procedures."

Bertie twisted her fingers together, startled by how cold they were. "If this is about the cannon—"

"That's just one instance in a long line of infractions," he said, his expression stern and unyielding. "The Stage Manager has complained for years, but time and again I let you go with just a reprimand or some minor punishment."

"Give me a bigger punishment. I'll clean the theater from top to bottom, fold the programs, polish the chandeliers, whatever you want. I can behave myself, truly I can. I'll be quiet as anything! You won't even know I'm here."

The Theater Manager's voice regained a bit of gentleness, which was somehow worse than his temper. "You're not the sort of girl who fades into the background. I had hoped you'd find your place with us, your niche, but I see now you must follow your stars elsewhere."

"But I belong here!" The last word came out a squeak. Fearing she'd cry in front of everyone, Bertie dug her black-painted fingernails into her palms.

"That's just the trouble, Bertie," he said. "You don't belong here. You're not a Player, you're not part of the crew—"

"You're a menace," the Stage Manager added, glowing with triumph.

"We've tolerated your exuberance," the Theater Manager continued, "in the expectation that you might contribute something valuable to the Company—"

Bertie leapt upon that tiny bit of hope. "If I could find a way to . . . to contribute, could I stay?"

The Theater Manager looked around at the countless shocked faces of the Players: Nate, Ariel, the fairies. Even Ophelia, standing in her puddle, looked vaguely dismayed. "No, my dear, it's best if you go now without a fuss."

"But you said it's because I'm troublesome, and that I don't contribute," Bertie persisted, chasing his logic as though it were a golden thread disappearing down a bottomless black hole. She caught it in her hand, wrapped her desperate, silver hopes around the metallic filament, and clung to it like a life-line. "What if I change that?"

"You've had countless chances over the years," the Theater Manager said.

Bertie could hear her pulse in her ears, like the slamming of doors. "I can change. I swear it, in front of all these witnesses."

The Players murmured variations of "that poor girl" and "he should give her a chance." Their whispers wrapped around Bertie's thread of hope and tugged at it.

They weren't the only ones on Bertie's tug-of-war team. Nate stepped forward, every muscle a threat. "If she goes, I go."

"Us, too!" Peaseblossom said as the boys chimed in their agreements. The idea, perhaps never before entertained by the majority of the Players, sparked a wildfire.

"You can't do that," the Theater Manager snapped, trying to douse the notion with cold water, but too late. "The Players can't leave the theater. It's impossible—"

Vicious wind rushed around Bertie, carrying with it the thousands of speculative—and in some cases, rebellious—whispers of the Company. The word-hurricane twisted about the Theater Manager, tugged at his coat, mussed his hair.

"I might be persuaded," he yelled into the onslaught, "to

reconsider an immediate departure." As the winds and the whispers faded, the Theater Manager looked at the Players, then back to Bertie. The reluctance in his tone might as well have been a neon sign. "If you can find an invaluable way to contribute, I suppose you may stay." His inflections on the words "invaluable way" gave every indication that he didn't think for a moment that she could manage such a thing.

Bertie tossed aside his lack of confidence in her. "Do you promise?"

After a very long moment, he nodded. "I give you my word."

The walls of the theater trembled in acknowledgment of the promise.

Bertie felt similarly shaky. "Thank you."

The Theater Manager checked his pocket watch again and closed it with a determined *snap!* "You have until eight P.M. tonight to decide what you will do. Please come to my Office at that time." Face half-lost to the shadows of the auditorium, he added, "I would strongly advise you to be on time, Beatrice."

"Understood," Bertie said.

The Theater Manager departed, and the whispers of the Players resumed, building to a crescendo. The Stage Manager tried to recapture everyone's attention.

"Quiet, please!" he shouted through his cupped hands. "Cue 'What Will Become of You'!" As the footlights flared to life, he brushed past Bertie with a smirk. "I've waited years to call this song in."

Wispy, gray gauze panels unfurled from the flies while the members of the Choruses arranged themselves in a tableau of plaintive misery: crouched, hands lifted in appeal. The orchestra launched into a dirge, and Bertie's chest vibrated with the pull of cello strings.

Then the Choruses started to sing:

> *What will become of you?*
> *The shadows are closing in,*
> *The velvet curtain's falling,*
> *Much to your chagrin,*
> *There is nothing you can do.*
> *The run you've had is through.*

A pause in the lyrics permitted the men and women to pair off, one movement flowing into another, like raindrops sliding down a window. Muscles strained as they dipped and spun, but their faces wore only mournful grace. The backdrop fluttered in a cold wind, and the end of Bertie's nose went numb to match her fingers. She shivered as their voices lifted again.

> *What will become of you*
> *When the lights go down?*
> *What will become of you*

When there's darkness all around?
The doors open to your future
But this curtain call's your last.
What, what will become of you?
Your time with us has passed!

They ended, as they'd begun, on the floor in various importuning poses. Bertie would rather drink gasoline and shove a lit match up her nose than applaud, but the Stage Manager didn't share her sour sentiments.

"Bravo!" he called, clapping with unfeigned enthusiasm. "Well done, indeed!"

The Players, wearing expressions that varied from uneasy to sympathetic, coughed and made their excuses before shuffling off Stage Left.

Bertie glared at the Stage Manager, wishing he'd spontaneously combust or at least get knocked unconscious by a wayward sandbag. "Where did you dig up that awful number?"

"An obscure little ditty, but so apropos to the moment," he said, cupping a hand over his headset. "Strike the set!"

The gray flats disappeared into the flies with a muted whirring noise, and the houselights came up. When the Stage Manager sailed away like a full-rigged ship, Bertie wished she could kick him in the mizzenmast.

"I have the chance to stay," she shouted, "and I'm going to make the most of it!"

"Nyaaaaaah!" added the fairies, making terrible faces at his retreating backside.

But the Stage Manager only laughed, a hearty chuckle that taunted her as he exited.

"I have the chance to stay," Bertie said again, this time to convince herself.

"Fool." Ariel crossed the stage, blazing bright with hunger. "You have the chance to leave, to see the world!"

"I don't want to see the world!" She backed away, trying to escape his voice—his beautiful, horrible voice—that tangled around her with streamers of excitement.

"Think of the places outside these walls, where the buildings aren't made of cardboard and the sunshine isn't electric." Ariel's words pulled Bertie closer. "You must want to see it, Bertie: the London that doesn't appear in *Peter Pan*, the Venice that exists outside of *Merchant*."

His eyes . . . his eyes! Bertie had never seen them glow so, alight with possibilities.

I could almost believe his every word when I look into them. . . .

"You could take me with you," he said, utterly beguiling.

Bertie looked up at Ariel, and her next words came with reluctance, for she only wanted to tell him yes, to give him everything he asked of her. "You heard the Theater Manager. That's not possible."

"I heard him." Ariel's too-beautiful mouth worked as darkness filled his eyes from corner to corner. Bertie could see her face reflected in their liquid black depths. "I also heard the panic in his voice when the Players began to whisper amongst themselves. I heard a man struggling against words, winds, desires, instincts. He's very much afraid of something, Bertie, and I think it's you. You're smarter than all the Managers put together. You could find a way to free me."

"Why should I find a way to free you?" Bertie, struggling against the spell of his eyes and his words, managed to take a step back. "You walked away from me a long time ago. You made it clear that I meant nothing to you!"

"The more time I spent with you, the more I dreamed of leaving." The butterflies' wings turned black as the air around them shifted. The muscles in Ariel's jaw flexed; each time he gritted his teeth, the lights flickered. He was three inches off the floor now, without the aid of wires, without the use of smoke and mirrors. "Now I know why: You're the key to my freedom, the one who can open the door."

Bertie choked on the accusation. "That's ridiculous!"

Still rising in the air, he looked at her as he had all those years ago, his face soft with yearning. "I watched you grow, like the flowers I've never seen—" But then it tightened again. "If you ever cared for me at all, you'll leave this wretched place and take me with you."

" 'This wretched place' is the only home I've ever known!"

"But there's something you haven't thought of yet."

Ariel paused for a perfect three-count. "Your mother is out there, Bertie. Somewhere."

Nate caught her by the arm, and the fairies grabbed handfuls of her hair; together, they kept Bertie from launching herself at Ariel's boots.

"How dare you use that as ammunition?" She fought against the vise of Nate's grip. "If I ever get my hands on you, Ariel, I'll take you apart. The Stage Manager will need more than the ocean set to wash the blood off the stage!"

"And I tell you that I won't be imprisoned here, written into the pages of some damned play for all eternity!" Ariel scowled, a thwarted prince with twin storms in his eyes. His hair crackled with static electricity, a shower of sparks poured from his hands, and the lenses in the lights overhead exploded.

Bertie raised her arms over her face and dropped to the floor as glass shards rained over them. Nate threw himself on top of her, shielding her from the worst of it. The entire theater rattled and reverberated as though in the throes of an earthquake, the noise a standing ovation that wouldn't end.

The building shuddered one last time before settling. In the ensuing silence, Bertie tasted dust from the floor and blood from where she'd bit her tongue. Everything smelled of ozone and singed velvet.

Nate eased off of her and peered over his shoulder. "He's gone."

The emptiness Ariel left behind took up more room than it should. Bertie stood and brushed the broken glass from her hair and clothing as the fairies complained in not quite undertones.

"What a diva!"

"Stupid, men can't be divas. . . ."

"Divo, then."

"That just sounds weird. Call him a jerk and be done with it."

Bertie rummaged in her pocket, locating her cigarettes but unable to find her lighter. Her knees wobbled, overcome with the fading vestiges of emotion and adrenaline, and she sat with a graceless thud.

"D'ye need a match?" Nate's voice was as soft as the linen shirtsleeve that brushed against Bertie's bare arm when he sat next to her.

"I need something, but a match will suffice for now." She took comfort in his solid presence and the scent of seawater. "This has been *such* a Monday! I wish I'd stayed in bed, and I wish yesterday had never happened."

Nate lit the cigarette, omitting the stern looks and lectures anyone else would have given her. He could hardly warn her of the evils of the demon tobacco as he lit his own pipe. Once it was started, he put his arm about Bertie's waist and gave her a bone-cracking squeeze. "It'll be all right, lass."

"Somehow I very much doubt that." *If I have to leave, I'll never see Nate again.* Bertie's free hand sought out his, her skin pale against his rope-roughened paw. "Do you think . . . do you think Ariel was right?"

"Most o' his words are naught but pretty lies an' truth twisted like ribbon candy, but which bit did ye mean?"

"That I could figure out a way to take someone with me?"

He shook his head. "Ye heard the Theater Manager. Players can't leave th' theater."

"But if they could?" Bertie tried to swallow, but her mouth was too dry.

Nate's grip on her tightened, and the passing seconds were knots tied in heartstrings. "Would ye want me t' come with ye?"

"Yes. No! I mean, I don't want to go, so what good is asking that question anyway?" She started to get up, but Nate caught her by the back pocket of her jeans.

"Sit yer arse down an' stop tryin' t' run away."

Bertie twitched but didn't try to get up again. "Ariel was right about something, though."

Nate assessed how firmly affixed her rear was to the stage before he nodded. "Th' bit about yer mother?"

"Yes."

"Do the play for him, Bertie!" Peaseblossom said. "He hasn't seen the new version."

Nate raised an eyebrow. "Ye've been stagin' it again?"

"I reworked the middle section," Bertie said with a shrug. "But I don't see how performing it now will help things."

"Maybe this time you'll get it right and figure out where your mother is," Peaseblossom said, her eyes dark and serious.

Bertie's argument died in her throat. "Someone cue the lights. The rest of you take a seat."

CHAPTER FOUR

How Bertie Came to the Theater, a Play in One Act

The lights faded up on a stool far Stage Right. Bertie entered from the wings, carrying a large prop version of The Book embossed with the words:

THE COMPLETE WORKS OF THE STAGE

She settled on the stool, cleared her throat, opened to the first page, and pretended to read. "My mother was an actress, and surely she was the star."

The curtain opened. A tight spotlight came up on a lovely young woman dressed in a sequined costume. Silver stars decorated her dark curls, and smaller stars glimmered in her eyes.

"She was an ingénue on the rise, a society darling," Bertie said. "Titled men filled her dressing room with roses and sent jewelry that sparkled like the night sky."

The spotlight expanded to include dozens of flower arrangements and heaps of diamonds. Glitter drifted gently from the rafters until the very air shimmered.

Bertie's Mother sat at a dressing room table, powdering her nose and brushing her hair. She addressed the audience. "One of them must have captured my heart. Was it a young lord with a castle on the hill and a coach-and-four?"

A tight spotlight came up on an aristocrat in a black coat and ascot tie.

"Was it the powerful businessman with a keen eye for finance and a generous nature?"

A second spotlight on a heavyset gentleman consulting a gold pocket watch.

"Or was it another? Someone without name or coin, but who had instead a heart filled with love for me?"

The third spotlight illuminated a young man dressed in shades of brown and gray. He turned his pockets out to reveal they were empty, then unfurled his fingers like a magician to produce a single red rose.

Bertie nodded. "I'd like to think so."

Bertie's Mother accepted the flower from him as the lights faded on the other two suitors. She stood up to put a print Sunday dress, a silver hair comb, and the red rose into a small suitcase.

"I left the theater," she said, "and traveled to a small cottage by the sea."

Scenery for a railway station replaced the dressing room. Smoke boiled across the stage, and sound effects hissed to imitate a train coming to rest. Bertie's Mother stepped onto a platform outfitted with a leather seat and a large, floating window. She placed her suitcase in the overhead luggage rack, sitting as the "train" left the station.

The compartment heaved and rocked in place, accompanied by a *chug-chug-chug* that blared through the loudspeakers. Silhouettes of buildings and light posts flashed on the back wall, followed by fences, trees, and the occasional cow. With a final hiss and another blast of smoke, the "train" came to rest.

The sign overhead proclaimed it AN ORDINARY STATION. Bertie's Mother alighted, and her young man greeted her with an embrace. They exited together as the lights crossfaded to an unassuming home in the countryside. Laundry danced on the line. A large tree provided shade. Bertie's Mother entered Stage Left. She collected the pasteboard clothes off the line and hung out stiff sheets and towels.

"I like to imagine she was a simple person," Bertie said, "with an uncomplicated life. She married her lover and raised a family. She looked beautiful, even when doing her chores."

Bertie's Mother smiled at the audience, her starry eyes sparkling in the spotlight.

"I picture her with my father, along with five or six of my brothers and sisters." Bertie paused to think for a moment before she added, "And a dog."

"Of course there was a dog," Bertie's Mother said.

Bertie's Father led a procession of six Children arranged tallest to shortest. The Family Dog, on all fours, sat on his haunches and barked with enthusiasm.

"Then I arrived," Bertie said, watching from the side of the stage. "The youngest. The darling. The apple of every eye."

Bertie's Mother reached under her apron and pulled out a wriggling bundle. The Family gathered around to sigh and coo. "Isn't she precious?"

"One day," Bertie said, "when I was but a babe of six months—"

"What do ye mean, when ye were a babe o' six months? Ye can't remember that far back if ye were an infant!" Nate said from the audience.

"Don't interrupt." Bertie lifted a hand to her eyes to cut the glare from the lights. The fairies and Nate sat Fifth Row, Center.

"I'd be willin' t' believe it, if ye were two or three years old," Nate argued. "But six months?"

"Who's narrating this story?" demanded Bertie.

He sighed. "Ye are."

"Then shut up. You didn't protest when I was discussing things that happened before I was born."

"All right, all right." Nate crossed his arms over his chest and scowled mightily. "But yer no doubt gettin' it wrong."

"Shush!" Cobweb, Moth, Mustardseed, Peaseblossom, Bertie, and Bertie's Mother hissed at him.

"As I was saying before I was so rudely interrupted, I was a wee child of indeterminate age," Bertie said over Nate's derogatory snort. "Life was ordinary and boring and lovely. Every morning my mother woke me with kisses, and every night she read me a fairy tale that ended 'happily ever after.' She missed her old life of greasepaint and curtain calls and applause, but she never said a word of reproach to me."

"At least Bertie would like to think so," said Bertie's Mother.

Bertie nodded. "And then one day, a visitor came to my parents' cottage."

With wheels yellow as the sun, a ruby-red caravan rolled onstage, its flowered curtains fluttering in the tiny window. Two mechanical horses pulled it, their shoes clanging and sparking against the stage. Dulled metal plated their flanks and sturdy legs, steam hissed from silver-velvet nostrils, and rich amber light poured from their eyes. A woman with hair and eyes like bits of the night sky leapt down in a swirl of emerald and black silk. Her skirts were embroidered with tiny golden moons, and a belt of jangling golden disks encircled her waist.

"The sky threatened rain," Bertie said. The brilliant blue of the cyclorama shifted to a pale gray. Thunder rolled, echoing off the back wall of the theater and setting the chandelier atinkle.

"Greetings to you, goodwife," the newcomer said. "Permit me to introduce myself. I am Verena, Mistress of Revels, Rhymer, Singer, and Teller of Tales, on my way to a distant castle to perform for the Royal Family. Perhaps you would be so good as to shelter me from the oncoming storm?"

"Of course," Bertie's Mother said with a nod. "You may use our barn if you like. I can offer you some fresh bread and cheese for your supper."

"That is most kind of you," said Verena. "A debt paid today is one that cannot be called in tomorrow, so I will give you something in return. Come to the caravan tonight at moonrise, and bring your youngest child."

"Itinerant performers probably don't wear emerald an' black silk embroidered wi' gold. It would get filthy wi' dust an' muck."

A pause. "It's called 'creative license.' This is a play, remember?"

The lights faded to near darkness as a silver-foil moon rose in the background. The Mistress of Revels kindled a fire of red, orange, and yellow ribbons that leapt high with the aid of a tiny fan. The plaintive and melancholy sound of a single violin wended its way through the auditorium. Verena crouched before the flames, adding her lilting voice to the lament.

A candle flickered in the cottage window, and the door opened. Bertie's Mother tiptoed across the yard to the caravan, carrying the baby in her arms.

Somewhere, the Family Dog howled.

"Sit down, goodwife, sit down." Verena beckoned, the many bracelets on her arm chiming a welcome. "I promised you payment for the meal, so I have. I can weave your daughter's story on this night's loom."

Bertie's Mother hesitated. The violin held a long, high note; as it descended the scale, she took a deep breath and joined the Mistress of Revels by her fire. "Teller of Tales, it's her Future I want told, not a pretty bedtime story."

"Bedtime stories are filled with fairy godmothers and toads who become princes," Verena said with a low chuckle. "You would wish more magic than that in her Future?"

"There are stars in her eyes," said Bertie's Mother with a shiver. "She'll have magic enough because of those cursed things."

Verena took Bertie's Mother by the chin, twisting her face to study her closely. "Your stars are still there. Faint, but there."

"She will want a life greater than this. I did, too, a long time ago," said Bertie's Mother. "But that life . . . you know as well as I that it's not all roses and curtain calls and champagne on Opening Night. It's ugliness and filth and greed. The bright lights mask the sorrow, but the sorrow is still there. I don't wish that for her."

The Mistress of Revels sat back, her expression solemn. "Will you try to keep her from it, goodwife? Will you tie her to the laundry line with your apron strings? Hobble her at the knees, crush her soul, and break her spirit to keep her safe?"

Bertie's Mother rocked, trying to comfort herself as well as the child in her arms. "Will she be happy?"

"Ah, there's a question, there's a question!" Verena took a pouch from her jingling belt and cast a handful of powder on the fire. The flames exploded upward, green and purple and blue-black like a beetle's wing. The Mistress of Revels's shadow on the back wall was an enormous, twisted chimera reaching into the future with curved claws. "Her destiny lies at the crossroads of imagination and trickery. Her future is bound with red velvet and gilt."

"That's a nice bit of showmanship, but you didn't answer my question. Will she be happy if she binds herself to that place?"

"Happiness," Verena said, "is subjective."

"I have nothing to send with her, besides a mother's love and best intentions."

Verena nodded her dark head. "It will be enough."

"Take her with you, then, to the theater. Take her . . . before I change my mind." Bertie's Mother walked swiftly to the cottage. When she opened the front door, a shaft of light fell over her empty arms, and a single tear shone on her cheek like a diamond.

A baby's cry drifted through the auditorium. The caravan exited Stage Right.

"I liked it better when you were a fairy changeling," said Moth as the scenery shifted yet again.

"That was six drafts ago," Mustardseed reminded him.

"Besides, how could she be a fairy changeling, stupid?" asked Cobweb. "She doesn't have wings!"

"Don't call me stupid, half-wit."

"Being a fairy changeling just didn't feel right," said Bertie. "This is my story, and I'll edit it however I please. It's more romantic to travel in a caravan. So shut up!"

"The Mistress of Revels did not immediately take me to the Théâtre, as she'd promised my mother," she continued. "No, along the way I learned to dance and sing and tumble—"

"When ye were six months old?" Nate interjected.

"After that," Bertie hedged.

"Oh, aye, when ye were *nine* months old."

"The journey," Bertie said over him, "was fraught with danger."

The caravan began to cross the stage.

"They hit a pothole!" shouted Moth.

The caravan hit a pothole with a massive thump and the screech of protesting wood. The rear wheel on the down-stage side of the cart rolled into the orchestra pit.

"Then the horses stampeded and drove over Verena with their big, metal-shod hooves!" added Mustardseed.

The horses leapt forward and flattened the Mistress of Revels against the floorboards.

"They were set upon by brigands!" yelled Cobweb.

Two dozen extras dressed as highwaymen leapt from the catwalks onto the stage, brandishing swords and twirling their moustaches.

"And then the caravan burst into—"

"No!" Bertie interjected before they needed a fire extinguisher. "No flames! Absolutely nothing caught on fire or exploded. Stop it, right now. You know how I feel about you sticking things into my narrative!"

Verena cleared her throat. "Excuse me, but about the brigands—"

Bertie shook her head. "There were no brigands!"

The group in question looked at each other, and their

leader sidled to the edge of the stage. "What do you want us to do, then?" he said in a loud whisper.

"Shove off!" Bertie said. "You were never supposed to be here in the first place."

"All we want is a few minutes of stage time!"

"Fine, then. Have it *your* way." Bertie raised her voice and pretended to read, "The brigands met a terrible fate at the hands and feet of the Mistress of Revels, for though she didn't look it, she was a black belt in jujitsu."

Cobweb laughed as Verena landed a series of flying side kicks. "I don't think you've ever used that line before."

"Violence makes for good theater," Bertie said. "Now, while there were no brigands, no potholes, no stampedes, and certainly nothing burst into flames, the journey was still fraught with danger. Near the city limits, Verena took sick with a Mysterious Ailment."

"Dying makes good theater, too!" That was Mustard-seed. "Is she going to die?"

"Now you've ruined the surprise!" Cursing mightily, Bertie jumped from the stool and glared at the fairies. "You all had better shut your pieholes until I'm done with this scene, or so help me, I'll never steal you another snack cake as long as you all shall live."

There was no back talk this time, just the sound of crickets chirping.

Satisfied, Bertie cued the last scene change. The caravan approached a wooden flat painted to look like the façade of the Théâtre. The Mistress of Revels descended slowly, carrying a basket.

"She left me on the doorstep of the Théâtre," Bertie said, "with only a note and my mother's best intentions."

"Dear Sir or Madame," Verena intoned. "I entrust this child to you. Her name is Beatrice Shakespeare Smith, and her destiny lies within this theater."

Bertie flapped her hand at her. "Just leave me on the doorstep already."

The Mistress of Revels nodded before setting the basket against the door.

"Blackout!" the fairies called, and the lights obeyed. "Curtain down!"

Nate's voice drifted out of the darkened auditorium. "I liked that version, especially th' bit wi' th' thieves."

Bertie stowed the prop copy of The Book backstage and lifted the Stage Manager's headset. "House lights up, please."

"I was just thinkin'," Nate said, "about how yer mother *is* out there, somewhere. Mayhap now's th' time t' seek her out."

While his tone didn't challenge her, his words certainly did.

"I could wander forever and never find her." Bertie

looked to the back of the auditorium, at the faint phosphorescence of the Exit sign as she went to join the others.

"But if ye stay here—"

"Not 'if' I stay. I'm staying." She offered Nate her hand and heaved him to his feet. "So that when my mother comes looking for me, I'll still be here to find."

CHAPTER FIVE

Sedition Amongst the Ranks

Bertie looked up at Nate through the blue fringe of her bangs. "Will you help me?"

He nodded. "With my last breath."

"A plan! We need a plan!" said Cobweb.

"*Vive la Révolution!*" cried Moth and Mustardseed as they jumped to attention.

Bertie held up both her hands. "If either of you start singing something from *Les Mis*, I'll drop-kick you into next week."

"Can we build a barricade?" Moth demanded.

"Not until I think of a way to become invaluable." Bertie paced the aisle runner between the velvet-upholstered seats. "What jobs are vacant?"

The fairies put on their thinking caps, which were red and pointy.

"You could do a lot of things!" Peaseblossom said after a moment. "Maybe Mr. Hastings needs help dusting the props?"

"I guess," Bertie said, unconvinced. "But Official Duster doesn't sound impressive."

"You could put spangles on costumes!" Cobweb said.

Bertie shook her head. "I can't sew without stabbing myself. Mrs. Edith wouldn't want blood on the fabric."

"You're good with hair," Mustardseed said. "Maybe you could try your hand at wig styling?"

"I don't think that could be considered an invaluable contribution," Bertie said. "Think harder."

After a few moments, Moth wriggled his toes disconsolately. "I'm afraid nothing more important springs to mind."

"Besides, there are no small parts," Cobweb admonished Bertie, "only small actors."

"I don't know about that," Mustardseed said, giving him a shove. "You're pretty small."

"What about yer play?"

Bertie turned to look at Nate. "My play?"

"How ye came t' th' theater. It's a play, no?"

She thought about it a moment. "I . . . I guess so."

Nate folded his arms in triumph. "That makes ye a playwright, then."

The idea had never occurred to her before, and it tickled like a quill pen. "A playwright?"

"Aye. Ye could be th' Théâtre's wordsmith," Nate said, looking mightily pleased with himself.

"Scribble something with dragons!" Moth crowed. "I always wanted to ride a dragon!"

"I don't have time to write an entire play from scratch," Bertie said, possibilities switching on like spotlights nonetheless.

Nate laughed. "Then ye start wi' how ye came t' live here. It's nearly done, ye said it yerself. Ye just have t' write it out an' show th' Theater Manager."

Bertie scowled. "There's no sense in showing him something that isn't finished. He'd toss me out on my backside."

"You didn't just write the play, Bertie," Peaseblossom said suddenly. "You ordered the Players about, shouted, and threw an artistic hissy fit. Do you know what that makes you?"

"A temperamental fusspot?" Mustardseed guessed.

"Crazier than a bag full of crazy?" Moth said.

"Close," Peaseblossom said. "It makes her a Director."

Cobweb scratched his head. "That person dressed in black, who sits in the back, smoking and giving everyone their motivation?"

"Wow," Moth said. "We've never needed one of those before."

"A Director." Bertie's skin tingled. "But what could I direct?"

"You want to start with something dramatic," Peaseblossom advised. "Something with impact."

"Somethin' yer fair familiar wi'," Nate said.

"Something funny," Moth added.

"No," Bertie said, "something tragic. The most famous of all of the Shakespearean tragedies—"

Mustardseed jumped up and down. "Your hair!"

"*Shakespearean* tragedy, Mustardseed."

"Oh, sorry about that. *Hamlet*, duh."

"But why would *Hamlet* need a Director?" Peaseblossom asked. "The Players have performed it thousands of times."

"Precisely the reason it needs a Director!" Bertie said. "It's *tired*. It needs to be made over into something spectacular. Something that will fill the seats and have patrons queued up in the street and put 'Sold Out' signs in the windows of the Box Office. *That* would be a real contribution, wouldn't it?"

"I guess so," said the fairy, unconvinced.

"Trust me, it will be brilliant," Bertie said. "We'll take *Hamlet*, and we move the production to a new time period and location."

"Like where?" Moth asked.

"I don't know," Bertie said, biting her lip. "Somewhere with kings and queens and political intrigue, but with plenty of wiggle room for fabulous costuming and sets. Like . . . Egypt!"

"Egypt." Nate sounded less than convinced now.

"Ancient Egypt," Bertie said with a bounce. "It's perfect."

Nate shook his head. "Yer definition o' 'perfect' an' mine must be diff'rent. An' 'tisn't goin' to be easy t' convince ev'ryone. Change isn't in th' Players' nature."

"It's in mine!" piped up Cobweb. "Could we wear spandex and blow things up?"

"That would be wicked!" said Moth. "Are there going to be explosions, Bertie?"

Bertie imagined the Stage Manager's face when he heard about the plan. "Most likely. We need to recruit support."

Nate nodded. "Sympathizers, aye. Where d'ye want t' start?"

"We need all the departments on board before we go to the Theater Manager," Bertie said. "Let's start with the easiest and work our way down."

"Mrs. Edith it is, then!" Mustardseed said, flying ahead of the group with a burst of speed and sparkles.

"You really think so?" Bertie weighed their options as they stampeded down the hall. "I would have said Mr. Hastings."

"Mr. Hastings likes you, but Mrs. Edith loves you," Peaseblossom said. "I know that's difficult to remember, when Mr. Hastings lets you run rampant through the Properties

Department and Mrs. Edith tries to make you behave your-self, but it's true."

"Fine," Bertie said, "we'll start with her."

"Ye might want t' think up a way t' explain yer hair be-fore we get down there," Nate suggested. "Unless ye actually asked permission afore ye pilfered her drawers."

Bertie put a hand up to her hair and muttered, "I'd for-gotten about that."

Nate gave her a sardonic look. "Ye could always lead wi' th' news th' Theater Manager's kickin' ye out. It might take her mind off yer head."

Walking into the Wardrobe Department was like opening an antique steamer trunk only to be buried alive in silk charmeuse, bobbin lace, and assorted bits of millinery. Adding to the whirl of color and fabric, Moth immediately sat upon the brass control for the overhead conveyor. A thousand years of history swept past Bertie on wooden hangers, gliding along the circuitous iron track overhead be-fore disappearing into the cavernous storage closet.

Nate ducked his head and disappeared into the swirling vortex of frock coats, bustle skirts, and flapper dresses. "I need t' look fer somethin'. I'll be right back."

"What? Wait . . . Moth, get off of that!" Bertie nudged the fairy off the control button.

By the time the sweeping dance of costumes glided to a

halt; Nate had disappeared. The hiss and sputter of the coal furnace at the far end of the room replaced the hum of the conveyor. Heat poured off the boiler in waves, its steam powering the sea of sewing machines and flatirons as well as maintaining the dye vat at an eternal simmer.

Mrs. Edith sat at the long, work-scarred table with a lapful of copper taffeta that gleamed when she moved. While the rest of the theater bespoke the easy grace and artistic flourishes of the art nouveau period, the Wardrobe Mistress remained a stiffly starched Victorian, from the high, severe collar of her shirtwaist and the wide leg-of-mutton sleeves, down to the hem of her floor-sweeping skirts. The only concession to her grudgingly admitted artistic nature was a broach of rose gold, rumored to be a gift from the queen. She could cow the most insolent of Chorus Girls with a single look, and her spectacles served as an indicator of her mood; just now they were perched on the end of her nose, permitting her gaze to skewer both her work and her ward.

"Do you have something you want to tell me?" The needle she held was more threatening than a sword.

Bertie flattened her back against the door, searching the darkest recesses of her brain for the correct answer. "Do you think I have something I should tell you?"

Mrs. Edith assessed Bertie's head and pursed her lips. "Cobalt Flame?"

Bertie relaxed a fraction of an inch and nodded. "Do you like it?"

"Strange as it is to say, it does suit you, although if you keep using stuff as strong as that, you'll be lucky not to go as bald as an egg."

The fairies exploded with snickers, punctuated by "Hey, there, cue ball!"

Mrs. Edith set aside the topic of Bertie's hair as easily as she shifted the fabric to the table. "I missed the call to the stage trying to get this seam finished. What's going on?"

"That's what I came to see you about." Bertie slid onto a stool next to the Wardrobe Mistress while wondering how best to break the news. *Simply, without overdramatizing it.* "The Theater Manager asked me to leave."

"That's not amusing, Bertie dear," Mrs. Edith said with a frown. "You shouldn't joke about such things."

"I'm not joking. He said I need to make my way in the world."

Mrs. Edith pursed her lips as she selected a gleaming pair of sewing scissors from the table, snipped an errant thread, and tossed it into the rubbish bin. "Why now?"

"I guess he's mad about the cannon." Bertie looked at her feet so that she didn't have to see the dire look on Mrs. Edith's face. She noticed small details: Her clunky Mary Janes were scuffed and needed polishing; her favorite pair of black-and-red striped socks sagged around her ankles. "But it wasn't just the hole in the roof. He said I don't have a place here. That I don't contribute anything."

Mrs. Edith reached for the ever-present teapot and poured herself a cup of oolong. "That hardly seems fair. You're just a child—"

Bertie shook her head. "That's the trouble. I'm not a child anymore."

The Wardrobe Mistress sighed into her tea. "No, you're not."

"He said that if I can find a way to contribute, I can stay."

"Did he promise it?" Mrs. Edith asked.

Bertie nodded. "I have until eight o'clock to get everything sorted out."

"By that, I assume you have a wild scheme already in place?" Mrs. Edith's cup returned to its saucer with a clink.

"I need to become a Director," Bertie said, "so I'm going to restage a play in a new time period and setting. I want to move *Hamlet* to Egypt."

The gleam in Mrs. Edith's eye was a welcome sight; it signaled the coming of pleated linen robes and gold embroidery. "You'll need costumes. When will this performance take place?"

"I'll ask for as much time to prepare as possible," Bertie said. "I should think I'll need at least a month."

"If not two," Mrs. Edith mused. "Write out a list and you'll get what you need."

Bertie threw her arms around the older woman's neck and pressed a kiss to her wrinkled cheek. "Thank you!"

Mrs. Edith was about to answer when Ophelia wandered in, still dripping water. "Oh, had you heard then already? I came to tell you the news."

"Yes, Bertie's told me all about it." Mrs. Edith eyed Ophelia's sodden dress. "You're going to catch your death. Let's get you into some dry clothes." She reached for the bell pull; before it finished tinkling, half a dozen assistants hurried into the room, carrying a clean gown, mops, and buckets of soapy water. They shoved Nate out ahead of them, making shooing gestures with their fingertips.

Bertie glared at him, wondering why he'd left her alone to plead her case. "What were you looking for?"

"It doesn't matter, as I didn't find it," Nate retorted. He dashed past her, gesturing to the fairies to follow as he whispered, "I'll explain later!"

"We have to go," Bertie said, edging for the door. "I still need to convince Mr. Hastings and Mr. Tibbs before I go to the Theater Manager with my idea."

Mrs. Edith, busy getting Ophelia changed, spared a moment to fix Bertie with a stern look. "You come back here before you go, and I'll see you're properly attired for a meeting with Management."

Bertie blanched, wondering what Mrs. Edith's idea of "proper attire" would encompass. "Yes, ma'am."

"And, Bertie?"

"Yes?"

"In my professional opinion," Mrs. Edith adjusted her glasses, "the blue hair would look smashing if you tinted the ends black."

As it turned out, they didn't have to go all the way to the Properties Department to find Mr. Hastings. Out of his natural habitat, the Properties Manager had the wizened look of a plant kept too long in a cupboard. The glass in his spectacles was cloudy with age, and the wire frames were worn thin from rubbing against his nose and ears, both of which had hair growing out of them. Every bit of his clothing, from the tweedy jacket to his corduroy pants, was infused with a thousand years of dust. Today he scuttled along, the awkward weight of an iridescent green glass hookah bouncing against his hip. Perched in Mr. Hastings' arms, with all its metallic bits and coiled hoses, it looked more like an enormous beetle than a water pipe.

"Give that t' me, Mr. Hastings." Nate assumed the burden of the hookah with a good-natured smile. "Steal this back from th' Scenic Dock, did ye?"

"I have the paperwork right here in my pocket," the Properties Manager said, a wee bit breathless. "The Stage Manager checked it out for the Caterpillar scene in *Alice in Wonderland* three weeks ago." He reached under his arm with his newly freed hand, presumably for the signature sheet. Instead, he produced a fan with a carved ivory handle and three-foot-long ostrich plumes that molted exotic puffs of white and pink. "Wait, no, that's from the last number the Ladies' Chorus performed. All bare legs and high kicks, it is."

Bertie laughed and got a feather up her nose. "Where's the hookah been since *Alice* closed?"

"Seems as though the Chorus Boys thought to open a hubbly-bubbly bar in one of the back dressing rooms." He scrutinized Bertie's face. "You weren't down there, were you?"

Peaseblossom looked scandalized. "She most certainly was not!"

Moth kicked at the twirling bits of down. "Yeah, we miss all the fun stuff."

Mustardseed eyed the hookah with due consideration. "We should try that out."

"Don't let me catch any of you touching this lovely thing." Mr. Hastings patted the water pipe with gentle affection. "My dear, could you please get the door?"

Bertie pushed it open with a small, happy sigh. The Properties Department was her true sanctuary, free from the threat of a scene change anytime the Stage Manager wanted to be tiresome. In fact, it was as far removed from the hot lights, the ever-shifting scenery, and the Stage Manager as she could possibly get.

The ceilings were low, the lighting dim, and no matter where she stood, Bertie couldn't see to the end of the room. The larger pieces of furniture were arranged closest to the entrance, thrones next to sideboards, steamer trunks next to rose-bedecked arbors. Beyond that, row upon row of metal shelving marched for miles. Bits of labeled masking tape and crumpled inventories adorned each shelf. Candelabras, platters of wax fruit, rolls of parchment, silver cigarette cases, and a hundred thousand other curiosities resided therein.

"This way," Mr. Hastings said.

Nate obliged and followed him down the aisle, lugging the hookah and hindered by the fairies' attempt to help him.

"I'll hold this hose," Moth said.

"No, let me!" Cobweb tried to elbow in front of him.

"Just get out o' th' way," Nate barked.

"Come along, Nate. Stop dragging your feet." Mr. Hastings scattered more feathers in his wake, having forgotten the fan under his arm, which trailed behind him like the back end of a peacock with only slightly less strut.

The fairies slashed and parried at the dancing plumes as the unusual parade made its way down the aisle, past Victorian statuary jammed higgledy-piggledy next to fin de siècle French perfume vials and Babylonian pottery.

Bertie nearly fell over the fairies when Mr. Hastings paused mid-aisle to consult the clipboard pinned to the shelving.

"Here we are," he said. "49B. Shoehorns, devils' pitchforks, hookahs."

Nate heaved his burden into the empty space between its glittering sisters of gold-on-rose and midnight-blue-and-silver. On the neighboring shelf sat Alice's "Drink Me" bottle. Bertie slanted a look at it; Mr. Hastings had let her sniff the contents once, and she'd never forgotten the combination of triple apple, rose, mango, Arabian coffee, cantaloupe, cola, licorice, and mint.

All that's missing is the hot buttered toast.

Bertie's stomach gurgled at the thought. As Mr. Hastings transcribed mysterious hieroglyphs onto the inventory sheet, Nate nudged her with his elbow and nearly sent her sprawling.

"They're all so beautiful," she said with a sideways glare for her cohort. "Maybe you'll let me pick a souvenir to take with me when I go?"

"What's all this now?" A frown cut Mr. Hastings' forehead nearly in half. "Where are you going?"

"The Theater Manager's asked me to leave," Bertie said.

"She's being thrown out into the cold, cruel world," Peaseblossom said in a funereal tone.

"Goodness gracious!" Mr. Hastings clasped his clipboard

to his thin chest like a shield. "That's terrible! Whatever is he thinking?"

"He's thinking that the Théâtre would be better off without me." Bertie patted his arm in what she hoped was a reassuring fashion. "I have one chance to change his mind. I just have to mount a production the likes of which they've never seen before!" She gave the Properties Manager her most winning smile. "How would you like to use all your Egyptian bits in a new staging of *Hamlet*?"

CHAPTER SIX

Window Dressing

My dear, you're not making a speck of sense," Mr. Hastings said with a frown. "Hamlet was from Denmark."

"Not in my version, he's not. Picture it: all the court intrigue—"

"With asps in baskets!" added Moth.

"Mummies everywhere!" said Cobweb.

"I have to make a contribution to the theater," Bertie said. "So I'm going to be a Director, which means mixing things up a bit."

"Ah, I see," Mr. Hastings said. "And once you've 'mixed it up,' as you say, you'll be allowed to stay?"

Bertie nodded. "The Theater Manager promised."

Mr. Hastings set off at a brisk trot, indicating they

should follow. "We'll need Egyptian artifacts, then. Third row on the left."

Bertie gloried in the golden treasures that filled the shelves, easily imagining the feline statuary and canopic jars sitting in pools of bronze and turquoise light. Mr. Hastings patted the wrappings on an ancient, dusty mummy.

"Isn't he a lovely thing," he said, then admonished the fairies, "Mind the dearly departed, please."

He shifted a layer of linen and released a cloud of gold-flecked particles. The fairies sneezed in unison, flying backward into the open sarcophagus with such force that the lid swung closed and locked them inside.

"I think they'll make excellent mummies as they've already had their brains removed," Bertie said, her voice raised for their benefit. There was much shrill, muffled protesting and thumping from within.

"My dear," said Mr. Hastings, "I doubt that esteemed gentleman wants company in his final resting place."

"Not exactly very restful if you keep opening it to admire him, is it?" Bertie released the catch, and the fairies escaped, vibrating like hummingbirds.

"Did you know there was a piece of bread inside that thing?" Mustardseed asked.

Mr. Hastings frowned behind his glasses. "That piece of bread was four thousand years old and came from a mortuary temple in Western Thebes."

Moth picked at his teeth. "It did taste a bit stale."

"Yes, and it was full of sand," said Peaseblossom.

Mr. Hastings retrieved the gnawed crust and sighed. "My dear, your friends are very hard on the antiquities."

Bertie gave the fairies a pointed look. "Sorry about that. It won't happen again. Now, about the play?"

"We'll start with the sarcophagi. Obelisks to the ceiling, although Mr. Tibbs will claim that's his department. I must get my papers in order." Mr. Hastings slammed the coffin lid shut again, then apologized to the long-dead with absent-minded civility. "Sorry, my dear."

The fairies snickered behind their hands, but Mr. Hastings didn't notice their mirth as he strode past them.

"Come along, all of you. No reason to dawdle. I need to locate the appropriate inventory lists and begin to cross-reference the artifacts. There are all the pieces from *Antony and Cleopatra* to unearth. . . ."

Bertie skipped happily as she followed him, clapping her hands, though Nate laughed at her ill-contained exuberance.

"I'm going to put the kettle on," Mr. Hastings said over his shoulder. "Would you all care to join me for a cup of tea?"

Bertie wavered, loath to diminish their momentum but tempted by the promise of nourishment. "I still have to secure Mr. Tibbs's support, and he's sure to be difficult."

"Perhaps some hot, buttered toast before you brave the lion's den?" Mr. Hastings suggested.

That decided it. Better to make her entreaty with a full belly. "Yes, please. That would be lovely."

"Actually," Nate said, "I have a small favor t' ask of ye, Mr. Hastings."

"What do you need, my pirate friend?" Mr. Hastings filled the kettle and set it on a hot plate.

"Bertie needs a talisman," Nate announced in the same way he might ask for a drink of water.

She looked at him askance. "I need a what?"

"I can't keep my eye on ye every second o' th' day, so ye need something for good luck an' protection."

"Just what do I need protection from, pray tell?" Bertie set her fists on her hips.

"Mostly yerself." Nate turned back to the Properties Manager. "Can ye think of anythin' that ye might have?"

Mr. Hastings blinked at the question, took his spectacles off, rubbed them around with his handkerchief, and returned them to his face. "I'm sure I can, except I'm not quite certain I understand—"

"She's goin' t' need a powerful charm t' pull off this crazy scheme, don't ye think?" Nate said.

"I cannot argue with that notion, but I'll have to check my lists for the most appropriate choice." Mr. Hastings crossed to the ceiling-high file cabinets arranged on either side of his rolltop desk. Opening the first drawer of the eighth tower, he extracted a single sheet of paper. "Let's see. Under 'talismans,' we have amulets, four-leaf clovers, money trees, mystic stars, rabbits' feet—"

"Ew. I'm not wearing some dead animal's paw around my neck," Bertie stated firmly over the appalled shrieks of the fairies.

Mr. Hastings continued, unperturbed. "There are also rosaries and scarab beetles."

"What are you playing at?" Bertie muttered at Nate, well aware that Mr. Hastings could research for hours, and she had no intention of listening to his entire catalogue in alphabetical order, cross-referenced by production use, purchase date, and historical significance.

"'Tisn't playin'." Nate might have said more, but Mr. Hastings made a pleased noise of revelation.

"What about a scrimshaw?"

The pirate grinned, his teeth a flash of white against the bronze of his face. "That'd be particularly appropriate, I think. I'll nip back an' fetch it, if ye'll tell me where 'tis."

Mr. Hastings squinted at the paper. "Aisle 88F."

Nate set off at a jog. Bertie shook her head over the entire idea as she retrieved her favorite toaster from the collection on a nearby shelf. Victorian vertical stands required open flames, and later electric models lacked the ornate worksmanship and array of push buttons she found most intriguing, though the fairies always moaned that this particular nickel-plated box took too long and sometimes burned the toast.

Bertie plugged it in and reached for the bread, safe-guarded from both vermin and fae in a tin picnic basket. "I really don't need a . . . what's it called?"

"Scrimshaw," Mr. Hastings said.

"Scrim, like the curtain?" Moth said, his forehead wrinkled with concentration.

"And Shaw is a playwright!" Cobweb added with a bounce. "Good ol' George Bernard."

"No." Mr. Hastings tapped the file in his hand. "All one word: scrimshaw. A carving on bone, an artform made popular by whalers in the nineteeth century."

"That would explain how Nate knew what it was," Bertie said, fitting slices into the toaster's mesh baskets. "Did he carve this one?"

"I did not." Nate had returned. A chain of dull, heavy metal dangled from one finger, its circular pendant gleaming in the late afternoon sunshine.

"Oh!" Bertie held out her hand.

Nate lowered the scrimshaw into it. The chain slithered over her fingers, significant and serpentine, and the bone disk settled against her skin, immediately warming to her touch. Whorls of gold ran through the medallion's rich patina and accented an engraving of the Théâtre's art nouveau façade.

The likeness of the building, reproduced on thick cream card stock for every program, every ticket, had been rendered on the bone with an expert eye to detail. There was the dome-roofed ticket booth, flanked by massive revolving doors likewise inset with stained glass and blooming vines of wrought iron. With robes flowing and never-to-fade flowers framing their lovely faces, gracious gilded statuary held the portico aloft in delicate hands.

Bertie rubbed her thumb over the scrimshaw's surface and marveled at the infinitesimal crosshatches that created the illusion of depth and shadow. "It's gorgeous."

Nate took the medallion back from her, swept her hair aside, and fastened the chain about her neck. The fairies and even Mr. Hastings crowded close to get a better look.

"It's pirate booty!" said Cobweb from Bertie's shoulder. He reached for it, but she shook her head at him.

"You're all sticky," she said. "Don't touch it."

"I'll give ye a warnin', too," Nate said. "Don't get it near saltwater."

"I'll have to stay away from the *Little Mermaid* set. The Stage Manager will be thrilled." Bertie started to laugh, but trailed off when he didn't join her. "What makes you say that?"

"Saltwater will call her." Nate reached out and stroked the scrimshaw's surface with his fingertip.

Bertie peered up at him. "Why are you being so cryptic? Who will the water call?"

Nate glanced at Mr. Hastings. "Th' Sea Goddess. Th' real one. That scrimshaw's carved from a bit o' her bone."

"Really?" Mr. Hastings began to flip through his paperwork. "That's fascinating!"

"That's not fascinating, it's disgusting!" The medallion's weight dragged at Bertie's neck. She reached for the clasp and did a frantic sort of dance. "Take it off."

"I won't, an' neither will ye," Nate said. "That's th' most powerful talisman I have ever seen. Close yer eyes a moment an' listen. What does it tell ye?"

"Are you drunk?" Bertie sputtered. "Have you been in the rum again?"

"Jus' do it." Nate used his sternest Giving Orders voice.

Without meaning to, Bertie let the rest of the room fade into the background. When she focused all of her attention on the medallion, something crawled over her skin and left it spangled with salt. "It feels very old and very sad, somehow."

"Duh!" said Mustardseed. "It's ivory from a dead animal. Of course it's sad!"

"Not in death, but in life," Bertie said, unable to look away from the engraving of the Théâtre. "The sadness seeped into her very bones and was locked inside."

"Exactly," Nate said. "I'll tell ye her story later. Just know fer now that a bit o' Sedna's bone is th' best protection ye could possibly have."

"Fine. Whatever. I don't have time to argue with you."
An acrid odor alerted Bertie—too late!—to the toast. The
fairies wailed over its loss, but Bertie shook her head. "Leave
it. We have to go convince Mr. Tibbs that I'm not a hooli-
gan. Will you be all right on your own, Mr. Hastings?"

"Yes, yes, of course." The Properties Manager frowned,
rifling through papers at a startling speed.

"Are you certain?" Bertie asked, already halfway to the
door.

He didn't reply as he turned back to his filing cabinets
and straightened his glasses. "I will have to make a notation.
I don't seem to have the provenance for that particular
scrimshaw in my paperwork. . . ."

"So?" Bertie held onto the doorframe.

Mr. Hastings looked up, startled. "Hm? Oh, are you still
here, Bertie dear?"

Wholly accustomed to his absentmindedness, she shook
her head and waved. "Never mind. We'll be back later . . .
and see if you can find me a basket of asps!"

"Are you insane?" Cobweb demanded as they headed for the
Scenic Department.

"For requesting asps?"

"For burning the toast!"

Bertie skimmed down the hall, fueled by success and

adrenaline. Sconces poured warm light on the rich mahogany paneling, but shadows, like creatures long of tooth
and nail, gathered in the narrow places. "We've more important things to worry about right now than food."

Mustardseed said reproachfully, "I'm certain you don't
mean that."

"She's under duress," Peaseblossom said.

"I don't care if she's under duress, over it, or alongside
it," Moth said. "Nothing in this world supersedes cake."

"Pie does," Cobweb corrected.

Moth glared at him. "Are you under duress, too?"

Bertie did her best to ignore both the fairies and the insistent thumping of the scrimshaw against her skin as she
planned her attack upon the Scenic Department. She would
need all her wits if she was going to convince Mr. Tibbs to
help her.

Considering the ongoing dispute between the Properties and Scenic Departments, it didn't help that Mr. Hastings had always favored her.

MR. TIBBS

(yelling)

If you can pick it up with your hands and move it, I'll
agree it's a prop! Anything too heavy to lift is a piece
of dash-blasted scenery and therefore belongs to me.

MR. HASTINGS

(standing his ground)

With enough leverage, anything can be lifted and
moved, my dear Mr. Tibbs.

MR. TIBBS

I'm not your dear anything, you upstart nincompoop!

MR. HASTINGS

Be that as it may, you bullying chimney stack, the vase
from the third act of *The Lake* most assuredly belongs
to the Property Department.

(He pulls out reams of paperwork.)

I will direct your attention to line 45A and the Stage
Manager's signature. . . .

MR. TIBBS

Signature or no, that vase is coming with me.

"Ye goin' t' need t' charm him," Nate said. "He still car-
ries a grudge against ye fer all th' times ye painted yer room."

"You don't have to remind me," Bertie said as she opened
the door and eased inside the Scenic Dock. "Yoo-hoo, Mr.
Tibbs!"

The Scenic Manager's lair was as tall as it was wide, stor-
ing the flats and backdrops of every set imaginable. Frosted
glass windows spanned the length of the room, and sunlight

flowed like molten gold over projects under construction. Just now, the room was eerily quiet, with a distinct lack of hammering, sawing, or any of the other thousands of noises normally associated with set production.

Bertie turned in a slow circle. "Everyone must be on a break—"

"What do you want?" a voice like an air horn blasted behind her. Bertie leapt aside, and Mr. Tibbs brushed past her as though she smelled.

If Mr. Hastings was a pale and shrunken stalk of celery, Mr. Tibbs was a livid beefsteak tomato. The Scenic Manager was round and red of face; he had plump cheeks and a wide slit of a mouth usually opened in a roar or, as it was at this moment, clamped around a malodorous cigar. He wore coveralls, trailed sawdust wherever he went, and the one time Bertie had seen him without his battered newsboy cap, she'd been simultaneously appalled and awestruck by the three strands of hair plastered over his bald spot. Today, she was glad to see his hat was affixed firmly in place.

"Well?" he bellowed in her face.

"I . . . er . . . that is . . ." Bertie stammered.

"Get out, get out," he said. "I have a schedule to maintain. Maintenance and production, replacement and refurbishment. You'll only be in the way."

"In th' way o' what?" Nate asked. "There's no one here an' nothin' t' do at th' moment."

"Shouldn't you be packing your things, young lady?" Mr. Tibbs stomped over to a half-painted flat and scowled at the bucket abandoned on the concrete floor.

"So you've heard," Bertie said.

"I heard, and it's about damn time."

"Probably," Bertie agreed.

The others looked at her as though she were crazy, while Mr. Tibbs exhaled smoke and suspicion. "What foolishness are you up to?"

Bertie didn't tie up her pitch with pretty words or a winning smile, knowing full well that neither of those things would have the slightest effect on him. Mr. Tibbs listened to the entire speech, shifting his cigar from one side of his mouth to the other.

"*Hamlet*," he said finally.

"In Egypt. Yes."

"Huh. That's quite the harebrained scheme. Nice try, girlie, but you're wasting my time. The Theater Manager will never give you permission for that."

Bertie felt her cheeks get hot. "He might, if I had your support. I have Mrs. Edith's already."

"And Hastings?" Mr. Tibbs demanded.

"He's agreed to help me."

"Oh, he did, did he?" The Scenic Manager glared at the sunshine as though it offended him, too. "Run along, and take your ridiculous plotting with you!"

About to burst with ill-timed anger, Bertie had a stroke of diabolical genius. "It's all right, Mr. Tibbs. I understand. In fact, I'm not even surprised."

"You're not, eh?"

"Oh, yes. Mr. Hastings said you'd be against it."

"He did, did he?"

Nate cut in smoothly. "Aye. He said that ye were stuck in yer ways, an' that ye wouldn't know a good idea if it bit ye on yer arse."

"Is that SO?" Mr. Tibbs demanded.

Bertie took a deep breath, crossed her fingers behind her back, and added her coup de grâce. "Mr. Hastings said not to worry, he'd manage the set decoration alone."

Mr. Tibbs nigh on exploded when he heard that. "What?!"

Bertie nodded, striving to appear both earnest and innocent. "He said something about obelisks being the responsibility of the Properties Department."

Not a lie! Even better!

If Bertie thought she'd heard every curse there was to hear in the Théâtre, she'd been wrong. Mr. Tibbs put the pirates to utter shame as he shouted that he wouldn't be bossed about and who did Mr. Hastings think he was anyway, his tirade punctuated by profanity and expletives the likes of which curled Peaseblossom's hair and left even Nate wincing.

"You'll have your obelisks!" Mr. Tibbs's shout rattled the

wrought iron curlicues that framed the windows. "Courtesy of the Théâtre Illuminata *Scenic* Department, and THAT is FINAL."

Bertie grabbed him by the hand and was shaking on it before Mr. Tibbs could realize he'd been had. "A pleasure to hear it, sir. You won't regret it, I promise!"

And then they ran for it, down a hallway that seemed far less gloomy and foreboding than it had only a short time ago. The fairies laughed and swooped, shoved at each other and dive-bombed Nate's head.

"Brilliant," Bertie shouted, holding out her arms and pretending to fly, too. "That's all major departments accounted for."

"That were a wicked bit o' trickery, my miss," Nate said, punching at the air. "Ye should be proud o' yerself."

The fairies whooped their approval as Nate gathered Bertie up to swing her about in triumph. Overcome by his enthusiasm, she gave him a loud kiss on his scruffy cheek.

He tastes like the ocean. And sweat. And—

Nate turned his head, his sandpaper bristles rubbing against her face. He inhaled very slowly, but a gust of cold air hit the two of them before he could say or do anything more.

Bertie twisted about in his arms, searching for the one she knew was listening. "Ariel."

Nate set her down and reached for his cutlass, but no

one appeared to challenge them. "He's not goin' t' be happy yer fightin' t' stay."

"Isn't that a tragedy?" Cobweb said.

"He'd better not try anything, or we'll let him have it, but good!" Mustardseed said.

Peaseblossom flew back to alight on Bertie's shoulder. "What are you going to do about him?"

"I don't have time to worry about Ariel now," Bertie said. "We still have to convince the Theater Manager, and I have an appointment for eight o'clock on the dot."

Nate looked from her disheveled hair to her dye-splattered shirt. "First, I think ye need t' consider a costume change."

CHAPTER SEVEN

Straitlaced

"The meeting will go well," Mrs. Edith said around a mouthful of pins. "I feel it in my bones."

"I'm glad you feel it in your bones," said Bertie. "Because my bones aren't the least bit certain about it."

"Tsk, dear. You're too young to be so cynical. Turn a bit to your left."

"Do you often feel things in your bones, Mrs. Edith?" Bertie wrapped her fingers around the scrimshaw and tried to ignore the jabbing of needles near her backside.

"All the time, dear. Theater people are a superstitious lot, and my bones are quite reliable, I assure you."

Bertie screwed her eyes shut and rubbed her thumb over the medallion.

Nate thought this would make a good luck charm. So let's see it do some magic.

"What do you think of our handiwork?" Peaseblossom demanded.

Bertie opened her eyes and confronted her reflection in the full-length mirror, which told her that the scrimshaw's luck had yet to have any influence in matters of fashion. "I thought we were going for something professional."

"It's pin-striped," Peaseblossom said, weighted down by a long strand of pearls and an offended expression.

"Classy!" added Moth.

"Like a lawyer going to court," said Cobweb with a nod.

"I guess," Bertie conceded. "But it's still a corset. And the skirt?"

"It's a bit short, but it's the best we could do with so little notice." Mrs. Edith tugged on the hem. "It's more decent than the costumes for the musical numbers, at least. Face front, please, and raise your arms over your head."

"Hold on." Bertie pulled the scrimshaw out of the way and obeyed, instantly sorry when the Wardrobe Mistress tightened the strings on her bodice. "Oooof!"

"The laces have stretched since you first put it on," Mrs. Edith said.

"No problem. I wasn't using that oxygen." Bertie thought of the almost-kiss she and Nate had shared in the corridor.

He said I needed to change clothes, but I doubt this is what he had in mind.

"Stand up straight," Mrs. Edith said. "Shoulders back and tummy in." She took the pearls from Peaseblossom and went to fasten them around Bertie's neck, encountering the scrimshaw hanging there already. "What's this?"

"My good-luck charm from Nate." When Mrs. Edith narrowed her eyes in scrutiny, Bertie amended, "Well, not really from him. He got it in the Properties Department."

Mrs. Edith sniffed her disapproval of both Nate and the scrimshaw's origins. "Anything a Player wears belongs to Wardrobe."

"What if it was an eye patch?" Moth asked.

"Wardrobe," Mrs. Edith said.

"And what about a baldric?" Cobweb wrapped a bit of twine about his waist. "For carrying a sword."

"That's a kind of belt, so it's Wardrobe."

"What about the actual sword?" Mustardseed said, his little eyes squinched up with concentration. "If it's sheathed, it's being worn."

"But if it's being used, it's a prop," Peaseblossom said.

"Some items," Mrs. Edith conceded, "are subject to interpretation." She nodded at the medallion. "You should take it off, dear. It interrupts the flow of your ensemble."

Bertie closed her hand over the scrimshaw. "I prefer to keep it on. I'm superstitious, too."

"Since when?"

"Since I might be homeless."

Mrs. Edith peered at Bertie over her spectacles. "We shan't let that happen."

Bertie sniffed heroically. "No, we shan't."

"That's right, my girl. Stiff upper lip." Mrs. Edith made her final adjustments to Bertie's clothes and posture. "Now, when you sit—"

Bertie put a hand to her waist. "I don't think I'll be sitting in this thing."

"Nonsense, of course you'll sit. Ease yourself into the chair and do your best to perch on the edge."

"Perch. Right." Bertie tugged at the front of the bodice and got her hands slapped for her trouble. "Anything else?"

"Spectacles!" Cobweb handed her a pair of cat's-eye glasses set with twinkling rhinestones.

"They don't even have lenses in them!" Bertie poked her fingers through the empty holes in the rims and waggled them at her accomplices. "Anything else?"

Mrs. Edith held up white gloves.

Bertie balked. "No way. The glasses are bad enough."

"You said the heels were bad enough!" said Mustardseed with a giggle.

"The heels *were* bad enough," echoed Bertie. "I wanted to look presentable, not like a Gal Friday."

Mrs. Edith didn't say anything, but she looked a thousand sorts of awful.

Aware further protests would be useless, Bertie took the gloves and smoothed them on, one at a time. The corset prevented her from heaving a long-suffering sigh. "When I swoon from lack of air, someone is going to have to cut me out of this thing."

Mrs. Edith looked to Peaseblossom, the least irresponsible of the four. "If she faints, cut her out from the back. Replacing the laces is simple, but if you slice through the boning, I will see that your wings are removed. With tweezers."

All four fairies paled. "Yes, ma'am!" they answered in one voice.

"Good. And as for you, my miss—"

Bertie pivoted on one heel and flashed her most mature, serene smile at the Wardrobe Mistress. "Yes?"

Mrs. Edith hesitated, and Bertie looked down in alarm.

"What? Am I coming out somewhere?"

"You . . . you just look so grown up." The older woman pulled an elaborately embroidered hankie out of her sleeve and dabbed at her eyes.

"Isn't that what we wanted?"

When Mrs. Edith didn't answer, Bertie forgot all the instructions about perfect posture and decorum. She threw her arms about the Wardrobe Mistress, inhaling the scents of lavender water, starch, and needle-thin silver; Mrs. Edith smelled of comfort and safety.

And home.

Bertie nearly choked on her fear. "What if he doesn't agree? What if I have to leave?"

Mrs. Edith's arms tightened around Bertie before the older woman pulled back far enough to look her in the eye. "That, my dear, is the worst-case scenario."

"Ariel said I should be excited," Bertie said. "That it's my chance to go find my mother."

Mrs. Edith's face tightened. "Ariel should keep his own counsel."

"That's what I told him," Bertie said.

"No, you didn't!" said Moth. "You told him to shut up."

"The only thing is—" Bertie paused, wondering how to word it, then gave up trying to be delicate "—if there's anything else you know, anything at all, about how I came here . . ."

Mrs. Edith took a deep breath and held it a moment. "I've told you all I can. You were left on the doorstep when you were very young."

"And you didn't see anyone, anything—"

"I would tell you more if I could." Mrs. Edith enveloped her in another swift, firm hug. "Now go on, dear. Break a leg."

Bertie had heard the phrase countless times over the years, but never directed at her. The well-wish settled alongside the carved bone disk, just between her collarbones.

"Posture!" Mrs. Edith admonished.

"Come on, let's go!" Bertie beckoned to the fairies. They rocketed to the door with handfuls of swiped sequins and beads.

"Miscreants!" Mrs. Edith narrowed her gaze at them and, by all the laws of physics, they should have burst into flames. The Wardrobe Mistress adjusted her glasses as though they were at fault and called to Bertie, "Remember, Management appreciates a well-polished presentation. Do your best to enunciate, and try not to stutter."

"I've never once stuttered!" Bertie said, indignant.

"Stage fright, dear," Mrs. Edith said. "It affects everyone, though you've never had the occasion to feel it before. Take deep breaths and you'll be fine!"

The door swung shut between them with a hollow boom that echoed down the hallway.

"Deep breaths." Bertie tried, but managed a quarter of a breath or perhaps a third. "Maybe she shouldn't have tightened my corset so much."

The five of them stood there for a moment. And another. Bertie shifted from one high-heel-shod foot to the other.

These shoes really are uncomfortable. It's no wonder the Chorus Girls are so cranky, if they have to dance in them.

"Are we going yet?" whispered Mustardseed.

"I think she's screwing her courage," said Peaseblossom, "to the sticking place."

"What are we sticking?" asked Moth.

"And where are we sticking it?" That was Cobweb.

"I think when we get there, you four should stay outside." Bertie set off down the hall at a purposeful clip.

The fairies protested as they flew to catch up. "But we didn't say anything rude yet!"

"Yet," Bertie repeated for emphasis. "The rude part is inevitable, and you're not the sort of supporting cast I need in a boardroom setting. We're talking about my future at the theater here, not a pie-flinging contest."

"There's going to be pie?" Mustardseed clapped his hands. "What kind?"

"She means she doesn't trust us to behave ourselves," said Peaseblossom. The hitch in her tiny voice was unmistakable as she landed on Bertie's shoulder.

"It's not that." Bertie tilted her chin toward Peaseblossom, taking care not to knock her off. "All right, maybe it is that. Just a little."

"Mostly the boys, though, right?" Peaseblossom whispered.

"Of course." Bertie pressed a hand to the cramp she was getting just under her ribs. "Walking in this thing is a pain in the—"

"Language," Peaseblossom said to cut her off.

"Spleen," Bertie finished.

Peaseblossom snickered. "I'll try to keep the boys occupied during your meeting, but you know how they are." She chased after the others, who'd raced ahead, reached the end of the passage, and disappeared around a right-hand turn.

"Yes," Bertie said, trying to keep up. "I know how they are."

"Beatrice."

Ariel's voice was ice down her back, despite its attempt at warmth, and his slim fingers wrapped about her wrist before she realized how close he was.

"That is quite the ensemble," he said. "Are you joining the Ladies' Chorus?"

"No." Bertie attempted to recover her hand from his grasp, but didn't quite manage it.

"A tryst, perhaps? A secret assignation?" Ariel tilted his head to one side, as though he needed one eye to be a quarter of an inch higher than the other to ponder the great mystery of her destination. "Tsk. Mrs. Edith will be disappointed all her hovering didn't succeed in strangling your puberty into submission." He led her in a turn, whistling soft and low. "Who are you meeting with, dressed as you are?"

"Nate." Bertie pulled back as far as she could. "We have a hot date aboard the *Persephone*, and I couldn't find a wench costume."

Ariel shook his head. "Try again."

Bertie remembered Mrs. Edith's admonitions about posture and drew herself up. "The Gentlemen's Chorus offered to help me remain at the theater if I gave them each a kiss."

Ariel tried on a smile and stroked her hand. "That's two missteps in this charming dance. Would you care to attempt a third?"

Bertie glared at him; if looks were blowtorches, he wouldn't have any eyebrows left at all. "I have a meeting with Management, remember?" She tugged again at the hand trapped in his. "Kindly let me go."

"Ah, Management." Ariel laced his fingers through hers, tucked her arm under the crook of his elbow, and began to stroll as though they were in a Promenade scene, French Countryside. Bertie sucked in a breath at the intimacy of the gesture, but he continued, "Have you ever been up to the Manager's Office before?"

"Once or twice," Bertie admitted. *Perhaps more. Perhaps every time the Stage Manager led me there by the ear to await judgment. And perhaps there's a wooden chair with grooves worn into it that exactly match the contours of my backside.*

Ariel laughed, soft and low. A cool breeze teased around the edges of Bertie's very short skirt, and when she inhaled, she could smell autumn leaves. She hazarded a sideways glance at him, watching the frosted fall of his hair shift over his shoulders. It was restless. Wild. *Just like him.* The tiny hairs on Bertie's arms stood on end.

Of course he noticed. "Am I making you nervous, Beatrice?"

"No," she managed, pleased she could match his cool tone.

Ariel laughed again, and now her goose bumps had goose bumps. "I think I am."

Troubled to realize he *was* making her nervous, Bertie reached up to touch the scrimshaw for comfort.

She'd heard of people who saw double after hitting their head or, in the case of the pirates, imbibing too much rum. Though she'd done neither, her vision blurred a bit, as if she were looking at Ariel through saltwater. He still held her arm, still had his head at an earnest tilt, but beyond that mask of calm and elegance was an Ariel-shaped mass of writhing, snakelike tendrils. Scarves and streamers moved swiftly, weaving in and out among each other, reaching out to tug at her clothes and pull her toward them. They spoke in silk-hisses of the desperate need roiling under the surface of his skin, and their whispers stole the breath from her lungs.

"Let me go!" Bertie pinched the fleshy inner curve of his arm with her fingernails until he released her.

"Whatever is the matter with the girl?" Ariel asked the empty hallway.

"I'm not falling for your Prince Charming act." She didn't back away, though she very much wanted to.

"Act?" Smooth as cream. "Am I not your handsome prince, ready to save you from this mundane existence?"

"I hadn't realized how badly you want your freedom." The corset helped put steel in her spine; Bertie felt very tall, very thin, and very much in control. "I'm sorry, Ariel, but

Players can't leave the theater, and there's nothing I can do to change that."

"I don't believe you." The air warmed with the promise of a summer storm. What little distance there was between them disappeared as he stepped even closer. "Aren't you trying to change things so that you can stay?"

Bertie opened her mouth to argue and realized he spoke the truth.

"I see the lady is speechless, for once." His lips twitched with the faintest suggestion of a sneer as he permitted his gaze to come to rest on her cleavage. "Such a pity your intellect didn't blossom with the rest of you."

Mrs. Edith had told her once that the costume made the character, but only now did Bertie understand what she'd meant. The corset was dainty, demure, pin-striped, and it wanted her to slap Ariel across the face.

But Bertie was more than the sum of her clothing, so she cocked her arm and punched him as hard as she could in the stomach.

Ariel staggered back, unprepared for such an assault. They stared at one another, Bertie ready to duck and weave if he decided to return the favor and Ariel holding a hand to his solar plexus until the air returned to his lungs.

Finally, he wheezed, "Given half a chance, I will free not only myself, but all who are imprisoned here. Know that."

Bertie jutted her chin at him. "Get out of my way, or I'll punch you in the jaw for an encore."

He bowed low, his eyes never leaving hers. "Milady."

"I am a lady, but I'm certainly not yours." Bertie pushed past him and ran up the stairs, two at a time in spite of her heels. She arrived on the landing gasping for breath, and when she strained her ears, she could make out the telltale echo of his mirthless laughter. Bertie exhaled as much of him as her lungs would release before setting off down the hall.

The fairies circled in a holding pattern outside the door to the Theater Manager's Office.

"Where have you been?" Moth demanded.

"We were just coming back to look for you," Cobweb said.

Peaseblossom reached out to blot a droplet of moisture off Bertie's forehead with a tiny bit of tissue. "Why are you all sweaty?"

"It's hot as hell downstairs," Bertie said.

And I just dodged the devil.

CHAPTER EIGHT

The Manager's Office

The door to the Theater Manager's Office was different from any other in the Théâtre. Bubble-trapped glass gave the illusion of privacy while permitting dim light to filter through, and black lettering spelled out his full name, although Bertie had never dared use it. She reached for the ornate, wrought-brass doorknob that gleamed with hundreds of years of turning and polish, then hesitated.

"Go on," Moth said, picking his nose as he hovered next to her. "I believe in you!"

"We all believe in you, Bertie." Peaseblossom blew kisses that sparkled like flecks of fool's gold.

Bertie squared her shoulders and knocked. A seemingly infinite amount of time spiraled out between the final hollow echo and the voice that answered, "Yes?"

"It's B-B-B-Bertie." *Mrs. Edith was right about the stuttering!* She took a deep breath and measured out her words in careful increments. "May I come in, sir?"

"Yes, of course."

Bertie looked at the fairies as she opened the door. "Stay. Put." She slid inside the chamber and shut the door firmly behind her.

Now that she was under the threat of exile, Bertie took in the familiar surroundings with new eyes. There was the enormous twin pedestal desk, the piles of paperwork, and the shelves full of books. The worn, yellow chintz draperies hanging at the windows had been deemed too shabby for use onstage some previous season. Cut-glass decanters of liquor sat open on the sideboard, and the sharp sting of brandy snaked through the haze of cigarette smoke.

The Theater Manager had his back to her as he inquired, "Would you care for something to drink? A soda, perhaps?"

"No, thank you, sir. This isn't a social call."

He turned, and his mouth fell open at the sight of her ensemble. To his credit, he recovered within a split second, rearranging his features into a bland expression.

The same could not be said for the Stage Manager. "Why are you dressed like a—"

The Theater Manager cleared his throat. The Stage Manager swallowed whatever word he'd intended to say, making a face as though it tasted rancid.

Bertie inclined her head at the two of them, striving to project grace and decorum. "I apologize for interrupting, but I did have an appointment." She perched creditably on the edge of a leather-upholstered wingback chair and took a moment to adjust her glasses.

The Stage Manager intensified his glare as the Theater Manager sat down behind his desk and steepled his fingers.

"What did you decide you want to do, Beatrice?" he asked.

Bertie took a deep breath and said, "Esteemed sirs, I'm here to apply for the position of Director."

"Director?" the Theater Manager said, not betraying anything in his expression. "Well. That's certainly . . . unexpected."

"It's poppycock!" snorted the Stage Manager, his ruddy cheeks hinting at the possibility of an aneurysm.

"What do you want to direct?" the Theater Manager asked.

"Mayhem," muttered the Stage Manager. "Scenes of utter chaos and destruction."

The Theater Manager tapped ponderous fingers against the desk. "Let her answer the question."

"I want to restage one of Shakespeare's plays." Bertie leaned forward in her enthusiasm and instantly regretted it when one of the corset's steel bones jabbed her ribs. She gritted her teeth and smiled again. "*Hamlet*, but transported to Ancient Egypt."

"Why would you want to do that?" The Theater Manager looked genuinely bewildered.

"If I don't change the show in some dramatic fashion, there'd be no need for a Director, right?" Bertie asked.

"That is certainly true," he conceded, "though you've yet to convince me why that's a good idea."

Bertie had pondered this very question at length while Mrs. Edith had dressed her, so she was prepared to attack him right where it would hurt most: the Théâtre's coffers. "When's the last time we sold out a performance and had standing room only?"

The Theater Manager pursed his lips. "I don't see how that's relevant. . . ."

"You will, once we send out the announcement about the performance. Half our patrons will be intrigued by the idea, and the other half will be outraged by such a presumption, but all of them will buy tickets and turn up. If my version is a success, I can restage other classic plays. By the end of the season, the theater could touch upon the highest point of all its greatness, the full meridian of its glory."

"All thanks to you," the Stage Manager said with sarcasm sharp enough to cut through her grand visions. "I suppose you haven't stopped to consider we haven't the time or budget for such nonsense."

"We don't need either," Bertie said. The conversation

was a dance: a step to the side, a glide, a pivot, a turn. "We have the script. We have the costumes, the props, the sets."

"We'll help!" piped up four voices from the keyhole.

"Ridiculous," said the Stage Manager. "Those creatures are nothing but a menace."

"Baloney!" said the keyhole.

Bertie closed her eyes and prayed to Peaseblossom. There was a short, noisy conflict on the other side of the door, followed by blessed silence.

"Do you see?" the Stage Manager shouted anyway. "She encourages blatant disregard for the order of things. Ask her about the earthquake."

The Theater Manager's eyebrows collided in the middle of his forehead. "Earthquake? I don't remember any earthquake."

Might as well be honest about it.

"It was a very small earthquake, really," Bertie said. "And that was some time ago."

"You don't say." The Theater Manager peered at her, as though seeing her for the very first time. "That would mean you have experience coordinating large-scale projects."

Bertie sat ramrod straight—Mrs. Edith would have been proud!—and nodded in her most reassuring manner. "I do, sir."

"An understanding of commitment," he said.

"Of course," Bertie said. "Do you have any idea how much commitment it takes to pull off an earthquake? Or commandeer a pirate ship? Or teach the starfish to dance the fox-trot?"

"I'm warning you," the Stage Manager interjected, "allowing her to become a Director would only make things worse. Think of the damage she's already done, then imagine how much more she might do!"

The Theater Manager pondered a moment and then said with crystalline calm, "I'm afraid I agree. I cannot sanction such a course of action."

Everything in Bertie plummeted: her hopes, her heart, her incredible posture. "But you promised!"

"It's not that I doubt your sincerity, Beatrice, or your enthusiasm," said the Theater Manager.

"Then might I inquire as to your objections in the matter?" Bertie was proud to manage civility when her first inclination was to shout and throw things.

The Theater Manager crossed to the window; when next he spoke, his voice reminded Bertie of the yellow silk obscuring the glass. "I fear too many changes may upset the delicate balance of this place. A balance I've strived to maintain, I will add, since the day you arrived here. The more time the Players spend with you, the more they transform, the more they exceed the limitations of their written parts.

Your closest friends come and go as they please with no thought as to the consequences. . . ."

"How does that hurt anything?" Her bewilderment pained her. Bertie's fingers sought out the scrimshaw for reassurance. "I don't understand."

When the Theater Manager turned to exchange a long look with his colleague, the medallion took their every unspoken word and transformed them into rustling leaves. Within seconds, the Office was a forest primeval, oak-aged secrets reaching their arms from floor to ceiling like a family tree.

The Stage Manager wove poison ivy words through the vision. "Don't tell her."

"She has to know, in order to grasp the importance of the situation," the Theater Manager said.

"What do I need to know? I wish you both would stop being so mysterious!" Bertie let go of the medallion and shook her head to clear it. "This has been my home for as long as I can remember. I want to make my contribution, and you promised me I could try!"

"I did promise you, Bertie, and the theater will hold me to that promise," the Theater Manager said. "But I fear the changes you make might permit the Players to leave."

"I don't understand." Bertie frowned. "You said that wasn't possible."

"A wishful falsehood." The Theater Manager's face looked

as tight as a clenched fist, but the words that followed were fingers opening to reveal a magician's dark coin. "What I am about to tell you must never leave this Office." He waited for Bertie to nod before he admitted, "A long time ago, one of the Players managed to escape."

The revelation stole her breath from her lungs, just as Ariel had in the hallway. Bertie had her suspicions, but she asked anyway. "Which one?"

"That part," the Theater Manager said softly, "isn't important. What *is* important is that you understand the gravity of the situation. That you proceed with the utmost caution."

"How . . ." Bertie licked her lips. "How did it happen?"

"If I knew, I'd have put safeguards in place."

That's why Ariel thinks I can help him escape! He's done it once before!

But all Bertie said was, "I just want to prove that I belong here."

"This will be a disaster of colossal proportions." The Stage Manager snarled his dissent. "Mark my words, we'll find ourselves standing in the smoking ruins of the theater. I'll have no part in it!"

The doorknob rattled. Another scuffle broke out in the hall.

"If you'll have no part in it, I'll give the cues myself," Bertie said.

The Stage Manager opened his mouth, closed it, opened it again, thought better of it, and shut it once more. He picked up his glass and attempted to finish off his brandy in one determined gulp.

Bertie couldn't resist adding, "I know the headset fits."

The Stage Manager choked. "Now see here, you pip-squeak—"

About the time he threatened her nose with his finger, Peaseblossom lost her grip on the situation with the boys. The door crashed open, and three irate fairies launched themselves at the Stage Manager. Cobweb and Moth pelted him with sequins while Mustardseed rammed beads into his ears.

"Dance!" they commanded, and dance he did, hopping with impotent anger and pain from one foot to the other as he batted his meaty hands at them.

"I'm sorry!" Peaseblossom wailed as she landed on Bertie's shoulder. "I tried, really I did."

"I know."

"Maybe I didn't try as hard as I ought when he started calling you names," the fairy admitted. "Serves him right, the nasty old turd. Punch him again, Moth!"

The Stage Manager howled and fled as the fearsome threesome gave chase. In their pursuit, they knocked over the crystal inkwell, and Moth flew straight into the door-jamb.

"Bugger!" he yelled, either in pain or at the fleeing man's back.

Bertie winced at the profanity, which was one of her favorites, and slanted a look at the Theater Manager to gauge his reaction.

"Look demure!" Peaseblossom coached. "And horrified."

Bertie arranged her lips in an O of surprise, raising one gloved hand to her mouth. "Such shocking behavior," she said, but didn't specify whose.

"Indeed." The Theater Manager righted the inkwell and wiped at the mess on the desk with a piece of blotting paper.

"Do let me help you with that, sir," Bertie said.

The Theater Manager flapped his blotting paper at her. "No, no. I wouldn't want you to soil your gloves. Or get a spot on your . . . er . . . ensemble. Mrs. Edith wouldn't be pleased at all."

"Quite the opposite," said Bertie. Peaseblossom shuddered, presumably remembering the threat about the tweezers.

The Theater Manager opened a leather-bound calendar and began to flip through the pages. "There is a bit of difficulty, I'm afraid."

Bertie leaned forward, trying to catch a glimpse of the rows and rows of his neat lettering, until the corset reminded her of her limited range of motion. "What is it?"

He tapped a single blank spot with his fingertip. "The only opening I have in the schedule for some time is this weekend.

You can have the Friday evening slot, which is slightly less conspicuous than a Saturday night performance, but better attended than a weekend matinée."

"That . . . that's in *four days!*" Bertie stared at him, aghast. "There's no way I can be ready with a new production in four days!"

"You said you have departmental support," the Theater Manager said.

"I do, but—"

"And the Players already know their lines," he continued.

"Yes, but—"

"So what, exactly, is the difficulty?"

"I-I-I . . ." There was the stutter again! Bertie swallowed her protests along with the superfluous vowels so intent on ruining her. "No difficulty, sir. Four days will be more than sufficient. I'll make the announcement to the Players, run through the show a few times with the new sets and costumes. Piece of cake."

"Glad to hear it," the Theater Manager said, nodding once. "Now, as to setting some measurable parameters for your success . . ."

"Measurable what's-it?" Bertie felt her forehead pucker like one of Mrs. Edith's gathered seams.

"What will constitute a success on your part in this challenge." His hand hovered over the mess on his desk until he located a fountain pen, then he began adding notations to a sheet of paper. "You were saying something about a sold-out performance?"

"Um," she answered, watching with a sinking feeling as he nodded, taking the monosyllable as her agreement.

"Standing room only?"

"I did say that, didn't I?"

"In addition," he said, not looking up, "I think a standing ovation might be in order, as proof that the audience appreciates your vision and innovation."

"Of course, sir." Bertie thanked the heavens and Mrs. Edith for the corset, which was the only thing holding her up at the moment. "A standing ovation, it is."

"We have never before had cause, in the history of the Théâtre, to hire a Director, God help us." He handed her a form that read EMPLOYMENT CONTRACT at the top in bold, black letters. "Sign at the bottom, please."

"And don't you dare get ink on that corset," said Peaseblossom.

Bertie took as deep a breath as possible and signed at the X.

Beatrice Shakespeare Smith

She handed both pen and contract back over the desk. "Well."

"Quite," said the Theater Manager. "I have no idea how

the Players are going to cope with changes in scenery and subtext, so you should get an early start tomorrow."

Bertie gathered what was left of her composure and shook his proffered hand. "Would you be so kind as to tell the Stage Manager he can be in charge of hand-delivering announcements to our patrons, season ticket-holders, and benefactors, something that will let them know about the new performance? They should go out immediately, if we want to sell out the show."

"I'll give him the assignment," the Theater Manager said with a dismissive nod. "Get some sleep. You're going to need all your wits about you."

Bertie walked to the door in something of a daze.

"Oh, and Beatrice?" he called after her.

Halfway into the hall, she turned back. "Yes, sir?"

"Best of luck."

Bertie summoned a brilliant smile that lasted only until she shut the door. "Famous last words."

"You're a Director now," Peaseblossom said with a tinge of awe in her tone. "How does that make you feel?"

"Sick to my stomach," Bertie said with great irritation. "Which way did the boys go?"

"Last I saw them, they were chasing His Royal Pain-in-the-Hind-End down the stairs."

Bertie kicked off her heels and went barefoot, wincing with each step. "I need to get out of this."

"The new play?"

"The corset." Bertie snapped her fingers. "Then we need to post a notice on the Call Board for the Players. Eight A.M."

"Eight in the morning is pretty early for this crowd," said Peaseblossom.

"The Theater Manager seemed to think we'd need an early start." Bertie tried to remember the last time she had gotten up before ten of her own volition and failed. "We're going to have to set my alarm clock."

"You have an alarm clock?" the fairy asked.

"Amend that statement to say I need to 'borrow' an alarm clock from the Properties Department. The Managers need to know about the rush order, anyway, and I can start by telling Mr. Hastings."

"They aren't going to be happy," Peaseblossom said as Bertie took the stairs two at a time. "Do you think you can convince them four days will be enough time?"

"I'm an alchemist; I'll make gold of it," Bertie said.

CHAPTER NINE

Divas and Drama Queens

Bertie's first indication that she'd overslept was the troupe of cancan dancers that brushed past her bed and hit her in the head with their rustling crinolines. The second was their tittering giggles. But even that was easier to ignore than Nate's hand clamped down on her shoulder.

"Lass." The nudging became more insistent as his other hand joined the first. "There was a notice on th' Call Board, an' they're all gatherin'. Ahoy. Wake up."

"Go 'way," Bertie mumbled in denial. "I set my alarm. It can't be time yet. Tell the Chorus Girls to bugger off." She turned over and burrowed deeper into the bedclothes.

"Ye have t' get up afore th' rest arrive."

Bertie cracked an eye at the clock, which told her in no uncertain terms that it hadn't gone off at seven as planned.

She went from mostly comatose to completely awake in less than half a second, bolted upright, and leapt out of bed. Nate sidestepped her mad bounce into the land of the living, but Moth and Cobweb slept on with their little bums hiked in the air and faces buried under the pillows. Peaseblossom tumbled down Bertie's pajama top. Mustardseed landed on the floor with a thump and a sleepy "bwaaah?"

"Ye know I'd rather hazard an ocean o' sirens than rouse ye from a slumber, right?" Nate asked.

"Yes, I know, and it's a good thing you did. Hairbrush, hairbrush, who moved my hairbrush?"

Bertie realized they were already in the middle of a scene change. Half her furniture and her clothes, carefully selected to look authoritative and directorial, were already gone. She raked her fingers through the brilliant blue rats' nest atop her head with a growing sense of futility and spoke down her pajama top. "We overslept. Wake up!"

Peaseblossom flitted free, instantly alert. "Get up get up get up get up!" She kicked Moth directly in the backside, which only nudged him three inches farther under the pillow.

Bertie shoved her feet into a pair of slippers, then grabbed for all four fairies and dropped them in the pocket of her plaid flannel sleeping pants mere seconds before her bed disappeared under the stage. "Who authorized this?"

"That would be me." The Stage Manager dispensed hot

coffee and smiles to the early arrivals crowded together Stage Right.

"I don't suppose you know what happened to my alarm." Bertie shoved her way through them to reach his table.

"No idea whatsoever," the Stage Manager said.

Bertie surveyed the pastries, coffee cakes, and mammoth silver samovar. "This is an impressive spread. Must have taken a while to set up."

"A bit of time, yes."

"You could have paused during your preparations to wake me up."

"I could have."

"But you didn't."

"Obviously." The Stage Manager held up an insulated cup. "Coffee?"

Bertie rubbed her thumb over the scrimshaw as she peered at him. *Another one wearing a mask, though it's as ugly as what lurks underneath.* He smirked, sending nasty, oily serpents to pluck at her composure, to push, to goad, to tug at the reins of her temper while the Players looked on.

Bertie let go of the medallion along with her plans to unleash a blistering diatribe that would only make her look ridiculous. Instead, she turned on a smile so sweet the cinnamon rolls were jealous. "Please."

Clearly disappointed she'd left the bait dangling on his

hook, the Stage Manager filled the cup to the brim and handed it to her. "There you are."

Nate joined them at the table as Bertie slurped enough coffee to make room in the cup for a healthy amount of cream and sugar. "Is everythin' all right?" His hand twitched toward his cutlass.

"Unspeakably fabulous. I was just getting some breakfast." She turned out her pocket to dump the fairies on the table. "Eat up, guys. You'll need your strength today."

Mustardseed landed on a jelly-filled doughnut with such precision that raspberry jam shot across the tray and dripped over the edge. "Oops! Did I do that?" Then he jumped on an éclair.

"Wait for us!" Moth and Cobweb hastened to skate in the mess.

"Make them stop," snapped the Stage Manager. "The food is for the Company."

"We're part of the Company!" Peaseblossom said. "We even have lines."

"Not a lot of them, but they're there!" said Mustardseed, discovering the sugar cubes.

The Stage Manager fixed Bertie with a gimlet gaze. "As the Director, you're going to need to maintain some semblance of authority."

"Authority, yes, but I'm not the boss of them." Bertie spoke around a mouthful of doughnut, old-fashioned cake with glaze, because she was a girl with simple tastes and because the cancan dancers had snaked all the ones with sprinkles, the hussies.

"Yeah, she's not the boss of us!" Moth and Cobweb stopped painting each other with jam war paint long enough to stick their tongues out at the Stage Manager.

"Yes, she most certainly is," he said.

"For argument's sake, let's say that I am," said Bertie. "I therefore direct them to make a lovely, lovely mess on your table."

"Nyah!" the boys jeered, and did just that.

And Peaseblossom—decorous, proper Peaseblossom— dropped her trousers to waggle her naked, pale bottom at the Stage Manager. Bertie laughed involuntarily, choked on her coffee, and nearly died as it came out her nose, but it was worth the searing pain in her nostrils to see the look on the Stage Manager's face. He spun away from the table and disappeared into the wings, presumably to retrieve his headset and his dignity.

"Wow," Bertie said. "Add Peaseblossom's rump to the list of things I never thought I'd see."

"Aye," agreed Nate. "That were truly appallin'."

Peaseblossom did up her pants and straightened her tunic. "I don't have to be perfect all the time, you know. Being the responsible one gets *tiring*."

"Tell me about it." Bertie grabbed another doughnut and

headed for the front of the stage. The realization dawned that there were too many Players milling about, sitting in the auditorium, gathering in the balconies. She turned to Nate. "What are Othello and Desdemona doing here? And Rosalind and Viola and—"

"Ye called fer everyone," said Nate.

Bertie shook her head in vehement denial. "No, no, I just needed the *Hamlet* cast."

"Oh, dear," said Peaseblossom.

Bertie pivoted in time to see the fairy slap herself on the forehead. Both of them winced.

"You didn't!" Bertie said, not holding out any hope.

"I did!" the fairy wailed. "I posted the call for everyone!"

A few of the Players peered at them with great curiosity, so Bertie tried to look resilient and indefatigable despite the pajamas and crazy bedhead. If she left to change her clothes now, the Stage Manager would spread rumors and misinformation the entire time she was gone, doing his best to make it look like a retreat.

"It's all right," she said, trying to believe it. "It's not the end of the world."

Peaseblossom peeked at Bertie through her fingers. "It's not?"

"I might as well make the announcement to the entire Company. They don't need to get it secondhand though the rumor mill."

"That's th' spirit," Nate said. "Now go an'...er...do whatever 'tis ye plan t' do."

"Thanks, Nate. Truly inspirational." Bertie tossed him the rest of her doughnut and absconded with the wooden crate from under the refreshment table.

Situations like this require as much stature as possible.

"Beatrice Shakespeare Smith!" Gertrude bellowed as she made her entrance, very late and hardly sorry.

"Thank you so much for joining us," Bertie said to the queen, dragging the crate to the front of the stage.

"What are you doing at the front of this assemblage?" Gertrude demanded.

It was the sort of question that didn't have any right answer, like "does this pannier make my royal butt look big?" Bertie sorted through her options, but not quick enough for Gertrude. The queen reached out to rap Bertie's pate with her ruby-ringed knuckle.

"I require your assistance. My silk overskirt must be mended before the next performance, my son is off sulking...." She paused and assessed Bertie's pajamas. "Your attire is most inappropriate, even for this early hour."

Bertie shook her head at the errant royalty. "Never mind my clothes—"

Gertrude snorted with enough force to set the velvet curtains flapping. "I'll have none of your excuses, miss. The moon shall find me dancing, or I'll know why." She turned away to take full advantage of the refreshment table.

"Please do help yourself to coffee before joining the rest of the Company." Bertie climbed onto the crate and cupped a hand next to her mouth. "Excuse me, everyone!"

Trying to capture their attention was like throwing pennies into a restless ocean; the words sank, unnoticed, into the churning waves of morning gossip.

"You need a bullhorn," said Moth.

"Or an air raid siren," said Mustardseed.

"You need a commanding presence and an air of authority," said Peaseblossom.

"Thank you, fairy godmother, I'll get right on that." Bertie signaled to Nate. "Will you gainsay me a whistle?"

"Not this time." Nate reached for the small, copper bosun's pipe that hung around his neck. "Which do ye want?"

"'All Hands on Deck,' just in case we have Players missing, followed by 'Word to Be Passed,' if you please."

Nate obliged with the high-pitched signals used to gather the crew and command silence for an order to follow. The noise was meant to carry from ship to ship; as such, it would have driven a dog under the bed, if there had been a dog, and if the bed hadn't already disappeared below the stage. The Players as yet unaware of Bertie's presence winced and looked around. Hero upset her coffee down her front, and Claudio tried to mop it up, doing more harm than good where her dress was concerned.

Bertie tried to ignore the suspicious looks now aimed at her. "Thank you all for coming this morning. I appreciate your punctuality and graciousness at such an early hour."

The Players complained to their neighbors in rumbling undertones. Though she couldn't see the Stage Manager, Bertie caught his muttered whispers of "whippersnapper" and "troublesome little baggage" in the slosh of conversation. When Nate crossed his considerably muscled arms, the crowd fell into a grudging silence.

"You know that I've been asked to leave the Théâtre." There was another rumble, this time with varying degrees of sympathy. Heartened that they did not cheer and throw half-eaten pastry at her, Bertie continued. "Now I have to prove to the Theater Manager that I belong here. That I can contribute something unique and valuable. So I'm going to become a Director."

The Players looked around in confusion. Bertie heard several voices overlapping as they spoke the same question. "What does that mean?"

Bertie rushed to answer. "I want to direct *Hamlet*."

A resurgence of protests, in large part from the characters not involved with that production. Lady Macbeth, in particular, was livid.

"I don't see why that play should take precedence over the classics!"

"You would think that," Gertrude said with a sniff. "Just because you've performed for the queen—"

"I *am* the queen!" bellowed Lady Macbeth.

"No, I'm the queen. You merely have aspirations for *him*." Gertrude pointed at Macbeth, who was holding up a cruller and muttering, "Is this a doughnut I see before me?" Then he noticed the raspberry jam on everything and started to shriek. With a glare at the fairies, the Stage Manager bundled him off into the wings.

"If I'm not to be involved in this production, why was I roused at this unearthly hour and forced to put in an appearance?" Lady Macbeth demanded. Others—the lovers from *Midsummer*, all the Henrys, and, of course, the Shrew—echoed the complaint.

"*Hamlet* doesn't even need a director," Katerina said. As others shouted in agreement, Bertie feared she was losing her grip on the situation.

Unexpected aid came when Ophelia appeared at Bertie's elbow. "You mustn't let them drown you out. Lead on, though it seems nobody marks you."

"I'll do that, thanks." Bertie focused her attention back on the milling throng, her gaze skimming over the Company. Nearly everyone was there, including a shadow that mingled with the Chorus members at the back: an apparition in smoke-gray just behind the cutthroats.

Ariel.

But Bertie could only address one problem at a time. "I know *Hamlet* isn't new, but we're going to restage it."

Even more confusion. "Restage?"

"What does that mean?"

"We're going to have to make a few adjustments," Bertie said, raising her voice.

"Adjustments?"

"What kind of adjustments?!"

Bertie almost had to shout to be heard now. "The production will be transposed in both time period and setting. I was thinking about Ancient Egypt—"

The clamor! Bertie lost her tenuous grasp on the situation.

"Impossible!" the Players cried.

"She must have gone quite mad!" someone pronounced in a voice that was silk-wrapped daggers.

Bertie was certain that undermining whisper came from Ariel. "I have not gone mad. The changes are possible."

The air elemental stepped free of the crowd. "Perhaps a demonstration?"

Bertie would have cursed him, except it was a valid point. She'd convinced Management that it was possible. . . .

But is it? Really?

"Of course." Bertie beckoned to the fairies and lowered her voice to the barest of whispers. "I need you guys to do a scene for me."

"Which one?"

"Any one. But you have to change it. Significantly."

Moth scratched his head. "Well, it's not as if we've never mucked around on stage before."

Mustardseed peered into the flies. "I hope we don't get smited by some theater god."

"How's this for smited?" Peaseblossom kicked him in the shins. "Which play do you want us to do, Bertie?"

"And what's my motivation?" Cobweb asked.

"Your motivation is to avoid death by strangulation," Bertie said. "Just do a scene from *Hamlet* and really shake things up. Dance the tango if you have to."

But before anyone could ask for a rose to put between their teeth, Ophelia drifted past the refreshment table and strode to Center Stage.

"There's rosemary, that's for remembrance; pray, love, remember: and there is pansies. That's for thoughts." The words were not altered, but she spoke them simply, without any trace of the madness the speech suggested. What's more, she addressed the entire thing to an oven-mitt puppet she'd fitted over her hand.

The puppet answered her in a falsetto that mimicked

her brother, Laertes. "A document in madness, thoughts and remembrance fitted."

Ophelia nodded to the pot holder. "There's fennel for you, and columbines." Only, instead of flowers, she scattered doughnut sprinkles over the stage. "There's rue for you; and here's some for me. Rue, rue, rue. Oh, yes! I rue the way things ended."

Bertie stared at her, torn between fascination and horror. "That's not the line. We're not changing the lines. . . ."

Ophelia faltered and looked uncertain for the first time. She wiped the improvised puppet's mouth with a napkin. "There's a daisy: I would give you some violets, but they withered all when my lover departed."

That time, everyone noticed the misquote. "It's supposed to be her father—"

"After he died."

"I seem to have forgotten what comes next." Ophelia held the puppet overhead to squawk, "Line!"

"How can she forget her own part?" Moth wanted to know.

"I don't know," Peaseblossom said. "Maybe talking to a pot holder muddled things up."

"If that throws her off, what's going to happen when she's standing in front of the pyramids wearing gold silk gauze?" Bertie thought of all the alterations she wanted to make to the costumes and the sets. "What if they all forget their lines?"

Ariel's voice, smooth and silky with conviction, cut

through the crowd. "Perhaps they need rehearsing to accustom themselves to the changes."

"She expects us to rehearse?" someone cried.

"I know my part. I'll not be bullied in such a fashion!"

"Please, if you'll only listen," Bertie started to say, but the Merry Wives of Windsor were already arguing with the Two Gentlemen of Verona.

Ariel flickered through the Players like a silver needle through cloth; one second he was next to the Ladies' Chorus, the next he'd moved on to mingle with the Tricksters.

A troublesome spirit, indeed.

Onstage, Julius Caesar and Marc Antony now jabbed at each other with their daggers while a gang war broke out in the orchestra pit between the Capulets and Montagues.

"Nate?" Bertie called.

The pirate moved forward. "What would ye have me do, lass? Cut their throats?"

She shook her head, much as she would have liked to see punishments liberally administered. "There's too many of them, besides which I need them intact."

"They came prepared fer a fight," Nate observed. "Goin' so far as t' bring blood packs an' false limbs."

"This is ridiculous," Bertie said, wishing she could hit someone. "How are we going to restage a play if we can't even get through the announcement without bloodshed?"

"Better to give up the idea. They'll never agree to it."

The Stage Manager pushed his mop through the mêlée, moving from one sticky pool of red corn syrup to another and looking smug.

Bertie wondered if he was right as the Chorus Girls alternated between screams of dismay over the red flecks on their skirts and calls of encouragement to the brawlers.

"They need a good coolin' off," said Nate.

It took a moment to process the suggestion, but then Bertie smiled and signaled to the fairies. They stopped tormenting Oberon and Titania long enough to hear her whispered request. Hooting with laughter, they departed in the direction of the Properties Department.

Bertie turned back to Nate. "If you'll excuse me a moment?"

"Aye." His mouth twitched with the promise of a hearty laugh.

Bertie shoved her way through a set of dueling Dukes to reach the Stage Manager. "I need a scene change," she said without preamble.

Startled, he jumped almost a foot. "I beg your pardon?"

"Did I stutter? I said I need a scene change. Let's try an evening in London." When he didn't answer right away, Bertie tapped her foot once, twice. "Shall I get the headset and do it myself?"

The Stage Manager winced at the suggestion. "No need. I can make things as you like them."

"Oh, I like them. Cue up a nice drizzle, too."

The Stage Manager stomped off into the wings, muttering and waving his arms over his head. Bertie returned to the front of the stage in time to meet the fairies with their brightly colored burden. She accepted the cherry-red umbrella and popped it open mere seconds before cobblestones appeared and the stage clouded with a lovely pea-soup fog.

Nate joined Bertie under her shelter, his broad shoulders protecting her from stray splashes as rain, ice-cold and miserable, began to fall. It dampened the battle-spark of those brawling onstage, and soon the Players fighting in the auditorium turned to gawk.

"Lamplight, please," Bertie called. "And cleanup!"

The gas lamps flickered to life as the rain-doused shivered. The main trapdoor Center Stage opened and water, fake blood, and one of the minor Players sluiced through.

"Disorderly conduct will not be tolerated," Bertie said in a bright, conversational tone. "The Players in *Hamlet* will reconvene at one P.M. for our first rehearsal."

There was coughing and the shuffling of feet, but no one offered any further words of challenge or resistance.

"Nicely done," Nate murmured. "Ye shot right across their bows. Now let's see if they'll heave to."

Bertie nodded to the Stage Manager. "I think we can turn off the rain now."

"Send them on their way, lass," Nate whispered, taking the umbrella, "afore they have a chance t' question ye again."

"You're dismissed," Bertie said with a majestic wave of her hand.

The working lights clicked on as the London scenery flew out. The Players scattered, some pausing by the refreshment table to take a soggy pastry or a cup of watered-down coffee with them. The Stage Manager shooed them away so that he could shove everything into the wings, pausing to give Bertie and her assistants an over-the-shoulder dirty look.

Ophelia followed him, wringing the water out of her clothes while still talking to puppet-Laertes. "I spend far too much time toweling off, dear brother." But the oven mitt didn't answer, as its mouth was full of her skirt.

Which left Bertie onstage with Nate. The fairies.

And Ariel.

CHAPTER TEN

Still Waters

"Haven't ye caused enough misery fer one day?" Nate unsheathed his cutlass and pointed it at Ariel. "I've half a mind t' save us some trouble an' slit yer throat afore ye can do more harm."

"Bring your lapdog to heel, Bertie." The clouds in Ariel's eyes manifested in a wind that tugged at his hair and white silk sleeves. "Perhaps then we can have a civil conversation."

"I don't recall askin' ye fer yer thoughts, ye scurvy bilge-suckin' spirit." Anger vibrated in Nate's chest and emanated outward until even Bertie's timbers were shivered. "Shut yer gob."

"What?" Even Moth, who was fluent in pirate-speak, had trouble with that one.

"Shut your mouth," said Peaseblossom.

"Geez, I was just asking!" Moth said, thoroughly offended.

"Put the sword away, Nate," Bertie said. "Please. We just got the stage cleaned up."

He only lowered the weapon. "Scum-ridden weevil shagger."

"Ooh!" Mustardseed grinned. "I'll have to remember that one!"

"The company you keep, Bertie!" Ariel's wind chased away the last of the London fog. "To think Mrs. Edith considered *me* the bad influence."

Blue tendrils of hair whipped Bertie's face. "What is it you want, Ariel?"

When his only answer was a smile, she reached for the reassuring weight of the scrimshaw. Without calling for a scene change, she stood on a precipice, above an ocean that covered everything in ever-shifting blue currents. Held aloft by all the winds of the world, Ariel reached out his hand to her, enticing her with promises, tempting her with freedom . . .

. . . trying to draw her over the edge. Either he didn't understand what he asked of her, or he didn't care.

He's air and I'm earth. I could try to fly with him, but I'd only fall.

Far below them both, Nate treaded water. He didn't call to her, didn't even beckon, but she knew without asking that he, too, wanted her to jump.

If I fall, the ocean will catch me.

The unbidden thought struck Bertie between the collarbones. She let go of the medallion and stepped back from both cliffs and sea. The ocean's roar faded, as did the winds, until she found solid footing on the wooden boards of the stage. "Get to the point, Ariel."

"I stand before you on my best behavior, Mademoiselle Director," he said with another one of his courtly bows. "I present myself for inspection and place my considerable knowledge and services at your disposal."

"Easier t' slip a dagger between her ribs if yer standin' close, eh?" Nate said.

"Ariel doesn't need anything so common as a dagger," Bertie said with mock solemnity. "His weapons are far more subtle."

"Subterfuge," said Cobweb.

"Artifice," said Moth.

"Lies and tricks and sleight of hand," said Mustardseed.

"Such big words from ones so small." Ariel shrugged lightly, a slight motion under silk. He wore the same immaculate clothes as always, his features were arranged in the same beautiful mask, but with the medallion still warm against her skin, Bertie could see hairline cracks radiate like spiderwebs across his surface. His winds were yet contained, but something had warmed them with hope, something that carried the promise of spring after a harsh, icy winter.

Suddenly, Bertie knew why he tried to charm her with

pretty smiles and words like sugar candy. "You saw things could be changed."

The rest of Ariel's mask splintered under the accusation, permitting his winds to escape in triumph. "Yes. Just as I knew they could be."

"I had nothing to do with Ophelia's unexpected performance," Bertie said. "Take it up with her. Or better yet, try it for yourself. Maybe you can shuffle right off to Buffalo, if you want it badly enough."

"Only when you order the changes do they happen." Words conspired with winds to wrap cloud-tendrils about Bertie's wrists and tow her toward him. "Somehow you're the one that makes it so."

Nate caught Bertie around the waist in the span of two heartbeats—his and hers—as his cutlass came up again. This time, the tip dug into the white skin of Ariel's throat. "Let's see if ye bleed like any other man."

No one moved. Bertie wondered if either Nate or Ariel breathed, so hard were they staring at each other. She put her right hand over Nate's and pushed down until the cutlass swung away. A crimson stain bloomed on Ariel's collar.

Nate smiled. "So ye can."

"Stop it, both of you," Bertie said. "I've had a difficult enough morning without refereeing another brawl. I need a shower and a decent breakfast. Definitely more coffee. And then maybe—just maybe!—I might have the fortitude to deal with you, Ariel. Until then, stay out of my hair."

"Yes, I see you have enough going on in that department." Ariel gave the top of her head a pointed glance. "Are you going to call in the ocean set again or use an actual bathtub?"

"Wouldn't you like to know?" mocked Cobweb.

"Pervert!" yelled Mustardseed.

"None of your business," Bertie said. "Now, I suggest you find something to do with your time that doesn't involve sabotaging my production."

Ariel managed a wounded look, aided by his bloodied throat and deathly pallor. "My dear—"

"She's not yer dear," interrupted Nate. "Sod off."

"Yeah! Sod off!" Moth shook his fist for emphasis.

"Very well." Ariel gathered his winds about him like a cloak and disappeared through a trapdoor.

"He does know how to make a dramatic exit," Mustardseed said. "You have to give him that."

"I don't have t' give him a thing, save a knife through th' ribs." Nate spat on the stage. "Th' son o' a parrot eater."

"Son of a parrot eater," Moth repeated. "Is that bad or good?"

"Buggered if I know!" Cobweb said.

"Oh, no, you don't. We are done being pirates," said Peaseblossom. "We're Assistant Directors now, and Assistant Directors do not bugger anything."

"Fat lot you know," said Mustardseed. "They bugger lots of things! They bugger left and right and every which way in between."

Nate nudged her. "Ye were gettin' a shower."

"Are you implying that I stink?" Bertie turned her nose in the direction of her armpit and sniffed gently. "Phew. Never mind. I do stink."

"We didn't want to say anything," said Moth. "But yes, you're a little ripe."

"So, do you want a shower in the Ladies' Dressing Room or something that will annoy the Stage Manager?" asked Peaseblossom.

Bertie pretended to contemplate her options. "Who wants to join me in a Turkish Bath?"

"I'll get the headset!" Peaseblossom hollered.

Nate frowned. "Won't ye get in trouble fer a scene change?"

"I'm a Director now," Bertie said with a grin as an enormous dome lowered from the flies. "I say it's research."

A large marble pool spiraled up from below-stage. A dozen fountains, each spurting warm water, slid into place along the back wall, which was decorated with an elaborate mosaic.

Nate gazed at the swirling picture rendered in stone, marble, and glass with something akin to awe. "That's th' Greek Chorus. What's it doin' in a Turkish Bath?"

Bertie spared it a glance. "All conquering empires have bathhouses." She kicked off her slippers as the final set decoration, an enormous water clock, landed Downstage Left. "And before you ask, that's Greek, too. Mr. Hastings told me what it was ... a long word ... starts with *c* ..." She snapped her fingers and came up with "Clepsydra."

"A water thief." Nate walked around it to better admire the doors and windows, spinning pointers and dials. "How'd ye remember such a mouthful?"

"I like a big word now and then." With great affection, Bertie reached out to pat the huge, elaborate thing, which already dripped the ancient precursor to *tick-tock*.

"Seems like a lot o' work for a bath," Nate said. "D'ye do this often?"

"No," Bertie said. "The steam is hard on the ceiling murals." On cue, vapor poured in from both sides of the stage.

"Whoo!" yelled Moth. "Time to get naked!"

Nate took a step back. "Er ... perhaps I ought t' be goin' now."

"Don't be ridiculous," said Bertie. "You could probably use a bath, too."

He shook his head. "Pirates don't really bathe."

"Liar. You wash all the time with seawater, and this is more pleasant, I promise." Bertie paused to peer at him. "Are you blushing?"

"No!"

"Yes, you are." Bertie grinned so hard that she stretched muscles in her toes. "Don't be such a prude! I promise not to look."

As Nate hesitated, Mustardseed flew between them, divested of pants and tunic. His tiny, naked butt disappeared into the steam as he cried, "Wheeeee! Balls out!"

"I think that's a rugby reference," Bertie said. "But don't quote me on that."

Nate shifted from one booted foot to the other. "Pirates don't play rugby, an' I don't think—"

"No, you really don't, so I'm not wasting any more time or hot water standing here arguing with you." Bertie turned toward the pool and pulled her shirt off.

"By all th' hells!" Nate ducked his head, presumably to give her some privacy.

Her pajama pants, socks, and underwear followed. "Should I take the scrimshaw off before I get in?"

"'Th' bath isn't filled wi' saltwater, is it?" he muttered, eyes still averted as a flush crawled up the nape of his neck.

"Nope." Bertie pinned her hair atop her head so the dye wouldn't turn the bathwater blue.

"Then leave it on. Ye need all th' protection ye can get right about now."

"If that's true, maybe you oughtn't leave me alone, so

helpless and vulnerable." Bertie slid into the soaking pool. "Anyway, you were going to explain about the necklace and the Sea Witch."

"Th' Sea Goddess, Bertie. Fer all that ye muck about wi' th' *Little Mermaid* set, ye should know about Sedna." There was a sigh, followed by the sound of his cutlass hitting the stage and the slither of linen that signaled he'd started disrobing.

Bertie caught sight of his bare shoulders as the steam shifted Stage Right. She had only a moment to admire them before the mist obscured her view, but that was more than enough to appreciate the fine lines of a nicely put-together man. Wondering if being in close, naked proximity to Nate was such a brilliant idea after all, she cleared her throat and tried to concentrate on innocuous things. "So enlighten me."

"Sedna was a princess once, in love wi' a young man." Two thumps that Bertie presumed were his boots being removed and tossed aside.

"That sounds promising." Bertie forced her muscles to relax as the heat of the water seeped inward.

The surface of the soaking pool shifted when Nate slid in at the other end. "She eloped wi' him, but her father came fer her an' dragged her back. Halfway across th' ocean, he threw her into th' sea."

Bertie flinched, both at the gruesome turn of events

and at the water splashed in her face by the frolicking fairies. "That's worse than King Lear. At least he only disowned Cordelia."

"Ye haven't even heard th' worst o' it," Nate said, his tone grim. "When Sedna held on to th' sides o' th' boat an' begged fer her life, her father chopped her fingers off, one at a time."

"That's revolting!" Mustardseed said, sounding utterly delighted.

Moth swam the backstroke past a barely visible Nate. "Then what happened?"

"Her fingers drifted away through th' water, some becomin' animals, an' others goin' missin'." The pirate sat in silence for a moment. "I used t' dream o' her. Most sailors do. She calls t' us in our sleep; hers is a song filled wi' loneliness an' longin'. She offers us jewels an' gold if only we'll go t' her. Comb her hair. Rub her hands where th' phantom fingers pain her."

Bertie watched the medallion drift through the water, the Théâtre's façade wavering like a naiad's dreams. "You said the scrimshaw was carved from a piece of her bone. How could you tell?"

He shuddered, sending ripples through the pool as though someone had cast a stone into the deep end. "It was like holdin' a shell up t' my ear. Th' sea called t' me through it."

"But how is it supposed to protect me? Because I know you didn't mean it to be just a good-luck charm."

"Sedna learned, in th' hardest o' ways, t' look beyond th' surface o' a man, t' see what hopes an' dreams an' fears lay nestled in his heart o' hearts. There are secrets here, hidin' behind th' lights an' th' playactin'. I want ye t' beware those who are not as they appear." The pool stirred again, and the steam had evaporated just enough for Bertie to make out Nate's silhouette as water sluiced off his shoulders. "I'm not certain a cannon misfire is th' only reason th' Theater Manager wants ye gone."

Bertie knew she should avert her eyes but found she couldn't. "He's giving me a chance to stay. Stop being over-protective!"

"It's not yer job t' give me orders, fer all yer a Director now. I'll do what I can t' keep ye safe."

"Why?" Bertie persisted.

"None o' yer business, missy."

"Don't you 'missy' me. You're barely old enough to grow a decent set of whiskers."

Nate made a rude noise. "If yer goin' t' be insultin', I'm fer shore."

Bertie made a point of squinting at his chest. "That's an interesting tattoo."

Nate slid into the water up to his chin as a familiar voice said, "I'm sorry, I thought I heard the water running."

"Ophelia." Bertie didn't have time for her silly drowning

habit right now. "Would you excuse us? We're trying to have an important discussion."

"In the bathtub?" Ophelia asked. "Without any clothes on, and without a chaperone?"

"I do my best thinking in the tub," said Bertie. "And you sound like Mrs. Edith when you nag."

Ophelia looked at Nate, who had his gaze firmly fixed upon the water's surface, and back to Bertie before she sat to dangle her bare feet in the bath. "Isn't this pleasant?"

Bertie glowered at her, willing the water-maiden to either leave or explode. "It *was*."

"You needn't glare at me so," Ophelia said. "I came to tell you something important."

The clepsydra counted off several seconds while Bertie and Nate waited in polite silence for her to continue, but Ophelia only smiled dreamily.

"What was it you wanted to tell me?" Bertie prompted.

Ophelia started a bit, as though the question had jolted her back into her corporeal form. "Oh, that! Yes. I wanted to warn you about Ariel."

Bertie stiffened. "What's he done now?"

"It's not what he's done," Ophelia said, "but what he could do."

Again Bertie waited for an explanation that was not forthcoming. She would have shaken Ophelia, were it not for Nate's presence and her own lack of clothes. "What could he do?"

The water-maiden looked left, then right, as though to reassure herself that no one could hear her piercing stage whisper. "He could escape."

Despite the temperature of the water, Bertie went cold. "What did you say?"

"Hm?" Ophelia lifted her foot; distracted by her dripping toes, she didn't answer.

Peaseblossom landed on Bertie's shoulder. "The idea's ridiculous."

"Ridiculous in the best possible way!" Moth said with a snicker. "Can you picture him tunneling out with a spoon?"

"Bedsheet ladder out the window!" said Cobweb.

Ophelia frowned. "I don't know about spoons and sheets, but if he tears his entrance page out of The Book, he'll be able to leave the Théâtre."

Bertie stared at Ophelia through air so thick with water vapor and revelations that it hurt her lungs. The fairies choked on mouthfuls of bathwater.

"Good golly!" Mustardseed sputtered when he was finally able to breath again. The others echoed his sentiments while Nate swore under his breath.

"Ophelia?" Bertie said.

"Yes?"

"Whatever would give you that idea? That someone could tear a page out of The Book?"

"Oh, that's not important," Ophelia said with a graceful wave of her hand.

"It's important to me."

The other girl smiled. "Because I did it once."

Ariel wasn't the one who escaped. It was Ophelia. "You ripped The Book?"

"I pulled out my page. The one I make my first entrance on." Ophelia shook her head as though clearing it of spiderwebs. "Then I saw the Exit sign." Her eyes flicked toward the neon-green light at the back of the auditorium. "I'd never noticed it before."

Bertie was afraid to ask, but she had to know. "Then what did you do?"

"I waited for a quiet moment," Ophelia said, wiggling her fingers, "and I slipped out."

"You went through the door."

"Yes."

"Into the lobby?"

"Yes."

"And then?"

"Out a revolving door."

Bertie swallowed. "You left the theater?"

"Yes."

An errant draft stirred the moist air, chasing most of the

steam into the flies. Bertie glanced at Nate, who looked as shocked as she felt.

"I didn't think it possible!" he said.

"Anyway, I just thought I should warn you." Ophelia stood, smoothed her skirts, and departed without explanation or apology, leaving perfect wet footprints in her wake.

All the words Bertie wanted to say stuck in her throat, like the bits of mosaic decorating the back wall. She thought the members of the Greek Chorus shifted to leer at her.

"Bertie—" Peaseblossom tugged at her ear.

"Shut up, Pease." Bertie had a million and one questions to ask, and none of them good.

"But, Bertie—"

"I mean it!"

"It's just—"

"Beatrice Shakespeare Smith!" Mrs. Edith strode onstage holding a plush bathrobe in one hand and a towel in the other. Her mouth was pinched together so tightly with displeasure that she looked as though she'd been sucking lemons. "The Stage Manager came to tell me you were bathing, so I thought I'd bring you these. And this is what I find!"

"It's not anything, really." Bertie reached for the robe, but her arm wasn't quite long enough.

"Then why are you sitting here *naked* and in the company of a *pirate?*"

"He was dirty, and I didn't see how it could hurt."

"Of course you didn't, because you never think these things through." Mrs. Edith draped the robe around Bertie's shoulders and heaved her out of the soaking pool with surprising strength. "When are you going to realize that you're not a child anymore? There are those who would take advantage of you—"

"Now, see here," Nate protested. "We weren't doin' anythin' improper."

Mrs. Edith pointed a bony finger at him. "You hold your tongue this second. I shall speak to the Theater Manager about this, you defiler of innocents."

"I defiled nothin'!" Nate jumped out of the pool and strode toward them. Mrs. Edith shrieked and clapped her hands over Bertie's eyes.

Bertie twisted away from the Wardrobe Mistress, glimpsing the full extent of what had so shocked her. Nate suddenly reconsidered his advance, turning and sprinting to his clothes. The water spangling his legs made it difficult for him to pull on his trousers, but he managed it. Bundling up the rest of his things, he nearly impaled himself on his cutlass, twisting it aside only just in time.

"Be careful, Nate!" Moth said. "You don't want to lop off anything vital!"

Red with more than just the heat of the water, Nate

strode past them with a muttered, "I'll come find ye later, Bertie."

Bertie turned a pleading gaze upon Mrs. Edith. "I know you're mad, but I need to speak to the Theater Manager. It's about something very important—"

"Out of the question," the Wardrobe Mistress said as she gathered Bertie's dirty clothes. "You are going to stay in your room, young lady, until your rehearsal. If you set so much as a toe off this stage, I'll know about it, and if I have to leave the Wardrobe Department a second time, there will be precious little chance of your costumes being completed before Friday. Am I making myself clear?"

Bertie nodded. "Yes, ma'am."

The formidable lady bustled offstage, muttering, "What in heaven's name has gotten into you?"

What has gotten into me? Fear, maybe? A whiff of life outside the theater, brought in by a wayward girl too crazy to know her own mind?

The Turkish Bath set disappeared whence it had come, and Bertie's bedroom took its place. Her gaze drifted to the far corner of Stage Left, just in front of the proscenium arch, where The Book glowed with serene and even light. The fairies at her heels, she crept to the pedestal.

"D'you suppose it's booby-trapped?" Moth asked.

"Trip wires," Mustardseed guessed, surveying it with a clinical eye.

"Laser-triggered alarm system," Cobweb ventured.

Bertie reached out one shaking hand and touched a fingertip to The Book, fully expecting red-lit alarums and perhaps guards armed with spears to descend from the rafters. But nothing happened to stop her, so she lifted The Book and hugged it against her chest, feeling very scared indeed.

CHAPTER ELEVEN

Chaos Is
Come Again

You need to disguise The Book if you're going to keep it with you," said Peaseblossom. "If the Players notice it's gone, they'll raise a ruckus."

"Right after the rehearsal, I'll give it to the Theater Manager for safekeeping." Bertie rummaged in her desk drawer until she found a piece of discarded silk. After a few minutes of cutting and folding, The Book's rich leather binding was obscured by fabric.

"Is that enough of a disguise?" asked Moth.

"It'll have to be." Bertie bypassed the black slacks and button-down shirt she'd intended for that morning's rehearsal, reaching instead for her jeans. "If I leave the stage now, Mrs. Edith will have a fit, and if she has a fit, that's just time taken away from her finishing the alterations on the *Hamlet* costumes."

"Are you really going to wear that ratty old thing?" Peaseblossom asked.

Bertie looked down at the shirt in her hand. It was one of Nate's cast-offs, the creamy cotton so soft, it was practically a security blanket. "I am."

"You don't want something more professional?" the fairy suggested.

"The last time I wanted to look professional, I ended up in a corset," Bertie said.

"What are we going to do about lunch?" Moth whined. "I'm famished!"

Cobweb sucked in his tiny gut. "I'm wasting away for want of cake!"

"We might not be able to get to the Green Room," Bertie said, marching over to the headset, "but I think I can manage some refreshments."

A French Patisserie landed Center Stage, all gleaming wood and sparkling glass. The fairies followed her inside with screams of delight, lured by the intoxicating scents of buttery pastry and caffè lattes. Bertie lolled against the marble counter and admired the copper behemoth of an espresso machine.

"Can I help you?" One of the Chorus Girls bustled in, wearing a candy-striped shirtwaist and a frilled apron.

Bertie looked from the tarts decorated with whirls of sliced apple to the croissants oozing chocolate from their middles. "Mr. Hastings outdid himself with this lot."

"Pick something with whipped cream," Moth prompted.

"Something that will explode when you take the first bite," advised Mustardseed.

"Explode and scatter crumbs," said Cobweb with his nose pressed to the glass case. "The crumbly ones are the best."

Bertie eyed thick sandwiches constructed on baguettes. "Maybe something without sugar?" The fairies jeered, but she was undeterred. "I'll have one with ham and cheese."

The girl rolled Bertie's sandwich in white paper, then used squares of tissue to arrange pastries in a pink box. After she tied strings around everything, she measured out freshly ground coffee and steamed milk to produce a cappuccino so exquisite, it brought tears of gratitude to Bertie's eyes.

"Thank you!" Bertie managed to gather up the sandwich, the string-wrapped box, and her brown paper coffee cup while still holding The Book under one arm.

Outside the Patisserie, the Players passed by in grand Parisian style: on bicycles, with much elaborate cursing and bell ringing. Bertie dodged the traffic, skipped down the stairs, and settled into a plush red-upholstered seat Fifth Row, Center.

The fairies rushed to keep up, apparently convinced she

was going to horde the bounty. Bertie took an extra moment to shove the silk-wrapped Book under her chair, and Moth groaned.

"Get to the food already!"

Bertie held the box up. "You want this?"

"Yes!"

"You sure?"

"YES!"

Bertie laughed and yanked at the twine. The fairies danced a jig on the armrests and pinched each other at the prospect of sugar. She left them to it, interspersing bites of her sandwich with appreciative sips of coffee before claiming a tartlet filled with lemon curd.

By the time the Stage Manager arrived at a quarter to one, Bertie and her comrades were already licking the last smears of dark chocolate off their fingers. The only evidence of their lunch was a trail of crumbs and the lingering scents of fresh bread and cigarette smoke, as Bertie had long since banished the Patisserie set.

"Good afternoon." He gave her a barely civil inclination of the head.

"Yes, it is," Bertie replied, toasting him with what was left of her cappuccino.

He glared at her with suspicion and held up his headset. "Have you been mucking about with this?"

Bertie widened her eyes as far as they would go. "I'm

here in a professional capacity this afternoon. You would do well to remember that."

The Stage Manager clapped his headset on and disappeared into the wings with a muttered, "Argh!"

The fairies giggled, and Bertie drank the last of her coffee just as another appeared over her left shoulder.

"I thought ye might need this." Nate took a hesitant sip from his own cup and grimaced.

Bertie accepted the cup and peered into it. "Is this from the Green Room?"

"Aye. Bilgewater 'tis today."

"Will it put hair on her chest?" asked Moth.

"Yuck! Girls shouldn't have hair on their chests!" said Cobweb.

"Hey, Nate!" Mustardseed popped his head up over the chair back. "We saved you a lemon tart!"

"Did ye, ye wee beastie?" Nate settled into the seat behind Bertie. "That must have taken tremendous restraint."

"It did!" Cobweb agreed with a wag of his head as the other boys pushed the nearly empty pink box under the seats.

Nate leaned forward to snag the piece of pastry before one of them stepped in it. "My thanks."

"Sorry about what Mrs. Edith said to you." Bertie sipped the coffee and confirmed it tasted as awful as it smelled. "That whole 'defiler of innocents' line was a bit much."

" 'Tis all right. I can't blame her, considerin' what it must have looked like." Nate concentrated very hard on his dessert. Bertie finished her bilgewater, not knowing what else to say as the Players trickled in, singly or in groups of two or three. Gertrude arrived with her entourage, which included minor characters from other productions.

"This is a closed rehearsal," Bertie said, jumping up from her seat and hurrying onstage. "You weren't called."

"But we want to see the changes."

"Like when Ophelia forgot her lines—"

"It isn't fair to keep us away!"

"No, no, no, no." Bertie herded them to the stage door. "Out. All of you."

"Excuse me, Mesdemoiselles." Mr. Hastings sidled through the clucking women, burdened with an assortment of Egyptian antiquities.

"What are you doing here?" Bertie closed the door firmly behind him, despite the protests of the banished.

"The Theater Manager thought you ought to have some properties to set the mood, and you did ask for asps."

Bertie looked over the dangerous assortment of daggers, vials of poison, and a basket that hissed a warning. "Plastic snakes, right?"

"Of course." Mr. Hastings adjusted his spectacles.

"Where do you want the pyramids?" Mr. Tibbs arrived, sneaking covert glances at Mr. Hastings' contributions.

Bertie blinked. "How many are there?"

"Three," he said, scattering ash on the stage.

"Arrange them as you see fit," Bertie said. "I trust your judgment implicitly."

"Is that so?" Mr. Tibbs shifted his cigar around his mouth, trying not to look pleased and failing. He stomped off past a distracted Ophelia, who wandered in the wings near Mrs. Edith. The Wardrobe Mistress appeared to be wrestling the sheet off the Ghost of Hamlet's Father.

Bertie turned to Peaseblossom. "What's Mrs. Edith doing?"

"She said she needs that sheet. Something about using it for a template to make his new costume."

The first of the pyramids landed Center Stage as the Danish Prince slouched in, eyes deceptively lazy.

"So glad you could join us," Bertie said. "I hope the call didn't inconvenience you."

Hamlet leaned against the flat and took a long drag off a cigarette. "Not at all."

"Put that out," Bertie said, though she longed to join him. "We have rules about smoking in the theater."

Hamlet rearranged his beautiful mouth into a scowl, dropped the cigarette, and ground it out. "Better?"

"Nearly. Now pick up your litter and put it where it belongs," Bertie said.

Hamlet gaped at her. "That's the Stage Manager's job!"

"If I see you make the mess, you get to clean up after yourself like a good little boy."

They glared at each other for a moment, and Bertie wondered if Nate would have had something to say if his mouth hadn't been full of lemon tart. In the end, the prince shrugged, picked the butt off the floor, and flicked it into a nearby wastebasket.

"There," said Bertie with an insincere smile. "That wasn't so hard, was it?" She turned to the rest of the assembled Players. "And let me take the opportunity to announce that henceforth, latecomers will be replaced by their understudies."

There was a collective intake of breath from the principals while every member of the Gentlemen's and Ladies' Choruses straightened.

"Can that even be done?" Peaseblossom whispered to Bertie.

"It's just a threat," Hamlet said.

"Try me." Bertie returned his cold stare, frost for frost. "Now, if I could have everyone sit down."

With impressive silence, the Players took their seats around the stage. Gertrude arranged the skirts of her practice costume. Polonius lingered next to the curtains. The Ghost of Hamlet's Father sulked near the edge of the center pyramid.

"Mrs. Edith couldn't have found a less distracting substitute than a pink sheet with flowers on it?" Bertie demanded of the fairies.

"I guess not," said Moth between hiccups of laughter.

Bertie watched the Ghost bump repeatedly into the wooden flat. "It's really screwing with his head."

"He'll get over it," Cobweb said.

"Let's hope so." Bertie moved to the front of the stage and raised her voice. "This afternoon, I'd like to start by explaining the changes we'll be making to our production. We've set the stage to help you envision Ancient Egypt."

"I thought something was foul in the state of Denmark," someone protested.

"Yes, but we're restaging it," said Bertie.

"Are we changing the lines?" came from the back of the room.

"We don't have to change the words to change the play," Bertie said. "We'll say Denmark, but the audience will know we mean Egypt. The Scenic and Properties departments will set the stage in shades of gold and lapis. Mrs. Edith will have Hamlet dressed as a young pharaoh."

Everyone nodded and murmured things like "I suppose so" and "I hope this works."

Coffee sloshed about in Bertie's middle, and she did her best not to think about the large quantity of baguette and whipped pastry cream she'd just snarfed down. "I also thought it would be interesting to reinterpret the poison theme. Asps are appropriate for the setting—"

"Snakes?!" That was a horrified Gertrude.

Bertie faltered. "Yes, snakes."

Gertrude shivered as though something had already wriggled up her stocking. "I don't work with reptiles."

Hamlet stopped leaning on the pyramid he'd been holding up since his dressing-down. "But think of the impact you could have, using live ones! Imagine Mother Dearest as a reincarnation of Cleopatra, with an asp clasped to her breast."

"Leave my breasts out of it, you little degenerate!" Gertrude threw her cup at him.

He dodged remarkably fast for a melancholy introvert. Most of the coffee ended up on Polonius, who shrieked and attempted to dry himself on the curtains.

"Let's just fetch out one of the dear creatures." Hamlet peeked into the basket and grinned. A premonition of doom slid through Bertie, but before she could stop him, the prince dumped out the slithering contents of the basket, and a dozen glittering, very-much-alive asps wiggled free.

Gertrude screamed and jumped onto her chair as the rest of the cast scattered to the outermost edges of the stage.

Bertie hopped from one foot to the other, trying to make sense of it. "Someone call a Snake Charmer!"

"Help!" Gertrude shrieked. "Murder! Sabotage!"

Yes, sabotage. Probably by Ariel's hand.

Bertie caught sight of the Stage Manager smirking into his headset.

Except it's not just Ariel who wants to see me fail. I have more enemies than Hamlet himself.

"A little help, if ye please!" Nate had leapt onstage to grab snakes and shove them back into the basket.

Bertie flapped at her sleeves until they covered her hands—hardly protection against a venomous bite, but it was better than nothing. She grabbed an asp by the tail and flung it at him, doing her best not to shriek.

"Well done!" Moth yelled, flying past her to help.

"Don't touch them," Bertie said, catching hold of two more and feeling her skin prickle all over as she dropped them in the basket. "I don't want any of you getting bitten."

Nate returned with a wiggling handful.

"Bertie!" Peaseblossom cried, pointing at the side door. "The Players are running away!"

Bertie raised her voice to a shout. "Everyone is going to take their places for Act One, Scene One, this instant!"

"What about the snakes?" Gertrude demanded, poised to make a grand exit. Her Ladies-in-Waiting agreed with clucks and murmurs of equal parts sympathy and vitriol.

"We got them," Nate announced as he clapped the lid back on the basket. "Every last one."

"We haven't any time to waste," Bertie said, standing on tiptoe to make her entreaty. "We need to make it through the play at least once this afternoon!"

Amidst grumbles and confusion, everyone moved into position while keeping a careful watch on the floor. Bertie went out into the auditorium and took a seat, signaling to Francisco and Bernardo.

The latter clomped over to stand in front of the center pyramid. "Who's there?"

The Ghost of Hamlet's Father shoved past him. "Whooooooooo!" He circled the astounded sentries with his costume flapping.

"That's not the cue for your entrance," Bertie said, addressing the pink-flowered sheet. "Excuse me! Stop that immediately."

He continued to flap around the stage like an enormous, psychotic bird. "Whoop, whoop, whooooo!"

"I think the costume change might have broken his head," Bertie said. "Can I get some help, please?"

Marcellus and Horatio joined Bernardo and Francisco. The four of them chased the Ghost around the pyramids and into the orchestra pit.

"Your cue," Bertie yelled over the din of overturned instruments and creative cursing, "is 'the bell then beating one.' Get backstage, and change out of that ridiculous thing."

The Ghost obediently ripped off his sheet with a flourish. Gertrude put a hand to her forehead and swooned against the nearest Lady-in-Waiting.

"Oh, please!" said Claudius. "You were married to him!"

Gertrude stopped overdramatizing long enough to glare at him. "So?"

"So, unless Hamlet was an immaculate conception, there's nothing going on there that you haven't seen before. Stop playing the dewy-eyed virgin." Claudius jabbed a finger in Ophelia's direction. "That's her job!"

"If you like her so much, why don't you marry her?"

"Maybe I will!" Claudius took Ophelia by the hand and began to kiss his way up her arm.

"Let me go!" Ophelia struggled, but she was no match for the portly king.

"Cad! Philanderer!" Gertrude closed her fan and hit Claudius with it.

"Hellcat!" he yelped even as an angry, red welt bloomed on his cheek.

Gertrude swung at Claudius again. When he turned to run, he collided with the naked Ghost, and the two men went down in a tangle of limbs.

"Line!" Hamlet yelled. "For mercy's sake, someone give me the line!"

Bertie watched with growing horror as the brawl expanded to include most of the Ladies-in-Waiting and Rosencrantz. Guildenstern abandoned the fray to lick all the swords in sight, testing for poison. Someone in the very back row of the auditorium snickered.

Bertie turned to see who would make such a noise and spotted Lady Macbeth. "This is a closed rehearsal! Get out!"

"Interloper!" Gertrude bellowed as she charged down the stairs after her rival.

Lady Macbeth shrieked and leapt for the aisle. Bertie managed to grab Gertrude by her sash, thwarting the attack.

"Unhand me this instant!" Gertrude turned to kick at Bertie through a swirl of satin petticoats and bad temper.

Retreating from the assault, Bertie stumbled, fell, and cracked her head on a wooden armrest. Two Gertrudes stuck their fans in Bertie's face.

"I hold you personally responsible for this anarchy," they screeched.

"Me? You hold me responsible, you stupid old *sow?*" Bertie clutched at her head and tried to clear her vision. "Get out, or I'll kick your sorry ass myself!"

"How dare you?" Gertrude puffed up to twice her already considerable size and thrust out her chin. "I will speak to the Management about your ineptitude this very second."

"You do that!"

The fairies converged on Bertie as she struggled to her feet. There were eight of them, then twelve.

That is, she thought, *twelve too many.*

Bertie put a hand to the back of her head. Pain lanced in one eye and out the other. Her hand came away smeared with red. "I probably have a concussion."

"Let me have a look, lass." Nate reached for her.

Bertie peered up at him through a haze of pain and tears. "Just stay away from me, all of you. I've had enough help for one day." She stumbled to her seat and pulled The Book out of its hiding place. "Clear the stage!"

No one tried to stop her as she fled into the corridor. The door hissed shut behind her, and hot tears pricked her eyes.

How long do I have before the Theater Manager kicks me out?

Bertie swallowed a sob, tightened her arms around The Book, and limped in the direction of the Properties Department.

CHAPTER TWELVE

Legato and Staccato

The Properties Department was unoccupied when Bertie arrived. Dropping to her knees, she shoved The Book under Marie Antoinette's chaise and muffled its golden glow with one of the pillows. Resting her forehead against the sofa cushions, she wanted to cry until there was nothing left, but tears were saltwater.

And an impromptu appearance by a pissed-off deity is the last thing I need right now!

The door behind her opened, and Mr. Hastings entered, squinting at a piece of his ever-present paperwork.

Bertie stood up so that he wouldn't catch her kneeling on the floor and ask what she was doing. "Hey, Mr. Hastings."

He adjusted his spectacles. "How did the rehearsal go?"

Bertie stared very, very hard at his stapler and refused to blink, refused to let the tears fall.

Except it wasn't working.

She reached up, closed her hand around the medallion, broke the chain with one swift jerk, and slid the necklace in her pocket as the first tear slid down her cheek. "Not well. I expect the Theater Manager will be here any second to throw me out."

Her nose was running now. Bertie went to swipe at it with her sleeve, but Mr. Hastings stopped her with a look and held out his voluminous white handkerchief.

"What happened?" he demanded.

Before Bertie finished explaining, the Properties Manager's shoulders shook with laughter that was silent at first, then a bit rusty, like he'd stored his sense of humor between the oxidized metal birdbaths and boxes of discarded iron finials.

"My dear, I am so sorry about the mix-up with the snakes! But do you honestly think you're the first member of Management to have difficulty with the Company?" He turned to put the kettle on the electric burner and reached for a tin of biscuits. "Every one of them, at one point or another, has ended up right where you're sitting."

Bertie picked through the biscuit tin until she found one dipped in chocolate. "Probably not the Stage Manager."

"Oh, yes." Mr. Hastings spooned tea into the chipped ceramic pot. "Even him."

"What about the Theater Manager?"

"Didn't start off as the Theater Manager. He wanted to write a grand opera."

That surprised a small laugh out of Bertie. "Really?" She paused to think about him as a playwright, and the quill-tickle returned.

"Wrangling this lot took all his time and effort, so he gave it up," Mr. Hastings said. "You'll try again, and you'll do better each time, I promise you."

"Uh-huh." Bertie shoved the entire biscuit into her mouth and poked between its plain butter brethren for another. "I had my audition, and I'm not getting a callback."

"What do you mean by that, my dear?" He reached for the cups.

Bertie chewed and swallowed first, because Mr. Hastings didn't appreciate it when she spewed crumbs on his desk. "It means I blew my chance at staying."

"You're a bit young to be so very cynical," Mr. Hastings observed.

"Mrs. Edith said the same thing to me yesterday," Bertie said with a lopsided shrug. "But I'm older than Juliet, and she was plenty cynical by the end of that mess."

Mr. Hastings winced. "Touché." He pushed a teacup at

her. "Drink up. It won't restore your soul, but it might settle your thoughts."

"Can you put some pirate rum in it?"

"I find myself fresh out," he said. "But would you care for a bit of unsolicited advice instead?"

She sighed and wrinkled her nose. "That depends. Is it the kind of advice that has me pulling myself up by the bootstraps and slogging my way to school barefoot in the snow, uphill, both ways?"

"Not quite." Mr. Hastings added a bit of lemon to his tea. He carefully stirred three times counterclockwise and ran the edge of his spoon along the thin porcelain rim of the cup. "It's more along the lines of badinage and persiflage."

"Persi-what?"

"Banter, my dear. You're exceptionally skilled at wheedling people into doing things they wouldn't normally do." He held up a hand to silence her when she began to protest. "Please don't argue. We both know it to be true."

"And if it is?" Bertie shoved another biscuit into her mouth and chewed viciously.

"Play to your strengths. Become the person you need to be. Put your Players at ease and persuade them to dance down the path of your choosing. The trick is to let the sheep think they are herding themselves."

"Sheep, eh?" Bertie said. "Has Gertrude heard you compare her to a farm animal?"

"Goodness, no," Mr. Hastings chortled. "Otherwise I wouldn't be alive to tell the tale."

"Badinage," said Bertie.

"And persiflage," Mr. Hastings finished for her.

"That's if anyone bothers to show up to the next rehearsal," she said.

"They'll be there. They're too curious to miss it." He reached over to the vintage stereo cabinet and dropped the needle on a thick, vinyl record. Instantly, the room filled with the guitar-song and castanets of a tango.

"Why, Mr. Hastings," Bertie teased. "I never would have figured you for an aficionado of the Latin dances. Shall I put a rose between my teeth?"

"I think you have more important matters to attend to at the moment."

Bertie sighed into her tea, not at all convinced that she could direct the next rehearsal or that there would even be another rehearsal once Management heard Gertrude's thoughts on the matter.

"I hate to ask," Mr. Hastings said, "but about the asps?"

"We got them all back in the basket."

"I should fetch them and examine the container. It must have been mislabeled. If you'll excuse me for a moment?"

Bertie nodded, finishing her tea and three more chocolate-covered biscuits as she mulled over his advice.

Become the person you need to be.

Mr. Hastings could well dispense such wisdom, but transformation wasn't as simple as sipping from Alice's "Drink Me" bottle.

Unless it is just that simple.

Before she could second-guess the idea, Bertie was out of her chair and running full tilt for Shelf 49B. There were the hookahs, in all their jewel-toned glory; one shelf up and over sat a faceted crystal bottle, etched with the infamous command.

Bertie wrapped her fingers about it and pulled the stopper out. The gently sloshing contents smelled of fruit and candy, coffee and mint, and something else, under all that, something sweet and dark and flower-filled.

Alice needed to be short to get through the tiny door.

Bertie caught her distorted reflection in the green glass surface of the Caterpillar's hookah.

And I need to become the sort of person who can command my cast. A person the Theater Manager thinks of as invaluable.

"Bottoms up." Sparing a second to pray she wouldn't shrink to the size of a dormouse, Bertie took the tiniest of sips.

And waited. In the distance, she could hear the record player lift its arm and lower the needle back at the beginning of the song. She didn't feel different, and judging by the metal shelving, she hadn't lost any height, either.

Maybe one more sip.

"I thought I might find you here," said a voice behind her.

Bertie choked. Tears streamed from her eyes as she twisted about, hiding the bottle behind her back. "What do you want, Ariel? Come to gloat?"

"Do you mind if I join you?"

"Actually, I do. I'd like three seconds to myself without noise, chaos, or crisis." *And you're all three.*

"That's hardly welcoming." Ariel treated her to one of his beautiful smiles.

"That's because it wasn't an invitation." Bertie put her nose in the air and tried to look down at him at the same time. "Besides which, Mr. Hastings will be back any second. He doesn't like you to be in here, you'll remember."

"Ah, there I am in luck. Mr. Tibbs has absconded with the asps, and it will take Mr. Hastings at least half an hour to get them back." Ariel's gaze drifted along Bertie's collarbones, over her shoulder, down her arm.

"On what planet would a basket of asps be considered a set piece and not a prop?" Bertie wondered if Ariel could, as his expression intimated, see right through flesh and blood to the forbidden bottle in her hand.

"I think he plans to hold them hostage until Mr. Hastings relinquishes that large armoire in the corner." Ariel reached behind Bertie, his fingers closing over hers. For a moment, he simply looked down at her. "What do we have here?"

"Nothing." She twitched, but he didn't let go.

"Let me have a look."

Fairly certain she wasn't shrinking, Bertie nonetheless felt a bit odd as Ariel removed the bottle from her grasp and lifted it to his nose.

I'm probably concussed from bashing my head on that auditorium seat.

"Did you already partake of some of this?" he asked.

"I did," Bertie said, refusing to sound either guilty for the transgression or scared by the coinciding flare of heat in her stomach. Her sudden, violent hiccup startled them both, and as the echo ricocheted off the farthest reaches of the room, Bertie laughed. "It's sweeter than I thought it would be."

Ariel tasted it and handed the bottle back. "It will change you."

"Exactly what I'm hoping for." Bertie took another sip. "No need to make it sound all dangerous and forbidden."

"I suppose Mr. Hastings has far more dangerous items tucked away in here," Ariel conceded. "Samurai swords and fusion bombs and silly teenagers."

"Did you come looking for me just to call me names?" Bertie dangled the bottle at him in an unspoken dare.

"It wasn't my only reason." He hesitated for half a second before taking it.

Bertie tried not to fixate on his mouth, but as he drank, the muscles in his throat worked, and from his throat, it was only a hop, skip, and a jump to the muscles of his chest. . . .

The record's single tune started again at the front of the room.

Ariel replaced the stopper and put the bottle back on the shelf. "I think that's enough for now."

Bertie concentrated on the music. "Methinks that's an accordion."

He tilted his head. "It's a bandoneón, which is like an accordion, but with more allure."

"How very European." Insistent piano trills tempted her feet. Guitar-song chased the wheezing notes of the bandoneón down the aisles in waves, and she followed them on tiptoe.

"Where are you going?" Ariel asked.

Bertie looked at him over her shoulder, noting the danger in every languid line of his body. For a moment, she thought she might indeed be tiny Alice, her sanity and reason shrinking down, down, down until they disappeared with a puff of hookah smoke. "I'm a caterpillar turning into a butterfly. Care to join me?"

A moment passed in which she thought he'd refuse, then—

"How could I resist such an invitation?"

"Glad to hear it," Bertie said with an unintentional sway. She righted herself even as Ariel's arms appeared around her. Her right hand sought out his left, and she wrapped her other arm around his neck.

"Just what," he asked, "do you think you're doing now?"

Bertie tossed her hair so that it flicked him in the face

before falling over her shoulders in a messy blue tangle. "Dancing with you, unless I'm much mistaken."

"I think it's customary for the man to lead," he said. The only thing that moved was his left eyebrow, which slid up about an inch.

"How did I know you would say that?" Skilled fingers strummed the unseen strings of a guitar. Castanets beckoned, and Bertie wanted to snap her fingers, stomp her feet, clap her hands. "Lead on, pretty boy."

Ariel gave her a look that contained a lot of something, but he didn't say a word. Instead, he adjusted her arms with light touches of his hands, all the while keeping his upper body pressed to hers.

"This song comes from the center," he said. "So we'll move the center first."

"The center of what?" The butterflies drifted out of his hair as he leaned over her. They fluttered through Bertie's already swimming head, brushed over something dark and sleeping, and roused it from slumber.

Ariel tapped her lightly on the small of her back. "The center of you."

"My cream filling?" she suggested.

There was a moment of complete stillness and silent contemplation before Ariel smiled. "Yes, Bertie. Move your cream filling first, and your feet will follow."

When the music started again, they joined it with gliding steps and the sensation of being carried along. By the notes. By the wind. She was flying—

With Ariel.

For the first few bars, their movements were inseparable from the melody. Then Ariel placed his foot alongside hers and twisted. The world spun around Bertie. The shelves wavered with the vibrato before disappearing.

She would have blamed his words, his voice for the enchantment, except he was—for once—not speaking.

Ariel snapped her out of the dip and twirled her away from him. Bertie trailed her hand over an ancient wall that should have been protected by shelves. Plaster dust flaked away under her fingertips.

Catching her by the wrist, Ariel led her down an aisle that was now a narrow Spanish alley. They skimmed over cobblestones and under wrought-iron balconies. Bertie didn't remember a costume change, but her black-heeled character shoes fashioned a rhythm that ran counterpoint to a double bass. Crimson skirts flared around her legs and slapped against her skin after an unexpected and spectacular turn.

Ariel wore black silk now. The minuscule portion of Bertie's brain that still functioned noted that, on Nate, the outfit would have looked ridiculous, but on Ariel it was liquid night poured over lean muscle.

She missed a step, contemplating his arms.

"Do try to keep up, Beatrice." Ariel steadied her with one hand as he reached out with the other to pluck a rose from an unseen vine.

"If you put that between your teeth, I'll die laughing," she warned.

So he didn't. Instead, he used it to trace the contour of her cheek, the curve of her neck, and down to the spot where the dress dipped low between her breasts. An azure glow slowly washed over the scenery while a red-gelled spotlight beckoned.

"How did we get here?"

"We haven't left the Properties Department." Ariel took her hand. Her heartbeat matched the thrum of blood in his veins, and his midnight eyes followed her every movement. "What you see are but figments of your overactive imagination."

Bertie instinctively reached for the medallion, but her neck was bare, exposed, the scrimshaw in the pocket of her jeans, which were also long gone. "You're toying with me."

"I assure you, I'm not," Ariel said, leading her in another turn, another dip.

Someone in the lighting booth decided to scatter the scene with white pinpricks of starlight that floated like sequins on strings.

"That effect," Bertie said, bent completely backward, "is

achieved with a mirrored ball and pin spots. I hope you appreciate it."

Ariel's breath met her skin. Bertie raised her head to find his nose level with her cleavage.

"Believe me," he said. "I do."

He tucked the rose behind her ear and trailed his hand around the back of her neck. Then she was upright once more, with both arms above her head. Fountain spray drifted over them, dampening Bertie's skirts and spangling her hair with blue-diamond brilliants.

Ariel circled her. His hand skimmed her collarbones, her bare shoulder, her back. He paused behind her, drew her close so that his lips grazed her ear. "Are you ready for the finale?"

Bertie barely nodded before he led her in a series of turns that left her disoriented and dizzy. The stage lights whirled around them, every point of reference blurring into a shifting kaleidoscope of color. The world fell away until the only thing that remained was his hands upon her. He dipped her back farther—

"Ariel." Bertie closed her eyes and let herself fall.

He caught her, and as the music reached a crescendo, he covered her mouth with his.

Her first real kiss. Then her second, and third. She lost track of how many there were; she was too busy drinking him in, winding her tongue around his. He tasted of everything and nothing at all as he lowered her onto the grass.

The lights dimmed until only a soft golden glow drifted over their skin. Crimson faded back to denim blue, black silk to white.

The rose remained, as did his weight upon her.

The record player reached the end of the song one last time. The paper speaker hummed and crackled with the absence of music. Then there was a soft click and silence.

Bertie drifted into the blackout with Ariel's name on her lips.

CHAPTER THIRTEEN

Suspicions and Superstitions

ertie?"

She curled into a ball and tried to pull the covers over her head, but there weren't any blankets within reach. A tiny hand touched her shoulder.

"She's sleeping, but she smells funny."

Bertie's nerves jangled, her skin crawled, and her eyeballs felt three times too large for their sockets. When she tried to lift her arm, every joint creaked in protest.

Strong hands stood her upright and held her there as someone sniffed at her mouth. "She's been drinkin' somethin'."

The low whir of wings flapping near her ear. "No fair! She didn't share!"

"We weren't here, stupid."

Their voices. So shrill.

"What time is it?" Bertie tried to swallow the fuzz on her tongue, wished for a glass of water, and gagged.

"Time t' pay th' piper." Nate's voice rumbled through her rib cage, but she still didn't open her eyes.

"It's also teatime!" Moth said. "How about a nice fry-up?"

With a moan at the idea of greasy eggs and sausages, Bertie buried her face in the soft cotton of Nate's shirt, burrowing until she reached warm flesh and short, wiry hair that tickled her nose.

Apparently, it also tickled Nate, as he made a discomfited noise and set her down on the chaise. "Leave off."

"I must have fallen asleep." Bertie winced at the late afternoon sunlight slanting through an upper window. The brightness slapped against her cheek in time with her pulse.

"You have to speak with the *Hamlet* Players," Peaseblossom said. "Call another rehearsal—"

Nate cut in. "What were ye drinkin'?"

Bertie didn't want to answer, but the edge to his voice demanded the truth. "Just a few sips from Alice's 'Drink Me' bottle. Ariel said—"

Mentioning Ariel was a misstep, as Nate's glare intensified. "He was here wi' ye?"

She rubbed her hand under her nose, unwilling to discuss what had transpired.

Nate moved her hair aside and nearly burned a hole in her neck with his gaze. "Where's th' scrimshaw, Bertie?"

"In my pocket."

Nate brought his fist down on the arm of the chaise hard enough to splinter its unseen, wooden bones. The fairies scattered, squeaking with surprise at the unexpected assault upon the furniture.

"I told ye not t' take it off."

Bertie held herself stiffly away from him, feeling as prickly as a hedgehog and wishing she had spines for protection. "I was afraid I'd cry on it. Tears are saltwater, Nate. Even a thickheaded pirate should know that."

"It was meant t' protect ye," he said, "from people like him."

"I don't need your stupid necklace for protection." Bertie pulled the medallion out of her pocket and shoved it at him.

"No, ye obviously do!" Nate jerked it out of her hand to contemplate the broken chain.

Every word was like a smack to the head. "Don't *shout* at me!"

"I'll shout at ye until some sense sinks into that thick rock ye call yer skull." He pulled a leather thong out of his hair and used it to tie the medallion around her neck.

"That's tighter than necessary," Bertie said.

"Ye ought t' be thankful I don't strangle ye wi' it."

The scrimshaw's familiar weight settled against her skin, and though she didn't mean to, Bertie took comfort in its gentle warmth. Bone-magic seeped into her as though on an incoming tide, filling her with foam and insight. Peering up at Nate, she saw the insecurities that gnawed at his innards and fell out of his pockets like scuttling crabs. "What are you so afraid of?"

Instead of answering, he shoved a carton of something inordinately foul into her hand. "I want ye t' eat this."

Bertie's stomach heaved at the smell of food, and she let go of the scrimshaw. "What is it?"

"Restitution," he said. "Time t' start payin' th' piper."

She sniffed at something that gave every indication of being soup.

The rice isn't so bad. I think that bit is chicken. But shrimp? Pickled something or other? And quite a lot of garlic?

Bertie closed her eyes and wished she would die just to be done with it. "I'd rather eat my shoe."

"Ye may get yer wish." Nate handed her a spoon.

"Where did you get this horrible stuff?"

"Th' galley cook made it fer me."

"As a remedy or a punishment?"

"Eat."

"I can't!" she wailed. "The shrimps still have their heads! Their little eyeballs are staring at me!"

Nate put his face very close to hers. He smelled of leather

and pipe tobacco, dark rum and soap from the Turkish Bath. "Eat it, afore I pry yer mouth open an' pour it down yer ungrateful gullet." He straightened, slapped his hand twice against his thigh, and strode away in high dudgeon.

"Start with the broth," Peaseblossom advised.

"I'm sorry about this afternoon. I shouldn't have run away." Bertie poked at the fouler things swimming in the soup and managed to isolate a spoonful of broth. When she looked up, Peaseblossom was hovering very close.

"It's all right," the fairy said.

"It's not. It's a mess." Bertie let the liquid dribble off the spoon.

Peaseblossom got close enough to tuck a stray piece of Bertie's hair behind her ear. The touch was like a kiss. "It's not as bad as it seems."

That went for more than the soup, Bertie hoped. She licked the spoon, didn't die, and tried it again.

The stomping of boots preceded a profoundly pissed-off swashbuckler. Nate shoved the bottle under her nose. "Is that what ye drank?"

She recoiled from the cloying, sickly-sweet smell. "Yes."

"Why ever would ye do somethin' that stupid?"

"I was hoping it would change me into a proper Director." Aware he watched her every move, Bertie took another sip of broth. "Instead it filled my head with useless nonsense."

"Did Ariel drink wi' ye?"

"Yes, and quite a lot more of it than I did, I'd like to point out."

"He'd have more of a head fer it than you. An' he should have known better than t' let ye do yerself such a mischief." Nate sat down on the chaise but left a careful space between them. "Are ye feelin' any better yet?"

"Yes, thank you." Bertie chewed a morsel of chicken and swallowed with caution. It stayed put, so she added a bit of rice and ignored the rest of the questionable mess. "I'm not eating the cabbage even if you threaten to cleave me in twain." She set the container down.

"I can live wi' that," Nate said. "But I can't live wi' th' idea o' ye gettin' hurt. Ariel's dangerous."

"I wish you'd stop fretting about Ariel." Bertie wondered how the air elemental's head was faring. If there were any justice in this world, he'd have the mother of all hangovers, too.

"I want ye t' stay away from him."

"That's nice," said Bertie, closing her eyes. "I'm hoping for world peace, myself."

"'Tisn't a joke, lass."

"My head is about to split open, Nate, so please do us both a favor and shut up."

The pirate jumped up. "What will it take for ye t' listen t' reason?" Grabbing her by the arms, he hauled Bertie several feet in the air.

Startled by the sudden movement as much as the change

in altitude, it took her a moment to locate her ire at being treated in such a fashion. "Put me down!"

"I can't stand aside an' watch ye drown yerself in him!" Nate held her there for a moment, maybe just to prove that he could.

"I'm going to be sick—" Part of Bertie wanted to make good on the threat and puke down his front, but if she started throwing up, she wouldn't be able to stop.

Slowly, by inches, Nate lowered her to the floor. "One o' these days, lass, I'm goin' t' still that mouth o' yers." He gently traced her upper lip with his thumb.

Before Bertie could think of a response to his threat, he turned on his heel and made his exit.

"Oh, my," said Peaseblossom.

"Gross!" yelled Moth. "Nate likes Bertie."

"Nasty!" That was Cobweb, who turned to Mustardseed. "Darling!"

"Sweetie!" returned Mustardseed. They tackled each other midair and made loud, slurping kissing noises.

Bertie sat hard on the chaise and put her hands over her knees to stop them from shaking.

Peaseblossom patted her shoulder. "He wouldn't ever hurt you, you know. There's more brains there than brawn."

"Pity he seems to have misplaced his brains." Bertie scrubbed her hands over her face. "That's it. I need coffee and a cigarette, and I don't care if getting them kills me."

She was halfway to the door before Peaseblossom called, "What did you do with The Book?"

When Bertie spun around, it took the room a full three seconds to catch up. She put her hands over her stomach. "I stuck it under the chaise." Peaseblossom looked horrified, so Bertie added, "For safekeeping!"

"Wouldn't a safe be safer?" Moth asked.

"You'd think," Mustardseed said.

"I need to take it to the Theater Manager." Bertie lowered herself carefully to the floor and stuck her hand under the chaise, her fingers expecting to meet gilt-edged paper. When they didn't, she flattened out against the ground. It was too dark to see much, but it shouldn't have been dark at all. The absence of golden, glowing light stabbed at her already aching guts. "Where is it?"

"Oh, no," moaned Peaseblossom.

"I put it right here." Bertie swept her arm back and forth through the dust, hoping against hope that she'd shoved it farther back than she'd remembered, that it was still there.

Because if The Book isn't there, someone took it.

Bertie heaved the chaise over. Wood splintered through velvet brocade, and she stared at the empty space.

"Mr. Hastings is going to be furious!" Peaseblossom said, gaping at such wanton destruction.

Bertie sat back on her heels, breathing hard. "We have bigger problems than Mr. Hastings if we don't find The Book."

"What do you think happened?" asked Mustardseed.

Bertie tasted restitution soup in the back of her throat. "I think Ariel found it."

Trusting him, even for one second, was the stupidest thing I've ever done.

"We need to find him." Bertie's brain scampered in circles around the missing Book, around Ariel's deception. It looped wider around Ophelia's blatherings in the Turkish Bath, around the ripped-out page, around her claim to have left the theater. . . . "He was listening."

"Who?" Moth wanted to know.

"Who was listening to what, and when?" Cobweb clarified.

"Ariel was eavesdropping on us in the Turkish Bath. That was him, his wind, that cleared the steam."

That's why he followed me to the Properties Department. Why he was so charming, so beguiling. Why we ended up on the chaise together.

And why The Book's nowhere to be found now.

"He told me in the hallway that given half a chance, he would free all who are imprisoned here. Now he has The Book. He could pull out every last page and release the Players. We have to stop him." Bertie had another horrible thought. "Unless he's done it already."

The fairies clutched one another.

Bertie snatched Moth from midair. "How do you feel? Any more free than usual?"

He paused to reflect. "Yeah, but only because I'm not wearing underwear today."

Cobweb and Mustardseed backed away from him. "You're going commando?"

Moth nodded. "I forgot to give Mrs. Edith my hamper this week."

"Aw, man! I want to go commando, too!" Cobweb said as he reached for his trouser buttons.

"Keep your pants on. We need to figure out if The Book is still intact." Bertie turned in a slow circle, her eyes coming to rest on a small window. She righted Marie Antoinette's chaise, shoved it under the window, and stacked two packing crates on top of it. Hoisting herself up onto the first crate, she nearly put her foot through it.

"Careful!" Peaseblossom hovered right next to her. "Don't fall!"

"I won't if I can possibly help it." Bertie climbed onto the second crate. Standing on tiptoe, she could just reach the window latch, but it wouldn't budge. "Get me something. A piece of fabric, a handkerchief—"

"A pillow?" Mustardseed suggested as he kicked a blue satin square.

Bertie nodded. "Sure, if you can carry it."

Between them, the fairies managed to get it aloft. Bertie grabbed it, ripped it open, and pulled most of the stuffing out.

"Oh, my! Was that really necessary?" said Peaseblossom.

"Yes," said Bertie as she wrapped her silk-swathed hand around the window latch. "It was."

With two grunts and a heave, the latch gave way and the window swung open. A gust of fresh air caught the fairies unprepared, sending them tumbling back. Bertie clung to the windowsill until her knuckles turned white as the crates swayed underfoot.

"Go on," she urged. "Try to fly through."

They looked at her like she'd suggested they tear off their own ears.

"Are you insane?" Moth asked.

"I need to know if he's pulling the pages out!" The boxes teetered again.

"So you want us to go . . . out there?" said Cobweb.

"Yes, please."

"No way!" yelled Mustardseed. "Who knows what's out there?"

"I bet I get eaten by a grue—" Moth paused, choking on his own spit and cowardice, then finished, "—a gruesome monster of indeterminate size and shape. I'm pretty sure I taste like chicken."

"You're bioluminescent," Bertie said. "Which means you taste awful. Now, come on." She stuck her hand out the window and waggled it around a bit. "See? Nothing there to get you."

"Yeah, to get *you*," Cobweb scoffed. "Because you're *from* out there."

Bertie snagged him from the air. "I'm sorry."

"For what?" he asked.

"For this," Bertie said, and tossed him at the window.

Cobweb squeaked when he hit the opening, but light and energy filled in the gap and prevented his exit. There was a sizzle and a zing, then he bounced backward onto the ledge, smoking faintly and smelling of burnt popcorn.

"That answers that, I guess," said Bertie.

The other three looked at her in horror as Cobweb smoldered.

"I suppose," Bertie said, realization dawning, "Ariel might only have torn out his own page and left the rest alone."

"You couldn't have had that brainwave a minute earlier and saved me a frizzling?" Cobweb demanded.

"Sorry," she said with a guilty start.

"What is going on here?"

Bertie twisted around at the sound of Mr. Hastings' horrified voice. The packing crates slid one direction and she went the other, thankfully landing on the arm of the chaise before rolling off and hitting the floor.

Mr. Hastings advanced on her, but not to help her up. "I repeat, just what is going on in here?"

Bertie stood, rubbing her tailbone. "Just a little experiment."

"You totally deserved that," Cobweb observed.

"Yes, I suppose I did."

"But Marie Antoinette's chaise! And this cushion!" Mr.

Hastings rearranged his glasses to examine the damage. "Why on earth were you fiddling with that window?"

She didn't utter a word, certain that anything she said would only anger him further.

"I see." Mr. Hastings opened the door for her. "Clearly it's inappropriate for you to be in here unsupervised. In the future, you'd best make your requests in writing."

"Yes, Mr. Hastings. You're absolutely right, and I . . . I apologize." Bertie sidled past him, unable to meet his gaze. Any other day, the banishment would have been cause for protests and tears, but today it was the final entry in a long list of horrifying surprises, filed under the heading: "Failure."

CHAPTER FOURTEEN

Divide and Conquer

"Mrs. Edith is going to give me the lecture about how clothes don't magically sew themselves," Cobweb said with a mournful sigh.

As they walked, Bertie assessed the damage she'd done. There were holes in his pants, and his shirt had burned completely away. "Sorry."

"Don't worry about it," said Cobweb, never one to hold a grudge against her. He peeked down the front of his trousers and perked up a bit. "Hey, I'm going commando now, too!"

Bertie stopped and pivoted so she could peer down the hallways that splintered off the main corridor. "We have to figure out where Ariel put The Book. Even if he's gone, he had to leave it somewhere. Mustardseed, you and Moth go check the pedestal, just in case he did us a favor and put it back."

"Aye, aye, Captain!" They sped off, pushing and shoving to be the first to reach the stage door.

"What can we do to help?" Cobweb demanded.

"I need you to think about other places he could have stowed it." Bertie turned in another slow circle, wishing she had the right sort of dowsing rod for sensing a wayward air elemental. "The Théâtre is huge. . . ."

"And it has four hundred and ninety-seven hiding places," Peaseblossom said. "I counted once."

"We've used most of them ducking the Stage Manager," said Cobweb.

"We don't have time to check even a fraction of those," Bertie said. "We need to get The Book back before Management realizes it's missing."

"Ophelia's crazy," Peaseblossom said, trying to be comforting and failing utterly. "She was probably making the whole thing up."

"You don't really believe that she left the theater, do you?" Cobweb asked.

"At this point, I'd believe anything," said Bertie.

Moth and Mustardseed returned, expressions gloomy. "It's not there."

"Of course it's not. That would be far too easy." Her gaze came to rest on the one thing that could summon Ariel to them faster than a tug on a recalcitrant dog's leash:

The Call Board.

"That's it!" she shouted, setting off at a run. "I'll put a notice on the Call Board. If he's still in the theater, he'll have to answer it."

"I know where there's paper and a pen!" Peaseblossom headed straight for the Green Room. In the back corner, she landed atop a tiny mahogany table and began jumping up and down on its brass handle.

"Out of the way." Bertie applied her upper-body strength and growing desperation to the sticky drawer, which flew open, scattering its contents across the carpet. She fell to her knees and rummaged through needlebooks, spools of thread, and other detritus before locating a scrap of parchment paper so old that it undulated across the floor like waves in the ocean. Under it was an ancient fountain pen, rusted of nib and nearly devoid of ink. Still, she managed to scrawl:

ARIEL:
Immediate call
to the stage
with The Book!

Bertie folded the note in thirds, not wanting any passersby to be able to read her message, and wrote Ariel's name on the outside, underlining it twice for emphasis and nearly ripping a hole in the paper.

"Come on, let's go." She turned around, expecting the fairies to be gorging themselves on sticky toffee pudding or swimming in a pot of cheese fondue, but the refreshment table was oddly devoid of nourishment; not even crumbs dotted the surface of the tablecloth.

"What the heck is up with this?" Mustardseed said, his fists on his hips and his eyes accusatory.

Bertie faltered. Even the fairies at their most ravenous couldn't clear the refreshment table so thoroughly. Worse yet, no coal fire burned in the stove, the bouquets rotted in their vases, and the clock had run down, as though the un-seen, grandmotherly caregiver had abandoned the Green Room. "Maybe the Mariners just came through here. You know what they're like when they disembark."

"Something feels very, very wrong about this, Bertie." Moth backed away as though the table crawled with ver-min, or worse, carrot sticks and broccoli. "Wrong-er than Mariners."

"There's nothing in the sugar bowl but dust!" Peaseblos-som said.

"I can't worry about that now!" Bertie stuck the foun-tain pen behind her ear and dashed back to the Call Board, pulled out a brass thumbtack, and jammed it through the note, wishing it was a sword she could use to skewer her foe. "Come on! We have to get to the stage to see if this worked."

It was the same route that the Players took every night of a performance: Open the backstage door, climb a shallow set of black-painted stairs whose edges were lined with phosphorescent gaffer's tape, wend around large coils of rope, brush past the heavy weight of the velvet curtains, traverse the red-gelled glow of the Stage Manager's corner where his headset hung on a hook. The space around the pedestal radiated cold. Bereft of The Book's golden light, the dust motes lay on the floor as though dead.

"Heigh-ho, Ariel!" Bertie strode onto the stage. "Come out, come out wherever you are, you bastard."

"How long before he gets here?" Mustardseed asked.

"Sh!" Bertie commanded, flapping her hands at them. "I think I hear something."

As one, they strained their ears, trying to discern anything unusual, anything that would indicate Ariel's arrival. Bertie thought she could just make out a low whistle when Peaseblossom jerked her to one side by her hair.

"Move!"

Eyes smarting at the assault, Bertie stepped back seconds before something smashed into the spot where she'd been standing. "What the hell?"

It was one of the sandbags Mr. Tibbs used to counterweight the scenery, ripped down one side and disgorging its contents onto the stage. A length of sturdy rope, frayed at the end, trailed behind it.

Bertie squinted into the gloom overhead. Though she couldn't locate the source of the sudden malfunction, her instincts pointed an accusing finger. "It has to be Ariel."

All four fairies launched themselves upward in pursuit, but she couldn't follow without a harness and someone to hoist her aloft. Instead, Bertie paced the stage, heaping foul oaths upon Ariel for stealing The Book, on Ophelia for putting the idea in his head, on the Theater Manager for trying to kick her out. . . .

"He's not up there," Mustardseed said as the fairies returned to encircle her troubled brow.

"We looked all the way up to the ceiling!" Moth said.

"How can he ignore a note on the Call Board?" Bertie demanded. "Unless—"

"Unless he's already torn his page out," said Cobweb.

"Unless he's already gone," Peaseblossom whispered, clasping her little hands together.

Bertie gripped either side of her head, as much to squeeze the thought out as to force some inspiration in. "Where did he leave The Book, then?"

"Beats me," Mustardseed said. It bespoke their disconcertion that the other boys didn't immediately take him up on the offer.

"Now what?" Bertie felt she'd used up all her ingenuity on the Call Board summons.

"When I lose stuff, I'm supposed to retrace my steps," Mustardseed said.

Cobweb landed on the stage just so he could jump up and down. "Oh! Oh! You could try acting it out."

"That's dumb. She doesn't have a script," said Moth. "You can't act something that doesn't have a script."

"Hold on." The idea fluttered through Bertie's head like one of Ariel's butterflies. "That might just work."

"It might?" said Cobweb, taken aback. Recovering, he turned and shoved Moth. "See? It might!"

Bertie borrowed the Stage Manager's clipboard and started to scribble on its top sheet with the fountain pen. It was difficult to remember everything that she and Ariel had said; some moments were hazy—*curse that "Drink Me" bottle!*—but Bertie thought she had most of it by the time she pulled the page off.

"I know everything except the end," she said. "Maybe if we act it out far enough, we can figure out what he did with The Book. I can play myself, but I need someone to be Ariel."

"Don't look at me," said Peaseblossom. "I don't do elemental."

"Or me," said Moth. "I don't do antihero."

Bertie sighed and held out the inky excuse for a script. "Someone has to play Ariel."

Nate entered from Stage Left. "I'll do it."

Bertie considered escape routes, praying this was a soup-induced nightmare while the fairies considered the recasting.

"You're a little tall to play Ariel," said Moth.

"And you have way too many muscles," said Mustard-seed.

"But you might be able to pull it off," Cobweb said, "if you can look really constipated."

Nate reached for the page in Bertie's hand, but she pulled it back and started to crumple it up.

"It was a half-baked idea." She struggled to sound dismissive instead of frantic. "There's no way it's going to tell me anything I don't know already. The ending has to be written out."

"We'll improvise that bit," he said.

"We haven't checked everywhere," she protested.

"I have." Nate reached for the makeshift script again.

"Why were you looking for Ariel?" Bertie demanded.

All of Nate's muscles flexed at once. "I was going t' wring his neck."

"For stealing The Book?"

"Fer—" Nate blinked as the conversation shifted gears. "He stole Th' Book?"

"Lose the sword!" suggested Moth, still trying to give Nate an Ariel-makeover.

"Ariel took The Book," Bertie explained with reluctance. "We need to get it back before anyone realizes it's missing."

"An' if he's not in th' theater?" Nate pried the script out of her grasp. "Mayhap he's torn his page out an' fled."

"Scene change," Peaseblossom said into the headset. "The Properties Department."

Shelves slid into place, each one burdened with a glittering assortment of props. The "Drink Me" bottle sat Center Stage, sparkling in a soft pink spotlight. A golden glow emanated from under Marie Antoinette's chaise.

"Nate," Bertie said, "I really, really don't want to do this."

"Ye want t' find The Book, aye?" He leaned forward until his stubble tickled her ear. "Then take yer place."

Bertie made a strangled noise of protest as he moved into the wings. Against the advice of every screaming instinct, she knelt at Center Stage.

Where's an asp when I really need one?

The lights cut to a blackout. A warm amber wash slowly faded up as Nate made his entrance, divested of coat, sash, and sword. While he couldn't quite manage the air elemental's catlike grace, his boots made nary a sound against the floorboards.

"I thought I might find you here," Nate said with Ariel's inflections.

"What do you want, Ariel? Come to gloat?"

"Do you mind if I join you?" Nate read.

Bertie-as-herself shook her head. "Actually, I do. I'd like three seconds to myself without noise, chaos, or crisis."

"That's hardly welcoming."

"That's because it wasn't an invitation."

"Skip ahead, skip ahead, skip ahead," yelled Peaseblossom.

Moth signaled the orchestra, and unseen musicians launched into the tango.

Bertie's lower intestine tied itself into a knot, but she followed her stage directions and stood up. "Shall we dance?"

Nate pulled her close. "I think it's customary for the man to lead."

"So lead on, pretty boy."

Bertie wished one of the trapdoors would open up and swallow her, but Nate-as-Ariel led her into a fluid tango, as full of grace as the original but without the hallucinations of Spanish buildings or jetting fountains.

The scrimshaw's bone-magic seeped into Bertie's chest, except she wasn't sure she needed it this time. Though Nate had assumed Ariel's demeanor and his words, though his eyes got progressively darker, he'd never stood before her so completely unmasked. He twirled her out just when he ought—

I may hold ye at arm's length. . . .

—and pulled her back when the music called for it.

But I want ye t' be mine an' mine alone.

"Are you ready for the finale?" Nate's voice tightened as he dipped her.

"No!" She tried to twist out of his grasp.

He held her fast and shook his head. "That's not yer line."

"Nate—"

The light poured over his shoulders. "I'm not Nate right now. I'm a spirit. I'm th' wind."

"You're not him."

"I am, in this moment. Just for now. Just long enough."

Nate-as-Ariel lowered Bertie onto the chaise, but the lips that met hers were only Nate's, light at first and then more demanding. Bertie twisted his shirt up in her hands and tried to shove him off, but either he didn't realize or didn't care.

"No," she said into his mouth. *Some other time, some other way. But not like this.*

He pulled back to contemplate her, expression unfathomable, then held up the crumpled piece of paper. "It says here that ye pass out. Would ye like some help wi' that?"

She shook her head. "No."

"Then close yer eyes an' pretend. Pretend it very hard."

Bertie squeezed her eyes shut. She heard Nate crumple the script and drop it, felt him slide to the floor to reach a hand under the chaise.

"Is it there?" she whispered.

"That," he said, "was not in th' script."

Neither was the finger that touched her lips as the lights dimmed to a blackout. When the house lights faded up, Nate was gone. The fairies sat in the audience, stunned.

"She kissed Nate!"

"Yeah, we were all sitting right here when she did it."

"But that means she kissed Ariel, too."

"Yuck! That's disgusting!"

"Just how many boys have you played tonsil hockey with in the last two days, Bertie?"

"Never mind that," she said. "What about The Book? Did Ariel take it?"

Nate reentered holding a large, leather-bound tome. "Aye, he did."

He held it out, and Bertie's heart gave a tremendous thump. "You found it!"

"No, lass. 'Tis but a prop." He handed it to her. Only then could she see that it lacked the proper weight, that the gilt edges were worn and the leather false.

Bertie tossed the false Book aside and turned over the chaise for the second time that day, but this time, not even dust decorated the floor. Rage ignited in her chest, and before she thought twice about it, Bertie pulled her foot back and kicked a hole through the bottom of the chaise.

"Oh, Bertie!" Peaseblossom said. "That's hardly the right way to get back into Mr. Hastings' good graces."

"I don't care." After the next swift kick, her shoe got stuck. Nate reached out to steady her, but Bertie abandoned her Mary Jane and her dignity to leap away from him. "You keep your hands to yourself!"

"Perhaps," he said, pausing for effect, "ye should have said that t' Ariel."

"You shut up." Bertie took her other shoe off and threw it at his head.

Nate ducked, and it bounced harmlessly in the wings. "I will not." He picked up the "Drink Me" bottle from the stage. "That little scene was an eye-openin' lesson in how ye spend yer free time." A muscle in his jaw clenched as he turned. With a fluid movement of his arm and a grunt, he hurled the bottle into the wings after her shoe.

Crystal smashed into an unseen bit of scenery and Bertie flinched, at both the noise and his angry display. She thought she could smell whatever was left of the magical elixir, and the scent made her stomach clench. "Feel better now?"

Nate turned around with an expression that said he wasn't done breaking things. "Not yet."

"Look, I know you're mad at me—"

"That goes wi'out sayin'."

"But I really need your help right now!"

"Ye need somethin'. A good dose o' reality, mayhap."

Bertie wished she had more ammunition, but she was out of shoes. "And you need to get over yourself!"

Nate threw words instead of punches. "Ye were thought-less. Reckless. Ye've put everyone in danger wi' yer stupid-ity."

"I don't need you telling me what I did was wrong." Bertie couldn't rid herself of the lump of anger lodged in her throat, though she swallowed again and again.

"I'll go get th' Theater Manager." He headed for the wings.

"No, Nate, please!" Bertie gave chase, nearly falling over him in the half-light backstage when he paused to pick up his personal effects. "Give me a while longer to look!"

"He needs t' be told!" Nate jerked on his coat. "Perhaps he can set things t' rights."

"But he'll cancel the performance!"

"Are ye addled in th' head?" The look he gave her said he clearly thought it was so. "There's not goin' t' be a perfor-mance wi'out The Book in th' theater. Ye'll be lucky t' see out th' day here, much less th' week."

Anguish stabbed at Bertie's vitals. To hear it so pro-nounced was harsher than any blow, and hot tears poured out of her eyes.

"Bertie, no!" Nate dropped his sword belt to snatch at her, at the medallion, but too late.

Saltwater hit the scrimshaw. Underfoot, the stage trem-bled. The scenic flats and curtains swayed.

"Earthquake!" Moth cried, but it wasn't.

Every door crashed inward, and tidal waves of seawater spilled down the aisles. The fairies launched themselves at the ceiling, evading the tsunami by mere inches. Nate wrapped his arms around Bertie only seconds before the violence smashed into them.

This wasn't the gentle ocean set, with lighting specials and sparkling sand and swimming in a harness. Waves buffeted Bertie from all sides, filling her nose and flooding into a mouth opened to scream. She thrashed against the water that closed over her head, against Nate, who tried to hold her still. When the sea calmed an infinitesimal amount, he began to swim, no doubt hampered by her weight but refusing to let go of her wrist.

Through stinging eyes, Bertie saw a shadow loom behind him: a creature of purple ink, glittering scales, and creamy yellow bone.

Sedna's voice was whale song and shifting tides and the vicious sorrow of a harpooned soul. "You have something that belongs to me."

Dark tentacles reached around Nate to snake over Bertie's shoulders and around her waist. She clung to Nate, but the Sea Goddess would not be denied. With hands that had starfish where fingers should be, Sedna pried Bertie from Nate's grasp before tossing him aside like a bit of rotting fish.

Her own lungs burning, Bertie knew all too well that he needed to breathe, but still Nate hesitated.

"Go!" she told him, but the words were only bubbles.

He turned and swam for the surface, and though she'd given the order, Bertie wanted to scream in protest.

"I will have the girl as payment for the tricks played upon me." The Sea Goddess eyed the scrimshaw. "Bone of my bone, magical bone. You've used its power more than once."

A few seconds longer and Bertie would have no choice but to suck the water into her lungs. She could see Nate already fighting his way back toward them, held at bay by the currents under Sedna's command.

He won't get to me in time.

The Sea Goddess peered at the medallion in fascinated horror. "It's been defaced! Mutilated and vandalized—" But when her starfish fingers touched the scrimshaw, churning foam and bubbles erupted all around them, shoving Sedna away with all the force of wind under water. The Sea Goddess screamed, "His magic! The blood, the bones. You are *his* child!"

Bertie twisted and kicked, praying she was headed the right direction. Moments later, she surfaced, spitting and coughing, dragging air into her aching lungs as she treaded water. Completely disoriented, she blinked, only to realize the brilliant nimbus of light wavering just before her was the chandelier. With shaking arms, Bertie pulled herself free of the waves, clinging to the beaded chains and prisms as she shoved her hair out of her face. "Nate!"

Below her, the water formed a whirlpool, sloshing against the balconies and casting salt-spray across the painted seraphim on the ceiling. Bits of the Théâtre's walls trembled and slid into the maelstrom with a series of shudders and splashes.

"Bertie!" Nate cried.

She turned to see him fighting the current only a few feet away. Without pausing to consider the madness of what she was doing, Bertie flipped herself backward. Dangling from one of the chandelier's brass arms, she reached for him. "Grab my hand!"

"I'm comin'!" Nate rasped, though Bertie could see the exhaustion in every line of his face, in every straining muscle.

"You're almost there!" She thought her legs trembled with the effort of holding on, but then the entire chandelier began to shake.

"I cannot take the girl," the Sea Goddess roared as she surfaced, "but I will have something for my troubles." A riptide dragged Nate under. "Come, my brave pirate lad."

"No!" Bertie dove in, desperate to catch hold of him. Her fingertips brushed over his outstretched hand as a glowing fish rippled past them through the shifting vortex of air and water.

No. Not a fish. His page from The Book!

One last wave seized Bertie and slammed her to the seafloor as the Sea Goddess caught hold of both man and page. Laughing, Sedna retreated with her prize, taking the ocean with her on an outgoing tide.

CHAPTER FIFTEEN

Ill Met by Moonlight

Bertie lay on the carpeted aisle, empty as a shell washed onto the shore. Warm blood containing the memory of salt trickled from her nose, and the weight of her sodden clothes dragged at her.

This is what Ophelia does to herself, each and every night.

As horrifying as the thought was, Bertie couldn't stop to sympathize. She crawled to the auditorium door with pain lancing through her lungs.

"Nate!" His name was a water-rasped whisper rather than a scream, but either way, there was no one to hear it. The lobby stood empty, its carpet dotted with briny puddles. Water ran in rivulets down the glass set into the revolving doors, and the occasional droplet fell from the painted Muses on the ceiling who wept for her loss.

The Sea Goddess was gone, and Nate with her.

Bertie shoved the auditorium door closed and welcomed the return of the gloom. Twisting about to sit, she rested her head in her hands. There was no sound except her ragged breath and the steady *drip! drip! drip!* of water from every side.

The fairies rushed to join her in the back of the theater. Mustardseed touched the door as though it might vomit the sea again. When it didn't, he kicked it soundly with his boot. "And stay out!"

Bertie closed her hand around the scrimshaw and twisted her fingers through the sodden leather thong. For ages it seemed she only sat and rocked, back and forth, her shoulders shaking with shock. "It's all my fault."

"Oh, Bertie," Peaseblossom said as she pushed the wet strands of hair out of Bertie's face. "Stop. Stop it right now. How could you know that would happen?"

"Nate warned me."

"He's the one who made you wear it."

"To keep me safe," Bertie amended.

"From stupid Ariel," Cobweb said.

"And all that disgusting kissing," Mustardseed said.

Peaseblossom patted Bertie on the shoulder. "Boys can be so dumb." That evoked a protest in three-part harmony, but Peaseblossom spoke over them. "It's true! You're dumb as rocks."

Bertie put her forehead against her knees. "This is all so

screwed up," she said into her jeans. "Nate's been kidnapped, Ariel's vanished. The Book is missing. Management is going to *kill* me—"

In the middle of her quiet tirade, the lights died. Bertie looked up, startled, and the fairies froze. A low red glow came up onstage, accompanied by a violin's haunting protest. A gibbous moon rose slowly against the back wall as mist poured in from the wings.

Someone had called for a scene change.

Bertie put a finger to her lips, waiting to see who—or what—would enter. A trapdoor opened, and a figure rose to Center Stage.

"Through the house, give glimmering light by the dead and drowsy fire. A puff of wind is what we need to rouse the flames from slumber."

The newcomer snapped his fingers. A thousand fire-streamers leapt into the air to scorch the overhanging limbs of a gnarled tree. Smoke billowed from behind its trunk in chemical clouds, while a sudden wind tore through the room with grasping claws. In seconds, the blistering combination of heat and air dried everything from the dripping seats to the blue-smudged tangle of Bertie's hair.

"It's Ariel," she whispered. "He finally answered the call." Bertie saw then that he held The Book in his slim, white hands. Already it looked thinner, its leather cover set at a sad angle, and she wondered if the lighting onstage was indeed red, or if that was just murderous rage spilling over into her vision.

"What's the plan?" Mustardseed wanted to know.

"Now would be a good time to jump him," said Cobweb. "We still have the element of surprise."

"For once, you're making sense." Bertie exhaled hard through her nose. "You distract him, and I'll smash his head in with one of those rocks."

Peaseblossom shushed her. "He's going to say something."

"This Book has powerful magic, stronger than I ever could have imagined." Ariel hovered next to the stones containing the blaze, reflections of flames dancing in the liquid black of his eyes. The smoke rose and twisted about him, tugging at his hair and his clothes, shifting, then settling about his shoulders like a cloak.

Bertie clutched the medallion and focused all her hatred and concentration upon him.

Show me what you really are, Ariel.

His form wavered; one second he was a great winged creature with glowing eyes and claws bared, the next no more than a breeze stirring the leaves. Then he was as he'd always been: terrifying and beautiful all at once.

"Perhaps," he crooned to the open pages, "the power of

the stage can overcome your hold over me." Moonlight painted him with a silver brush as he held The Book aloft. "I call upon the winds of the world to stir the oceans and cover the sky with clouds. Uproot the trees, unseat the mountains, and cause the earth to groan. We shall, like mighty magicians, release the dead from this grave." Thunder and lightning, but Ariel's voice rang clear over the din. "I am one of the dead; let nothing bind me."

He opened The Book to a random page, gripped it in his fist, and tore it out.

"No!" Bertie's scream of protest was lost as everything shuddered: the carved moldings, the proscenium arch, the massive chandelier. She ran down the red-carpeted aisle and tried to make her voice heard over the noise. "Take your entrance page and go!"

Ariel looked both surprised and ashamed for all of a millisecond before a familiar half-smile slid into place. He shook his head. "Don't you think I've tried that? Mine is the only one that won't come out."

"I don't understand. . . ."

"No," he said softly, "you don't. Not about any of it."

"Ariel—"

"Hush," he interrupted, "I will show you." He turned the pages of The Book until he arrived at one that seemed brighter than all the others. His fingers curled under the edges, gripped it until his knuckles shuddered in protest. He wrenched at it with visible effort, but it wouldn't budge. When he released the paper, not a single wrinkle marred its surface. "Do you see?"

Bertie was afraid to ask, but the question voiced itself. "What will you do?"

Ariel didn't answer. Instead, he flipped through The Book, grasped another page. When he tore it out, the heavy curtains on either side of the stage fell in velvet puddles.

Bertie reeled as though he'd stabbed her. "Ariel, stop! The theater's magic is bound to The Book!"

"Precisely why I am going to tear the pages out, one by one, until its magic is broken, until it can no longer hold me."

Bertie threw out her hand as though she could summon The Book to her by will alone. "Give it to me, Ariel, before I break every bone in your body!"

"Every bone!" echoed the fairies as they rushed forward.

"Tell them to stay back, Bertie," Ariel said. "Or I'll summon a wind merely for the pleasure of pulping your friends against the nearest wall."

"Do as he says." Bertie never took her eyes off Ariel.

The fairies ducked behind a chair with great reluctance, but Bertie took deliberate steps toward him. Ariel held up his hand, gathering the winds behind him. She fought against the rising vortex of noise and chaos, but the power rushed over his shoulders to shove at her as though every wind fan and storm machine had been turned on.

"I said stay back!" he warned her.

"So help me," she screamed into the tempest, "I'll see you in chains before I let you destroy this place!"

Ariel shouted something in response as he disappeared behind the massive, wooden waves that rolled in from Stage Right. Bertie tried to crawl over them, then around, but the water rose higher as wheels and gears spun and clanked.

"Come back here!" she shouted.

"Pull for shore, sailor!" cried an offstage voice. A boat filled with oar-wielding Mariners entered Stage Right.

Prospero, wizard hat askew and beard streaming in the wind, pointed a bony finger at Bertie. "Have you seen Ariel, girl-child?"

"Yes!" She punctuated the word with wild gesticulating. "He went behind that wave! Someone grab him!"

Prospero peered over the scenery. "There's no one there. Don't play games with me! Do you know who I am?" He puffed out his chest with self-importance.

The fairies landed on Bertie's shoulders, no longer obliged to stay back.

"You're supposed to be Ariel's master," Moth said.

"If this was a class, you'd be flunking," said Cobweb.

"What are these creatures babbling about?" the wizard sputtered.

"Ariel stole The Book," Bertie said. She heaved herself

over the side of the boat and landed in a tangle of hemp rope tied in intricate knots. "I need to get it back."

The Mariners shrank away from her. "Wummin aboard's bad luck!" As one, they jumped out, shouting, "Splash!"

Without anyone to row, the boat shuddered to a halt. After a series of ominous creaks, it fell thoroughly apart, disgorging its two remaining passengers onto the stage. Bertie landed hard on her backside, but Prospero somehow managed to leap clear of the wreckage with a dexterous swirl of pale blue robes.

"What sort of foul spell was that?" he demanded.

"It wasn't me!" Bertie stood with a wince, though she had more to worry about than a few bruises on her elbows and bum. "Ariel's tearing out the pages, and it's destroying everything. A sandbag already tried to kill me."

"The rarer action is in virtue than in vengeance." Prospero stroked his beard, trying to look wise.

"Try telling Ariel that," Mustardseed said.

"Never mind that vengeance is more satisfying," Moth muttered.

"Tearing the pages out, you say?" Prospero asked.

The walls shuddered again. Dust sifted over them as ancient boards shifted and settled.

"He's trying to free himself." Goose bumps crawled down Bertie's arms. "He was penned as your servant. Your slave. Maybe he can't get his page out because you need to set him free?"

"Pah!" Prospero's exclamation involved quite a bit of spit. "You speak folly, girl-child. I set Ariel free every performance."

"It's not enough for him." Bertie wanted to scream and stamp her foot at him, but with her shoes off, there wasn't really a point. "He wants the freedom to come and go as he pleases."

"Mostly to go," Peaseblossom said.

"Ah." The word rolled out of the wizard like an incantation. "Our revels now are ended. These our actors, as I foretold you, were all spirits, and are melted into air, into thin air."

"Please," Bertie implored, "just use whatever magic you have to release him."

Prospero held up his hand in a gesture intended to command the attention of the audience, to halt the breath in every chest. "Graves, at my command, have waked their sleepers, opened, and let them forth!"

"Big deal," Cobweb said. "Everyone in a grave here is a Player!"

"Then I shall raise the dead elsewhere." Prospero marched to the edge of the stage and took a suicidal leap into the orchestra pit.

"Wait!" Bertie called. "Where are you going?"

He strode up the red-carpeted runner. "I would see the cloud-capped towers, the gorgeous palaces, the solemn temples, the great globe itself!"

"No, no, no!" Bertie shrieked. "You're taking that line out of context!"

"Yeah!" yelled Moth. "The next bit is about it all being an insubstantial pageant!"

"And such stuff dreams are made on!" Peaseblossom said. "The outside world isn't about dreams!"

"Not good ones, at least," Cobweb said.

But Prospero didn't mark them as he shoved open the door under the green Exit sign. Blinding white light cut through the semi-gloom, and everyone blinked at it as the outer doors revolved with whispers. The lobby door slammed shut, and Prospero was gone.

Bertie closed her eyes and shuddered. "How far do you think Ariel's gotten? Tearing out the pages, I mean."

"I'll see thee hanged on Sunday first!" screamed an off-stage voice. The words were followed by one of Bertie's shoes, launched at the head of a laughing man in a shabby crimson doublet.

"*The Taming of the Shrew*, I think," said Peaseblossom.

Petruchio kissed his fist and waved it at the disembodied voice screaming epithets at him in Italian. "Nay, look not big, nor stamp, nor stare, nor fret; I will be master of what is mine own!" When he turned to Bertie, his expression altered not a whit. After an elaborate bow, he grasped her by the hand and pulled her close. "But ho, what a comely lass waits here. Perhaps you are a flower waiting to be plucked."

Bertie turned thirty shades of red and wondered just what he would do if she slapped him a good one across his florid cheek. She tried to withdraw her imprisoned hand. "I think perhaps your attention is misplaced."

Petruchio only leered harder, if that were possible, and leaned close, ruddy whiskers all abristle and breath reeking of cheap wine. "Kiss me, little flower, and let me sup of your sweet nectar."

Two great, beefy lips headed for Bertie's cheek. Recalling the Mistress of Revels and her jujitsu skills, Bertie screamed, "Kee-yaw!" and drove her foot sideways into his kneecap. Petruchio's leg, unappreciative of the onslaught, went out from underneath him at what appeared to be a most uncomfortable angle. The fairies cheered while Bertie stared at the writhing Player, both appalled and impressed by the outcome of her defensive maneuver.

"Let that serve as a reminder to you," she said, "to mind your damn manners."

"Strumpet!" Petruchio cried, struggling back to his feet. "Spongy milk-livered canker blossom! Jarring dog-hearted flirt-gill!"

"Wow," Moth said in appreciation.

Encouraged by the feedback, Petruchio added, "Currish rude-growing baggage!"

Bertie towered over him when she stood up straight. "That's enough name-calling from you, pipsqueak."

Still muttering all manner of ill-natured insults, Petruchio hobbled from the stage, down the runner, and jerked open the Exit door. He, too, disappeared into the blinding light, no doubt in search of a blossom more amenable to sharing her nectar.

Another shudder underfoot. The fountain pen, forgotten in the interim, rolled onstage and came to rest by Bertie's stocking-clad toes. She bent to pick it up, her mind fuzzy with shock, adrenaline, and despair, but then an idea flared like a white-hot spotlight. "I need more paper."

"Another note?" Moth said with a groan.

"No," Bertie said as her thoughts tumbled over each other like drunken acrobats. "Another script. I can't change what's been done, but if I write down what I want to happen, it might come true!"

"The Players do what's in the script." Peaseblossom sucked in her breath.

Bertie paced the length of the stage, unable to keep still. "I'll do it the same as I did for my own play. It really isn't any different from *How Bertie Came to the Theater*, right?"

"Sure!" Moth said, covering his head. "Well, except where the bits of the ceiling keep falling on us."

"No need to add the potholes this time," Cobweb said. "I think Ariel's got the destruction angle covered."

"Just try to do better than you did on the script for the tango scene," Moth said, "because that didn't work out very well for anyone."

Bertie staggered to a halt. Caught up in the chase, she'd banished the horror of Sedna's appearance and Nate's kidnapping to the farthest recesses of her brain. Pain flared up at the memory, and for a moment Bertie thought that she might be sick all over the stage. "Nate—"

"Focus!" Peaseblossom smacked her lightly on the cheek. "Recover The Book, then we'll think of a way to get Nate back. You'll have to keep your wits about you. This will be a sword fight, but with words."

"Even if Ariel doesn't show up for the duel," Bertie said, her pen at the ready, "I have to try to guide what happens next, without plague, pestilence, or potholes."

The fairies took up the rallying cry with gusto. "No potholes!"

"Peaseblossom, bring up a spotlight! Boys, go find the clipboard!"

"Got it!"

Bertie uncapped the pen with suddenly sweaty hands and caught the clipboard as they flung it at her. She braced it against a knee, her words a scrawl, but she didn't consider penmanship overly important at a time like this.

The lights fade up on a forgotten corner of the stage. A figure lurks behind the transparent scrim curtain. One by one, he pulls the pages from a purloined tome.

A ripping noise.

The stage heaved as though it rode upon the back of an enormous, bucking horse. Bertie's pen flew out of her hand and vanished into the darkness that lay in wait for her beyond the spotlight. At the far back of the stage, an indistinct figure manifested.

"Write faster!" Peaseblossom urged from the wings.

"I can't! I dropped the pen!"

"It's over here!" Cobweb yelled, shoving it back into the light.

Bertie snatched it up and scribbled as fast as she could.

An angry mob convenes onstage; as one, they surround him.

There was shouting, followed by scuffling noises and the sound of an ill-whipped wind. But louder than anything else was the continued destruction of The Book. The rip and tear filled Bertie's head until she could hardly think. Somewhere far below the stage, the very earth screamed in protest.

The madman tries to fight them,
but finds his powers diminished from
the harm he has already caused.
The crowd overwhelms him and binds
his hands with twine.

Ariel's wind faded and died a quiet death. Bertie could make out other sounds now: the chants for justice, the heavy breathing of a captured animal.

As one, they bring the
criminal to stand trial.

The scrim parted to reveal Ariel surrounded by the members of both Choruses. They'd bound his arms behind his back; his head lolled forward, and for a moment, Bertie wondered if they'd killed him.

Not that she'd care. "Where's The Book?"

The crowd parted to make a path. The lighting shifted to a single beam cast from above.

"I tried to warn you." Ophelia stepped forward, carrying The Book in her hands.

"You told him how to destroy it!" Bertie shouted at her. "This is your fault!"

Ophelia opened the leather cover as a single tear ran down her pale cheek. "There's only one page left."

"No!" Bertie shook her head, lifted the clipboard, and struggled to scrawl different words across the paper. "That's not in my script. I can change it."

"Blackout," Ophelia said as she was thrown into darkness.

"Blackout," the others echoed before they, too, disappeared.

"Damn it, no!" Bertie couldn't see to write any more, but still she moved her pen across the paper. "No, not yet!"

She tried to change the ending, tried to write the pages back into their resting place, tried to write Ariel's bloody, violent death by her own hands, but the only word she could manage was:

BLACKOUT

CHAPTER SIXTEEN

Pins and Poking-Sticks of Steel

When the house lights came up, Bertie took what remained of The Book from Ophelia, tracing her hand over the cover and noting the lack of weight, the sense of insignificance and utter inconsequence. Her heart cried out against what she already knew was true:

He managed to destroy it.

Everyone took a step away from Ariel, as though afraid the heat from Bertie's murderous gaze might spill over and burn them, too.

"I couldn't get my page out." Ariel spoke softly. "All the other pages came out, each with greater ease than the last. Why was my own impossible?"

Bertie's hand, the one holding her pen, twitched. "Do you realize what you've done?"

"I failed." The words fell like drops into an empty bucket. "I wanted to be free, but The Book would not release me."

With a noise like white thunder, a gilt cherub toppled off the wall next to the stalls. Cracks ran rampant through wood and plaster, reaching across the floor and walls with covetous fingers.

"At least I managed one thing," Ariel said. "The Théâtre will fall."

Bertie wanted him to beg for mercy. She wanted him to weep and cry out for forgiveness. She wanted him humbled and groveling, just so she could deny him. She would bring him down low, but to do so, she would have to keep the ceiling from caving in upon them.

Clutching the leather cover of The Book against her chest, Bertie closed her eyes and forced herself to think of paper. Of trees. The scenery changed without anyone touching the headset, the lights shifting to reveal a grove of ancient oaks. Immense roots crept over the stage; Bertie could feel them extend into the very heart of the theater and farther still into the earth. Massive trunks and branches reached through the darkness overhead to stay the destruction.

Bertie opened her eyes to consider him. "I should kill you now, Ariel. Slowly. By inches. In the most painful way I can imagine."

"Carve his heart out with a sword," suggested Moth.

"A poison-tipped one," said Mustardseed.

"A slow poison," intoned Peaseblossom, "that will turn his guts to black oozing liquid while he begs us to put him out of his misery."

"Then slice his belly open and stir his innards with an iron rod," said Cobweb.

Ariel's breath came out in spurts and sputters. "Bloodthirsty little imps, aren't they?"

"They're being merciful, in my opinion," Bertie said. "The trouble is that I don't think it's possible for you to die." The fairies clamored for retribution, but she held up her hand for silence. "Just because he cannot be killed doesn't mean he won't be punished. Someone bring me a sword."

It appeared within seconds, fetched by a member of the Chorus. Men and women alike now wore dark robes with hoods drawn up. Shadows obscured their faces, and they formed a half-circle to witness the tribunal. One held the scabbard as Bertie unsheathed the weapon, and metal-song rang in the stillness.

Ariel shuddered then, an involuntary reaction that satisfied her only for an instant. Holding what was left of The Book close to her chest, Bertie brought the blade up to rest cold steel against his neck.

It's time for another sort of tango.

"Where are the pages, Ariel?"

"I destroyed them," he said.

The hooded figures murmured their disbelief while the leaves in the massive trees rustled a protest. The scrimshaw hummed as Bertie leaned in close enough to delicately sniff him. Sweat and desperation slicked his skin, carrying something fetid on a moisture-thick breeze.

"You smell of lies, Ariel."

"I swear upon my life, I destroyed them."

"Forgive me if I don't take you at your word. Now kneel."

He did as he was told in a fluid motion that should have been impossible with his hands bound behind him.

Bertie put a foot against his back, shoving until his cheek kissed the stage. "If you know what's good for you, you'll stay down."

Anticipation rippled through the gathered crowd. Bertie motioned to the nearest pair of hooded figures and handed her sword to the larger of the two.

"If he so much as inhales with too much enthusiasm, slit his throat. It might not kill him, but it will certainly slow him down."

"Threaten all you like, but the pages are gone." Ariel twisted about to smile at her. "You won't ever get them back."

She might have panicked at the idea, except he'd tipped his hand. "You said that you destroyed them."

"I scattered them on the winds," he said.

Bertie moved in front of him and held the medallion up

so he could see it. "Do you see this, Ariel? This piece of bone cost me Nate. He's gone, stolen from this place, because he wanted me to be safe, because he wanted me to look past the surface to what lies beneath. So I'm going to do just that. I'm going to strip away your every lie."

Not waiting for his protests or promises, Bertie knelt in front of him with the medallion warm between her fingers. She looked past the delicate features, the composure and grace, to stare into the liquid black of his pupils. In the dark, she found the soul-winds he rode, peeled back the currents like so much gift wrap, and there she spotted the windmill.

"Oh, Ariel." Bertie managed a short laugh at his cleverness before issuing her command. "Call in the *Man of La Mancha* set."

"No!" he cried out.

"Not another word," Bertie said as she stood, "or I'll burn your butterflies to ash. Spirits of the air wouldn't take kindly to fire."

He made a choking noise of protest but didn't speak again.

Peaseblossom peered into the flies. "What about the trees? They're holding the ceiling up."

"Keep them in the background," Bertie said. "We can't risk moving them out completely."

The canopy of branches overhead parted, permitting an

enormous windmill to descend. It landed with a hollow thud. The impact sent a spiral of cracks skittering along the wooden floor, though long, luxuriant grasses soon obscured the fault lines. The stalks swayed in the breeze as the windmill began to rotate.

Bertie clasped The Book to her chest and held her breath. "Please let this work. Please."

Everyone waited. Another rotation of the windmill's sails marked the passing seconds like a madhouse clock. Bertie's hair unfurled over her shoulders and gathered in snarls. Caught in the same breeze, a single piece of golden paper fluttered down from the windmill and tumbled across the stage. It glowed with its own faint but undeniable light. Bertie leapt upon it and scanned the words:

ALL'S WELL THAT ENDS WELL. ACT I, SCENE I.

"It's a page from The Book." Her words spread like wildfire through the dry grasses as everyone took up the whisper. A second page fluttered down. Bertie caught it mid-flight and unfolded it.

LONDON. A GALLERY IN THE PALACE.

"This one's from *Henry the Eighth*!" Bertie smoothed it out and placed it with the other one as dozens of pages fluttered loose from the windmill's sails. "We need to gather all of them! But be careful!"

Everyone shed their cloaks and set to work.

"Mr. Hastings would love this," Moth said, dropping three more pages on Bertie's head.

"We might have to get him up here. This is ridiculous." At first Bertie tried to identify each page and sort them into some semblance of order, but she gave up as the pile in her arms grew. "All these couldn't have fit in The Book."

"That was part of the magic," Peaseblossom acknowledged, then broke off to yell, "Cobweb, stop trying to tip that thing over! You're only supposed to *tilt* at it."

Bertie glanced down at Ariel. He had his eyes closed, but she knew better than to think he was praying. "I think that's all for this set."

"Where to next, m'lady?" Mustardseed mopped his brow.

Bertie stared hard at the prostrate air elemental, remembering how he'd tried to tempt her after the Stage Manager announced she was to leave. She heard his beguiling, mesmeric voice say, "The London that doesn't appear in *Peter Pan*."

"Bring in the London set again."

The city returned just as they'd seen it at the *Hamlet* rehearsal, with cobblestones, pea-soup fog, and gaslight. The Company looked about them in confusion when no pages appeared.

"Maybe the garbage in the gutters?" Ophelia suggested.

"We're not that historically accurate," Bertie said, thinking of the rows of shelving the Properties Department would require to hold that much trash.

"Then where?" Moth demanded.

The lights shifted as ghostly actors streamed onstage. Flower girls offered their bouquets to the gentlefolk. Jack the Ripper stalked his prey while Mr. Hyde chased Dr. Jekyll. The Queen and her courtiers took the air. Shades of the past, dressed in all manner of top hats and gowns with swishing petticoats . . .

Made of paper.

"Get their clothes!" Bertie ordered. "They're wearing the pages!"

The Company blinked at her, then looked more closely at the costumes. Origami-folded flowers decorated hats and filled Eliza Doolittle's basket. Moth and Cobweb chased three Darling children flying in their pajamas until they procured a paper top hat and teddy bear. The fairy that accompanied them had a page folded into her wings. Peaseblossom and Mustardseed wrestled her to the stage and extracted it along with quite a lot of pixie dust and tinkling profanity. Mustardseed seemed quite smitten, though she gouged up his face with her tiny, glittering fingernails and bit him for an encore.

"Hurry!" Bertie commanded. "I don't want a single page loose when the lamplighters come around." She shuddered at the idea of fire.

But there were other hazards to consider first. It took three members of the Company to divest Mr. Hyde of his waistcoat. Her Royal Majesty was so loath to part with her overskirt that Ophelia was forced to sit upon her and wrestle it off. A miserly gentleman tried to bat the fairies out of the air with his umbrella when they went after his coin purse.

"Be careful!" Bertie yelled at them. "Don't rip anything!"

"Mrs. Edith is going to raise a ruckus," Peaseblossom noted. "We're dismantling her work."

"I'm not certain these are hers," Bertie said. "Have you ever seen paper clothing in the Wardrobe Department?"

"No," Peaseblossom admitted. "But who made them, then?"

Moth jumped up and down on their captive's back. "Did you do this?"

Ariel shook his head. "I scattered them, but the theater did the rest."

"Did we get them all?" Bertie asked him, holding the medallion. "Answer me true."

"Life's but a walking shadow, a poor player that struts and frets his hour upon the stage and then is heard no more," Ariel said as though against his will. "It is a tale told by an idiot, full of sound and fury, signifying nothing."

"Macbeth's line," Bertie mused. "Nothing, nothing . . . You speak an infinite deal of nothing. More than any man in all Venice." She turned to Peaseblossom. "We need to go to Venice."

"Scene change!" the fairy called out.

There was an immediate blackout. Bertie felt the Players gather around her, the rush of air as one set of buildings flew out and another replaced them. There was the rustle of pages and the sickening lap of water against docks.

When the lights flooded up, Bertie indulged in a laugh that bordered on hysteria. "Truth has indeed come into sight."

The age-worn buildings that lined the back wall, the gondola they sat in, the water of the canal itself were all made with pages from The Book.

Ariel lay prostrate in the bottom of the boat. "I guess I should be thankful I wasn't left on the stage to drown in paper."

"That's only because no one asked me my preference." Bertie sucked in a deep breath. "We need to strike the set."

"Mr. Tibbs will have our guts for garters!" Moth said, appalled.

Bertie overruled the protest. "I'm the Director, and I need the pages. *All* the pages. Take it apart. That's an order!"

Everyone dove overboard and swam in all directions at once. Two of the girls shinnied up the barber poles and pulled off the stripes. The burlier men dismantled the other boats. Ophelia sat in the gondola, very still, with her eyes closed.

"You don't want to jump in?" Bertie asked her.

"The weight of words is far heavier than water," Ophelia said. "They would drag me to the bottom and hold me captive there."

As though to prove her wrong, Macbeth backstroked through the vellum waves. "Will all great Neptune's ocean wash this blood clean from my hand?"

Moth considered the proffered appendage. "Nope, you still have jam on you."

Mr. Tibbs entered Stage Right, scattering cigar ash and sawdust in his wake. He came to a dead halt when he spotted one group tearing down the back wall while three other members of the Company captured canal water and stacked it into piles. "What in the name of the sweet god's suspenders is going on here?"

"We had a little incident." Bertie put herself in harm's way between the irate Scenic Manager and the nearly demolished set.

"Who authorized constructing scenery out of paper?" Mr. Tibbs chomped down on his cigar so hard that he bit the end right off. Peaseblossom caught the smoldering chunk before it could hit the page-covered floor, whisking it off to the ash can with her little nose wrinkled up.

"I'm afraid he did, sir." Bertie nudged Ariel with her foot. "Such a silly thing to do, I know. But who can understand the mental workings of such impractical creatures?"

Mr. Tibbs dismissed the captive air elemental with a wave of his hand and another flurry of sawdust. "This is a cursed waste of time and glue, as well as a fire hazard!"

"Just what I told him, sir," Bertie said. "Yet Mr. Hastings seemed most taken with the idea. He even took one of the gondolas down to the Properties Department to examine the craftsmanship."

"He did!" The revelation gave Mr. Tibbs pause. "The nerve of that sticky-fingered shoplifter! Something as large as a gondola is a piece of scenery!" He twitched, clearly conflicted.

Bertie hastened to reassure him. "If you want to reclaim it, I'll supervise the cleanup here, sir."

"I'll be back in just a minute! And I'll tolerate no more of your shenanigans, miss!" Mr. Tibbs turned on his heel and marched off.

Bertie sent a silent apology in Mr. Hastings' direction and hoped Mr. Tibbs wouldn't return anytime soon, as she was quite sure there were a few more shenanigans to get through.

"We got all the papers that were here," Mustardseed said.

Moth shook his tiny head. "But I'm sure some are still missing."

"Yeah, I feel pretty free," Cobweb said, "and it's not just the lack of underpants."

When Bertie reached for the scrimshaw one more time,

the words of the Sea Goddess drifted through her head, un-bidden: *His magic! The blood, the bones. You are his child!*

Bertie had devoted countless daydreams to her mother, but now there was an unnamed "him" to suddenly consider. *My father.*

It was too big an idea; it wouldn't fit inside her already crowded head. She tried not to think of it, tried not to think of Nate, of where he might be or what might have happened to him by now. Longing for the quiet, reassuring presence that would have dispatched all this turmoil with one solid blow of his cutlass against Ariel's neck, Bertie forced herself to concentrate only upon the prone figure before her. "Are we still missing pages, Ariel?"

He didn't answer.

"Where, oh, where have you hidden the rest?" Bertie looked about them. With Venice completely dismantled, the cracks in the stage floor were once again visible, as was the half-circle of ancient trees. Bertie reached out to stroke the gnarled bark, watching as a single, yellow leaf fluttered from the rafters, drifted in a downward spiral, and landed at her feet. She peered up at the thousands of leaves rustling in the boughs of the ancient trees. "They're up there."

The fairies disappeared within the branches, causing pages to rain down upon the stage.

"Be careful!" Bertie yelled.

"We are!" answered four voices. After that, the only noise came from paper fluttering through the air.

"Tricky, Ariel. Tricky, tricky, tricky." Bertie knelt next to him. "But not tricky enough."

"You can't be sure you have all of them," he muttered.

"Oh, yes," Bertie said. "I feel it, Ariel. Not in my head, or my heart, because you taught me not to rely on those. But I feel it." She leaned very close to him, until her lips brushed against his ear. "I feel it in my *bones*."

CHAPTER SEVENTEEN

Once More Unto the Breach

With The Book's leather cover still in her arms, Bertie felt a sudden sympathy and kinship with Juliet upon waking to find Romeo poisoned. She held what remained, the cooling corpse of something beloved, wishing to all the gods that she could turn the hourglass over and set things to rights.

The scene onstage was a *tableau vivant* of gloom and despair. The Ladies and Gentlemen of the Choruses gazed helplessly at the pages, stacked in some places on the stage as high as their waists, countless more filling the orchestra pit and half the seats in the auditorium.

"Fixing this is gonna take a metric buttload of glue," Moth said.

"Are you insane?" Bertie asked. "All of these won't fit back between the covers. It's physically impossible."

"Maybe you could write them back in," Mustardseed said. "The scriptwriting worked to capture Ariel."

Bertie's heart leapt at the idea and plunged just as suddenly. "My words don't affect The Book, remember? I kept trying to rewrite the ending of the scene so that The Book wasn't destroyed, but we still went to blackout. We'll have to find another way to fix it."

"It's not going to be easy." Peaseblossom shook her head. "It's a magical object."

"Or it was," Mustardseed said. "Now it just looks like a pile of recycling."

Bertie surveyed the pages piled around her. Feeble fingers of power reached out, struggling to prevent further destruction to the Théâtre.

But how long do we have before that power fades?

"There's still magic here," she said. "I just need to figure out how to use it." Picking up one of the pages, Bertie held its edge against The Book's inner spine and willed it to stick. When that didn't work, she added, "If this page goes back in, I won't make a mess on the stage ever again."

"Wow," Moth said, impressed by the enormity of her offering, but nothing happened.

"Maybe it wants something more than that," Peaseblossom said. "A bigger sacrifice."

Bertie closed her eyes. "If the pages go back in The Book, I'll stop smoking."

"Double wow!" Cobweb said, peering over her shoulder. "But it's holding out for something else."

"I could offer to clean up my language." Bertie tested it, but the only page firmly fastened was the one with Ariel's entrance—

—and just under that, a page from Macbeth.

"What the hell?" Bertie demanded.

"Ah, ah, ah, you said no more cursing!" Moth said.

Cobweb shook his head. "She said no more cursing if the page stayed in, and it didn't—"

"There are two pages in here now," Bertie interrupted.

"Impossible," Ariel said.

She tested the page, but it was stuck fast and it glowed with twice the light of the ones scattered about the floor.

SOUND AND FURY, SIGNIFYING NOTHING...

"This wasn't here before, was it?" she demanded. "I'm not imagining things, am I?"

"No," Ophelia said. "The only page Ariel couldn't get out was his own."

"Then how—"

In the distance, a door slammed.

"Uh-oh!" the fairies said in one voice.

The Stage Manager stomped into the grove. "What in the name of the Bard is going on here?" He looked from Ariel bound on the floor to the lopsided piles of paper and finally to Bertie. "Who authorized this?"

"You mean the scene change?" Bertie said. "I did."

He squinted at the pages. "This isn't from your topsy-turvy version of *Hamlet*. What's going on?"

"We're just rehearsing." Bertie tried to shift the leather cover of The Book out of sight, but too late.

The Stage Manager leapt at her with an oath. "What have you done?"

"I didn't do anything!" Bertie gestured to Ariel. "Our friendly neighborhood air spirit stole The Book and ripped its pages out."

The Stage Manager's mouth worked in silence for a moment before he recovered enough to ask the dreaded question, "When?"

Bertie hedged. "We just discovered it."

"When did Ariel take it?"

Bertie tried to think of a plausible lie, but Ariel lifted his head and divulged, "When your Director left it under a sofa in the Properties Department."

The Stage Manager looked back to Bertie. "You touched The Book?"

"I took it to *protect* it from Ariel, but he destroyed it anyway!"

247

"Wait until the Theater Manager hears what you've done." The Stage Manager raised his voice so that everyone could hear his pronouncement. "I told him over and over again that you were a troublemaker. A destructive little menace. Perhaps now he'll listen. See if you're not out on your backside within the hour!"

"Is that so?" Bertie walked over to the Chorus Member standing guard over Ariel and retrieved her sword. She turned and flicked it over the Stage Manager's shirtfront, slicing through the fabric. "Call me a destructive little menace again."

"It's the plain truth!" The Stage Manager scrambled away from her.

"Shut up." Bertie followed him. "Or the next thing I cut off will be an ear."

"The Theater Manager will hear about this!"

"Don't say I didn't warn you." Bertie poked a hole in his earlobe. He squealed like a piglet, clapping his hand to the wound and falling to the stage alongside Ariel. "I will not be threatened. Ever again. Not by you or anyone else."

"Beatrice." The Theater Manager strode onstage. "What is going on here?"

Bertie let her sword arm fall. "A little housekeeping, sir."

The Theater Manager looked from Ariel to the Stage Manager to Bertie's bloodied sword. "This doesn't look like *Hamlet*. Why are these men playing captives?"

"Because I threatened to kill them if they moved." Bertie lifted the leather husk of The Book and held it out to him. "This is how Ophelia escaped before."

The Theater Manager sucked in a breath. "She's done it again."

"It wasn't her this time." There was another shudder underfoot, and a shower of sparks fell from the overhead lighting as Bertie pointed down. "It was him."

"The only page that would not come out was my own," Ariel said with a groan.

"You were written a slave," the Theater Manager said slowly. "I suspect that someone else must free you. Someone who wields more power than Prospero. Someone who can unlock the fetters of the written words that bind you here."

Ariel looked at Bertie, a thin edge of triumph in his gaze. A howl built in his throat before he cried, "I knew it. It *is* in your power."

Bertie pointed her sword at him. "Even if the Théâtre falls down around my ears, I'll never set you free—"

"Silence!" The way the Theater Manager said it made it so. "When I gave you my permission to change things, I warned you this might happen!" His unprecedented ferocity lashed out against Bertie's anger and anxiety.

She returned his glower with a glare of her own. "And you should have told me it was Ophelia who escaped! But we can trade blame and accusations later. Right now you have to tell me how to fix The Book."

His right hand spasmed. "I don't know the answer to that, Bertie."

Her gaze slid immediately to the water-maiden, standing still and silent on the fringe of the gathered crowd. "How did you get your page back into The Book before?"

Ophelia stepped forward to answer the summons, albeit reluctantly. "I . . . I don't know."

"Come now," Bertie coaxed, struggling to keep her voice even and calm. "Think back. You must remember your return."

Ophelia bit her lip, eyes clouding as the darkest depths stirred. "I . . . was in the lobby. The Stage Manager was there."

"Why does that not surprise me?" Bertie wished she'd cut his ear all the way off and not just pierced it for him. "Then what happened?"

Ophelia grasped Bertie's hand, her grip iron and ice. "Everything was red with blood."

"It took a blood sacrifice to get your page back in?" Bertie blanched at the idea.

The Stage Manager whimpered, no doubt fearful Bertie would put his head on the chopping block without a second's hesitation.

"And the page?" Bertie whispered.

"One minute I had it, the next it was gone." Ophelia

looked bereft, her next words no more than flower petals strewn on a grave. "Do you doubt that?"

"What do you mean?" Bertie said with a frown. "I don't doubt you, if that's what you're asking."

"It's my first line in the play," Ophelia said. "I heard the words echo in my head, so I asked him that very question. . . ."

"She's forgotten what really happened, if she ever knew." The Theater Manager shook his head. "I don't know how her page was returned to The Book, or I would surely tell you how to fix this."

The scrimshaw revealed the truth in his words to Bertie as the sun reflected on a still pond, but when she looked harder, the water wavered. Secrets swam under his surface; some were delicate things, no more than an air bubble breaking, while others were hard and dark and sharp. One of them jabbed at her as he said, "I, too, wanted to be a playwright. But you already have more power over the written word than I ever did."

"Not by choice." Bertie stepped back before she could stop herself.

"No," he said. "Perhaps not. All the same, it's yours, and with it the responsibility. You are the only one with the ability to repair The Book, and you must do so with haste. I'm not sure how much longer your trees will keep this place standing."

As though to illustrate his point, another hunk of plaster

slid down the wall of the auditorium and landed in the aisle. Whispers filled Bertie's ears:

The Theater Manager. *You're the only one with the ability. . . .*

Ariel. *I knew it. It is in your power.*

Even her Mother, speaking to the Mistress of Revels about the stars in an infant girl's eyes. *She'll have magic enough because of the cursed things.*

Some unseen, golden scale tipped, and Bertie lifted her chin.

It is not in the stars to hold our destiny but in ourselves.

She thought of Nate, and the "Drink Me" bottle back-stage, broken into smithereens, its power to change less potent than the determination already unfurling inside her. Variegated vines wrapped around her bones, steadying her, planting her feet in a stance favored by Commanding Generals and Pirate Captains. "Do me one favor?"

"Yes?"

"Get him out of my sight." She pointed at the Stage Manager.

The Theater Manager grimly nodded and heaved his colleague up. "Come on, old chap. We'd best get out of the way."

Bertie turned, ready to dispense orders. "Ophelia?"

The water-maiden stepped forward. "Yes?"

"I need you to fetch the Managers."

"Of course." Ophelia didn't drift away this time. Instead, she walked with purpose, her steps firm and steady upon the floor.

Bertie looked down at Ariel. "What am I going to do with you?"

He raised an eyebrow at her. "Another tango, dear heart?"

"Something involving hot pokers and salt in your wounds would be more apropos, but I don't have time for that now. What we need is a brig, or a nice scummy dungeon."

"Those wouldn't be able to hold me."

"That sounds like a challenge to me." Bertie reached for her clipboard. "Yours is the last page in the book; without it the theater cannot survive. And though you can't tear it free yourself, you can certainly stir up more trouble. I guess I'll just have to write you into imprisonment. I hear tell I have some power over words." He started to protest, but she raised her voice. "Someone dim the lights."

Bertie uncapped her pen and started to write.

CHAPTER EIGHTEEN

Tribunal

The blacksmiths meet under the light of the new moon.

The trapdoor opened Center Stage. A forge spiraled into place with the groan of wood and metal-shudder. A luminescent moon rose in the background on wires so thin, it appeared to float.

When the Blacksmiths entered, Bertie shook her pen at them. "Be careful about the sparks. The Book's pages have been through enough already."

The men took their places around the forge and waited for her to write another direction. Bertie let the tip of her pen bleed a puddle of ink before she thought of what to write next.

*They fashion a collar of earth
and fire and water: punishment
enough for a creature of the air,
to be so shackled.*

The Blacksmiths started to pound on glowing metal in three-quarter time. Smoke spiraled up like a ballerina dancing *en pointe*. There was the unmistakable boiling hiss of hot metal hitting water.

"They bring him forth bound, as befits a criminal," Bertie said.

Two Chorus Members hefted Ariel to his feet, though he struggled.

"The villain is still weakened by his misuse of the magic," Bertie continued, determined and merciless. "So he cannot stop her when the Righter of Wrongs places the collar around his neck and binds him to the place that he hates most of all."

"It is ready," the largest Blacksmith said.

Bertie set the clipboard down on the stage and reached for the collar; it glowed brighter with the growing power of her enchantment even as the forge's heat faded to a dim memory. "If you please."

"You'll need a witch to bless it," he said through his beard.

"I am the Witch," Bertie said. "I am the Writer of Words and the Changer of Scenes. The truth spills from my mouth, painting this world the color of my choosing."

The Blacksmith nodded and placed the collar in her hands. The warmth in the metal, like ember-glow, spread through Bertie's fingers as she took one step toward Ariel, then another.

His eyes begged her—for mercy, for something—but she didn't hesitate to place the band around his neck. The moment the two ends touched, they sealed shut, and he moaned.

"You are bound here, Ariel, to serve and protect the Théâtre. Your page is still in The Book, and so shall it remain."

He writhed as though he could hardly bear the weight of her sentence upon him. "I hope it all crumbles to dust."

"I believe you wish that." Bertie tapped on the collar so that the metal vibrated. "But as long as you wear this, your page cannot be torn from The Book. By anyone." She raised her voice. "Can everyone hear me? None shall be persuaded to free this creature."

"We hear," they said.

Bertie nodded to the ones that held his arms. "You can untie him now."

Ariel remained on his knees, neck bowed, hair tumbling over his shoulders to obscure his face. "Bertie." Her name on his lips was a plea.

"Get up," she said.

Against his wishes, Ariel stood.

Bertie pushed his hair back until she could see his eyes. "If I tell you to dance a jig, you will. If I ask you to mop the floors with your tongue, you will. Is that quite clear?"

"Yes." He lifted his eyes to meet hers. "Was the collar really necessary?"

Bertie gestured to the pages that littered the stage. "You tell me, Ariel. Tell me that you didn't do your best to destroy The Book. Tell me that you won't try to sabotage us again at the first possible opportunity. And if you speak, let it be the truth." When he could not, Bertie stepped back and tried to ignore the remorse already pricking her. "You brought this upon yourself."

"Quoth the jailer," he said.

"It's the truth," Bertie said. "You betrayed us all."

"The truth is in the mouth of the orator, and your truth is not mine."

"Save it, Ariel. . . ." Bertie's voice trailed off as she realized that neither his hair nor his clothes moved with his customary wind.

He stood coffin-still, as though carved from stone instead of poured from quicksilver. "Do you really hate me so much?"

"I hate what you did, Ariel. Help me to make it right."

"I won't deny you," he said, "because I cannot. But don't think for a moment that I do it for you or this place."

"Understood." Bertie hardened her heart against him.

"What would you have me do first?" Ariel asked with a stilted bow.

"Go find me a quad-shot cappuccino." Bertie turned her back on him, as clear a signal as any that she no longer considered him a threat; harder to admit, she feared she would cry if forced to look upon the defeated slump of his shoulders one second longer. She heard him move away and counted to three before she turned around.

Ariel was gone. At her feet, two of his red-and-gold familiars lay on the stage. Bertie knelt next to them.

I killed them, and Ariel's probably passed out backstage because the damn collar strangled him.

Bertie tasted something foul in the back of her throat. For a moment she thought she might throw up, but one butterfly twitched its delicate antennae and the other fluttered its wings. With a shaky sigh, Bertie gathered them up before someone could squash them. Once in her hand, they recovered enough to crawl into her hair and perch there, like brilliant barrettes.

The fairies flew back onstage at full speed, preceding Ophelia.

"I got them, Bertie!" the water-maiden called.

Sure enough, the Department Managers were heading toward Bertie like a cavalry at full charge. The triumvirate collectively goggled at the pages, the assorted damage to the house, and Bertie's thoroughly disheveled appearance.

"What on earth—" Mrs. Edith started to say before words failed her.

"It looks worse than it is," Bertie promised.

"I don't see how that is possible," Mrs. Edith said, "because it looks very, very bad indeed."

"It's not her fault!" Peaseblossom rushed to Bertie's defense. The other fairies chimed in and, with a jumble of cross-corrections and one fistfight, they managed to bring the Managers up to speed. Bertie didn't interject so much as a peep of disagreement, even when they suggested that she'd cut off the Stage Manager's head and fed it to a crocodile.

"The magic is breaking," she said at that juncture. "We have to find a way to get the pages back in The Book before the Théâtre falls apart."

Mr. Hastings pursed his lips, scanning the amount of paper piled onstage with a professional eye. "They should be filed straightaway, with every page in order."

Mrs. Edith waved a pair of scissors under his nose. "Anything I can't fix with my glue gun isn't possible to fix."

Mr. Tibbs chomped on a replacement cigar and glowered at them. "You're both off your heads. Get this rubbish off my stage so I can start repairing the floor."

"It isn't rubbish, my dear Mr. Tibbs," protested Mr.

Hastings. "Were you not attending? These are pages from The Book, for pity's sake!"

"I heard. Someone has got to clean this mess up, and right smart, too—"

"That's enough!" Bertie shouted over the top of them. Everyone fell silent, as startled by the order as by the authoritative steel in her voice. "The only thing holding this place together is the last page, if I guess correctly."

"Pages," Peaseblossom corrected.

Bertie had nearly forgotten. "That's right. There are two in The Book now."

"But how'd the second one get in there?" Moth wanted to know.

"I don't know." Bertie turned to the second page, running her index finger along the words. "Sound and fury, signifying nothing."

"It's a famous speech," Mustardseed said.

"That's true. But why *this* famous speech? Why not the balcony scene, or Hamlet's speech to the Players?" The butterflies opened and closed their wings, stirring a tiny wind in Bertie's hair. "It was the one that Ariel quoted, right before we went to Venice."

Cobweb wrinkled up his little forehead. "So?"

"Ophelia!" Bertie pointed at the nearest stack of pages. "Pick one up and read it to me."

The rest of the Company ceased milling about aimlessly

and suddenly looked very alert indeed as Ophelia cleared her throat.

"A little more than kin, and less than kind." She paused. "It's Hamlet's first line."

Moth zoomed in, trying to be helpful. "You're not reading it with the correct inflections."

Ophelia tilted her head, a wicked gleam appearing in her eyes. When next she spoke, it was in perfect mimicry of the Danish prince. " 'Tis not alone my inky cloak, good mother, nor customary suits of solemn black. Nor windy suspiration of forced breath. No, nor the fruitful river in the eye!"

The page in her hand faded around the edges. Bertie whispered, "Keep going!"

"Nor the dejected 'havior of the visage," Ophelia bellowed. Bertie could see the water-maiden's hand through the paper now. "Together with all forms, moods, shapes of grief—"

The page vanished completely. The Managers yelped, the Chorus Members swore in amazement, and Bertie opened The Book. She was almost afraid to look, but the missing page was back inside, bound firmly, she found, when she tugged ever so gently at it. Underfoot, the largest of the cracks in the floor sealed over.

"That's it! *That's* how we get the pages back inside!" Bertie hugged Ophelia around the neck. "You were brilliant!"

"Thank you." The other girl turned a lovely shade of

pink, the first color Bertie had ever seen on her that didn't come from a pot of rouge.

She couldn't linger over the transformation, though. "Peaseblossom, take the boys and put a notice on the Call Board. I want everyone onstage immediately. We have to *act* the plays back into The Book."

"All the plays?!" Peaseblossom looked aghast. "Do you have any idea how long that will take?"

"Do you have any idea how long the Théâtre will remaining standing if we don't do it?" Bertie asked.

"No," the fairy answered.

"Neither do I, but it's a better option than leaving the pages all over the stage to molder and rot, with the magic scattered everywhere and the theater reduced to rubble. Right?"

"I guess so," said Peaseblossom. "At least it will give the Chorus Members something to do besides wander about."

Bertie crooked a finger at Mr. Hastings, Mr. Tibbs, and Mrs. Edith. "I need you three to get back to your Departments and hustle up the necessities for the performance. It's still going to happen."

Before they could even twitch, the door at the back of the auditorium slammed open and everyone jumped. As someone stalked down the aisle, Bertie lifted her hand to block the glare from the footlights.

"Thanks a lot." Hamlet lit a cigarette and sagged against the wall.

"Sarcasm noted," Bertie said. "You're thanking us for what, exactly?"

"For whatever enchantment you performed to pull me back into the theater."

"We didn't do anything," said Cobweb.

Bertie silenced the fairy with a look before she returned her attention to Hamlet. "You left."

"Yes." His floppy hair fell into his eyes.

"Why?"

"I was going to find a girlfriend who didn't need medication," he said, with a lazy smile for Ophelia.

Bertie was going to tell him not to be such a jerk, but Ophelia surprised all of them by making a rude noise. "I deserve far better than you, you know that?"

Hamlet gaped at her, and Moth took the opportunity to pose the question Bertie was already wondering. "Where did you go?"

"Some sort of drinking establishment." Hamlet took a long drag and flicked ash on the carpet runner. "I'd just ordered something called a Hefeweizen."

"And then what?" Cobweb took up the interrogation, trying to sound tough.

"The woman next to me offered to pay. Very forward of her." Hamlet thought it over and added, "She was far too old for me. One-and-twenty, if a day, and I very much doubt that her virtue was still intact."

Bertie sighed and tried not to think about how good it would feel to punch him in the nose. "And after the middle-aged harlot offered to pay for your drink?"

"I felt a prickle in the back of my throat. Words echoed in my head. My words, but not my voice, if that makes any sense." He took another drag off his cigarette. "'A little more than kin, and less than kind.' Then I wasn't there any-more."

"You walked out of the bar?" Bertie said.

"No. I just wasn't there anymore. I wasn't anywhere. About the time I was thinking what a terrible bore eternity in limbo was going to be, I realized I was in the lobby." Hamlet detached himself from the wall, taking quite a lot of plaster dust with him, and ambled toward the stairs that led up to the stage.

"*That's* how Ophelia came back," Bertie said. "Someone said her opening line." Then she made a noise like the Mouse King squeaking.

"What is it?" Peaseblossom demanded, looking alarmed.

"Man overboard!" Bertie bellowed.

The fairies looked about them in confusion. "Where?"

Bertie clutched The Book to her chest and fixed a pierc-ing gaze upon the Exit door. "Man overboard, man over-board! Work, damn it."

"Nate's line!" Peaseblossom said, comprehension dawn-ing. "We can get him back!"

"We can!" Bertie hugged her hopes close. "Man overboard!"

"Man overboard!" the boys shouted.

"How long did it take," Bertie demanded, turning to Hamlet, "between the throat-prickle and reappearing in the lobby?"

"A few seconds only," Ophelia answered for him. "I finished reading his lines, the page reappeared in The Book, and he was transported to the Théâtre."

"Man overboard!" Bertie waited, counting to ten. Her heart thudded in time with the passing seconds. "Man overboard!"

Peaseblossom tried to look hopeful. "Sedna probably took Nate miles and miles away, so it will take longer than a few seconds to bring him back."

"That must be it." Bertie refused to believe it wouldn't work. "Assign his line to one of the Players and have him repeat it until Nate walks through the door!"

"Will do!" The fairies disappeared from sight.

Hamlet edged closer to whisper in her ear. "You are quite fetching when you're domineering."

Bertie elbowed him swiftly in the gut. "Don't you dare put the moves on me, Mister Melancholy. Start acting those pages back into The Book, and if I see you so much as twitch toward that Exit door, I'll poison you myself."

CHAPTER NINETEEN

Toil and Trouble

By the time Ariel returned with Bertie's coffee, a sort of controlled pandemonium reigned. The Danish Prince and a group of Chorus Members read pages from *Hamlet* as quickly as they were found, while everyone else sorted and stacked the rest into their play-appropriate heaps. Each seat in the theater housed its own pile, and the constant motion of the Players was a gliding court dance set to the music of shuffling paper.

"Hurry up," Bertie yelled at the swarm onstage. "Don't make me order a beating. . . . What time is it?"

"Early in the morning," Peaseblossom said. "Very, very early."

"Thank you, official timekeeper."

"And so reigned the tyrant, Beatrice the Terrible." Ariel

managed to stay out of arm's reach while handing her the coffee. He did a double take when he spotted her borrowed hair accoutrements, but said nothing about the defection of his butterflies. "What did I miss?"

"We found a way to undo the damage you did." Bertie gestured that he should sit on the floor, since all the available seats were occupied.

His posture was less perfect than usual when he obeyed. "Brava."

Bertie sucked on the cappuccino as though it were the Elixir of Life, as well it was by then. She was so tired that her bones ached.

Ariel waved a hand at the surrounding chaos. "I see you organized the troops. Excellent demonstration of time management."

"If I need my butt kissed, I'll ask for it," Bertie said.

"What do you want kissed instead?" he asked.

"Shut up."

He obliged.

"I don't like this any more than you do, all right?" Bertie said.

He nodded and pressed his lips together in an exaggerated silence that thoroughly irritated her, but everything irritated her right now. Bertie shoved the now-empty cup at him and stomped off.

"What are *you* looking at?" she snarled at a member

of the Ladies' Chorus who was sorting out *Titus Andronicus*.

"Nothing!" Three pages fluttered to the ground, and the girl rushed to pick them up.

Peaseblossom returned before Bertie could yell and kick things. "Hey, boss lady!"

"How are we progressing?" Bertie demanded.

"We can't find any more *Hamlet* pages, but I'm pretty sure we read in all the entrance lines." Peaseblossom pointed at the stage. "All the Players from that show are present and accounted for, at any rate. I checked them off against the cast list twice."

Bertie opened The Book. Counting under her breath and then checking again just to be sure, she whispered to Peaseblossom, "All pages from *Hamlet* are back in. I guess it just takes the entrance lines."

"That's good," Peaseblossom said, "because there's something else you need to know."

Bertie sighed. "More bad news?"

"No, no. Not really *bad* . . ." Peaseblossom's voice trailed off.

"Just tell me what it is."

"We're sorting more pages than just Shakespeare."

"What?!"

"It's *The Complete Works of the Stage*, not *The Complete Works of the Bard*. So it's not just the Shakespearean plays, it's—"

"All the plays ever written." Bertie's legs wobbled, or it might have been structural damage to the building that made the floor tremble.

"Breathe!" Peaseblossom advised. "It will be all right. Really it will. Why don't we just leave it at *Hamlet*? Why does it have to be all of them?"

There was a shudder overhead, another shower of plaster, paint, and frescoed ceiling.

"That's why, Pease," Bertie said, shaking the dust out of her hair. "Besides which, even if the Théâtre weren't falling apart, what would you propose we do with the pages in the meantime? File them? Cart them off in boxes? Even Mr. Hastings couldn't handle this mess."

"Then the plan is still the same," the fairy said. "It's just going to take longer to get it done, is all."

"We have to finish before Friday night." Bertie forced herself to sound calm and firm.

"That gives us the rest of today, tomorrow, and most of Friday," Peaseblossom said, trying to sound upbeat. "We need to maximize efficiency, so let's run multiple plays at the same time."

Bertie looked at seat after seat filled with the various scripts. "Finish sorting the pages off the stage, and then have two platforms lowered in, three if we can fit them. I want every available Player acting around the clock until further notice. Is someone still saying Nate's line?"

"One of the minor Players," the fairy said. "It just needs time to work."

But Bertie felt the hope, round and gold, slipping away from her like a coin thrown into a wishing fountain. She clung to it with determination.

"I know you don't want to consider it," Peaseblossom said, her voice soft, "but Sedna's magic may be stronger than the Théâtre's. She is a goddess, after all."

"I don't care. Keep trying."

"Will do!" Peaseblossom said before she darted back toward the stage.

"Bertie!"

"What now?" Bertie glowered at the new arrival. "Mustardseed, if you tell me one more thing has gone wrong, I will hurl myself off the second balcony."

"Okay," he said. "Nothing else has gone wrong."

She debated leaving it at that, then yielded. "Are you lying?"

He squirmed a bit and pulled his vest over his face. The next words were muffled by quilting and embroidery. "Depends on how you define the word 'wrong.'"

"What is it?"

He peeked at her with an eye as bright as the black button next to it. "Nothing. I mean, I just noticed that Ariel's . . . er . . . gone."

Bertie looked around; sure enough, Ariel was nowhere to

be seen in the flurry of activity. "I didn't actually forbid him to leave the immediate vicinity. I should have, but I didn't."

"Do you want me to look for him?" Mustardseed asked.

"It would be a good idea to find him before he does something stupid, yes," said Bertie. "Tell him I said to get back in here and that's an order."

"Got it!"

Bertie sat down on the floor and closed her eyes. For the moment, no one was looking her direction, pulling on her sleeve, or calling her name—

"Bertie?"

So much for that.

"Yes?" She cracked one eye open.

"You look tired," Ophelia said.

"I am tired," said Bertie. "And there's really no end in sight, is there?"

The water-maiden's smile was rueful. "I did try to warn you. About The Book, that is."

"Yes, you did." Bertie motioned to the place next to her. "You can join me, if you don't mind sitting on the ground."

Ophelia settled herself with a graceful folding of limbs and arrangement of skirts. "I wanted to apologize."

"For what?"

"For all this. I might have done better, explaining the dangers, but clarity sometimes eludes me. It's like a silver fish swimming through the water." She caught hold of Bertie's hand, quicker than any of the asps could have struck. "Sometimes I catch it! And sometimes it slips out of reach."

Bertie frowned. "It's all right. You did your best for—"

"A crazy girl?" Ophelia suggested, letting go of Bertie's hand.

"You're not crazy."

"No," Ophelia agreed. "Not today. Today, I have the fish firmly in hand."

Good grief. Bertie would have made her excuses and ducked off to supervise the bedlam, but curiosity pricked at her. "When you tore your page out, where did you go?"

Ophelia looked at the wall opposite, but seemed to see something much farther away than the water-stained velvet wallpaper and sagging moldings. "On a vacation by the seaside. When all this is done, you should do the same."

"If I go on vacation, it won't be to the seaside," Bertie said.

"Oh, but it was lovely." Ophelia took an ivory comb out of her pocket and began to plait her hair, weaving in flowers and shells with thoughtless dexterity. "What I remember of it, that is."

Feeling suddenly unkempt, Bertie attempted to tidy her wayward blue snarls with her fingers. "What *do* you remember?"

Ophelia finished the braid with a loop of gilt ribbon and

a tidy knot instead of the fussy bow Bertie had expected. "The calls of the seagulls. Endless blue water."

"Don't you get enough of the water here?"

Ophelia held up her comb. "May I?" When Bertie nodded, the other girl teased through the mess with ivory tines, untangling the knots and twisting curls about her fingers.

Bertie closed her eyes. Mrs. Edith often combed her hair, an efficient pass with a brush accompanied by a good-natured smack on the head when Bertie didn't hold still enough for her taste. But this was soothing. Hypnotic.

Another ten strokes and I'd bark like a dog if she asked me to.

Ophelia broke the spell by repositioning the butterfly barrettes and patting Bertie on the shoulder. "There you are. I see Ariel headed this way, so if you'll excuse me?"

"Of course."

Ophelia's skirts fluttered as she walked down the aisle, and flower petals drifted in her wake to mingle with the pages.

"She's a thing of loveliness." Ariel lowered himself to the floor.

"I didn't give you permission to leave," Bertie said.

"Ah! But you didn't tell me that I couldn't."

"Enough with your double negatives, miscreant. Where did you go?"

"To refill this, O tyrannical one." He handed her another paper coffee cup. "I figured I might earn my way back into your good graces by keeping you in quad-shot cappuccinos until you are awash in caffeine."

"Ah. Good." Bertie nodded, feeling stupid. "Thanks."

"Where did you think I went? Gallivanting, perhaps? Persuading an unsuspecting damsel to remove my shackles?"

"I didn't have much time to think about it, to be quite honest." Bertie sipped the foam off the top of the coffee. "But it made me nervous all the same."

"Would you like me to stay in your line of sight at all times?" His dark eyes regarded her. "Ask and ye shall receive, Milady."

"No, I think I'll just have Mustardseed shadow you," Bertie said.

"Have you so little faith in your word-spell?"

"It's the first time I've condemned someone to eternal servitude," Bertie snapped. "Stop questioning me."

"Questioning you? I wouldn't dream of it." Ariel made a great show of squirming around to get comfortable. "So what did Ophelia want?"

"What's it to you?"

"I harbor certain concerns about her, the least of which is that she's a few bricks short of a cartload."

"That's singularly unkind," Bertie said. "And you're hardly the person I would ask to judge rational behavior."

"All that imagery with the flowers is unnerving," he said.

"White carnations symbolize innocence, faithfulness. And pure love. Ardent love. You've seen how she feels about Hamlet."

"It's less than ardent," Bertie admitted. "But her flower obsession isn't a reason to cart her off to the loony bin."

"There you are!" Mustardseed careened overhead and landed with a splash in the middle of Bertie's coffee.

With an exclamation of annoyance, she fished him out before he could drown. "Watch where you land, please. I was drinking that!"

Mustardseed sputtered foamed milk and pointed an accusing finger at Ariel. "I searched everywhere for you!"

"I'm always in the last place you look," Ariel said.

"Don't change the subject." Mustardseed shook like a tiny dog, throwing droplets of cappuccino all over Bertie's jeans.

"I wasn't attempting to change the subject, but if it makes you feel better, I'll shut up," Ariel offered. "I've had a lot of practice at it today."

Mustardseed, who'd no doubt been working up to a good "shut up," wrung out his shirt and stomped off to join Cobweb.

"Explain something to me?" Ariel said, his voice low.

Bertie picked up her coffee cup, considered the questionable content of the now-murky depths, and put it back down. "What?"

"Your admirer. The daring swashbuckler." Ariel slanted

a look at her. "You said he was stolen away. How did that come to pass?"

"I am not having this conversation with you." Bertie scrambled to her feet and fled, but Ariel kept pace with her.

"Indulge my idle curiosity," he coaxed.

Bertie flinched when she thought of her tears hitting the scrimshaw, the auditorium instantly ocean-filled. She slammed through the door and into the deserted hallway. "He was kidnapped."

"Ah." Ariel said only the one word, but it was more than enough. "He's being held against his will somewhere?"

Bertie pressed her back to the Call Board and her fists to her eyes. She didn't want to imagine the lair of the Sea Goddess, nor Nate in shackles. "Yes."

Ariel grasped her hands with his own and pulled them away from her face. "It's not your fault, Bertie."

She kept her eyes on the floor, refusing to meet his gaze. "It is. I summoned her."

Ariel put a finger under her chin and coaxed her to look up. "You would free him if you could."

"Yes." The word was more than a promise.

Ariel's smile was all things wounded and rueful. "Yet you won't do the same for me."

"It's not the same thing," Bertie whispered.

"Why not?"

"Because I don't trust you, Ariel."

He pulled her close. "Someday, I will win your trust, and you will be the one to set me free. I know it."

"I won't." Bertie recoiled from both him and the assertion she would do such a thing. "Not ever."

Ariel made no move to touch her again, though his words were a caress. "Don't make promises you won't be able to keep."

CHAPTER TWENTY

But a Walking Shadow

Bertie didn't let him corner her alone again. For the next forty-eight hours, she positioned herself in the center of the noise and chaos, well guarded by the fairies, constantly surrounded by unwitting chaperones. Even now, the morning of the performance, a stream of minions carried props backstage while carpenters smashed bits of scenery in and out of place. Mrs. Edith and a horde of fluttering assistants seemed to be everywhere at once as they pinned, trimmed, and hemstitched costumes.

The Players kept at their lines, and every page acted back into The Book repaired a bit of the Théâtre. The healing was as noisy as the destruction had been. Dust swirled and coalesced to reconstruct plaster statues and moldings. Gilt paint spread like gossip. Rents in both fabric and wood knit themselves back together. Bertie led the cast of *Hamlet* through rehearsal after rehearsal, and with each run-through, the Players coped better with the decorative changes. But Bertie still fretted over every dropped cue, every misstep. If the play was a failure, she could blame the lack of time to prepare compounded by the constant stream of interruptions and the shouting that threatened to deafen them all.

"Get out of the way!"

"Line! Someone give me my line!"

And always, the never-ending litany of "Bertie! Bertie!"

"The next person who calls my name gets a boot to the head," she told Peaseblossom just before a scenic flat came crashing down on Oberon and Titania.

"Bertie!"

"That's my cue." She ran for the stage and arrived just as Mr. Tibbs and the Stage Manager levered the fallen pyramid off the fairy king and queen. "I know the acting was bad, but attempted murder is a bit much."

"I beg your pardon!" Oberon struggled to his feet and still managed to look haughty with a scrape down his cheek. "There wasn't a single thing wrong with my performance."

Bertie corrected him. "Certainly you're the ultimate personification of the Bard's vision for the fairy king, but I've noticed a few changes for the worse since you started reading entrance lines."

"Such as?" Titania righted herself and sulked as hard as someone covered in glitter and flower petals was capable of sulking.

"Overacting, posing and posturing, giving in to inherent ego, hogging the limelight, upstaging one another. . . . Shall I continue?"

Titania didn't look the least bit abashed. "Perhaps we wouldn't have to overact if you could do something about these people running amok."

"The people running amok are loading the scenery for the performance scheduled to take place tonight."

"The scenery normally moves of its own accord—"

"Yes, but normally *Hamlet* doesn't take place in Egypt, does it? The show must go on, but that's contingent upon your ability to move your royal backsides and finish reading the entrance lines you were assigned."

"The impudence!" said Titania.

"The rudeness!" said Oberon.

"The schedule!" Bertie repressed the urge—for the hundred millionth time that day—to run everyone through the nearest wood chipper.

Surely they have one in the Scenic Dock? I can be the Demon Director of Whatever Street the Théâtre is on. Double bonus points if the Stage Manager has a heart attack when he sees the resultant mess.

Bertie's homicidal thoughts must have showed on her

face, because Peaseblossom spoke out of the side of her mouth, "You can't kill them. You need them."

"For now," Bertie added in an undertone before she raised her voice. "I'm sorry that pyramid landed on your head, but it's not like someone yoinked your brain out through your nose."

"Did someone call for mummification?" Moth appeared, armed with a buttonhook. "We'll prepare you for eternal slumber, internal organs removed and body wrapped in gauze, for one low, low price!"

"But wait!" Cobweb added. "If you act in the next five minutes—"

Bertie shooed them offstage and let the Fairy Court go back to swaggering. "Don't I have enough to worry about, without the two of you contributing to the commotion?"

The door to the auditorium opened to admit the latest recaptured character. Bertie whirled around, only to suffer fresh disappointment.

Come on, Nate. You've had time to crawl back from the ends of the earth. What's she done to you?

"Bertie!"

She turned to find Mr. Tibbs's cigar in her face. "Yes?"

"You tell that little shrimp-tail of a Properties Manager that the necropolis is part of the scenery, and I'll thank him to leave it alone!"

"Necropolis?" Maybe she needed more coffee, but she'd already had four, and her entire body was starting to vibrate.

"You know! The necropolis! 'Alas, poor Yorick.' The Graveyard scene?" Mr. Tibbs returned her blank gaze with impatience. "Are you playing the fool, or have your brains turned into pudding?"

"The Graveyard scene. The necropolis." Bertie nodded and did her best to look knowledgeable. "I remember now. My apologies, it's just that I've had more than enough of bones lately."

"Enough bones or not, you tell Hastings to keep his sticky fingers to himself!" Mr. Tibbs stomped off Stage Left.

Peaseblossom appeared. "Bertie!"

"Yes?"

"We have a little problem," the fairy said. "Rosencrantz and Guildenstern are in the middle of a violent argument with the Properties Manager in regard to their daggers."

Before she could ask, Mr. Hastings shoved a handful of paperwork under Bertie's nose.

"I will not put up with this nincompoopery!" he proclaimed, so angry that he was purple in the face. He stood ramrod straight for once, three full inches taller than usual. "Forms should have been filled out in triplicate, but these miscreants showed up at the Properties Department and started pulling weapons off the shelves without so much as a by-your-leave. I want them all returned immediately!"

"Mr. Hastings, I'm so sorry. I must have missed the daggers on the requisitions list. It's completely my fault." Bertie put her hand on his arm, turning on every bit of her charm. "Surely there is something we can do about this."

He held himself as stiffly as a bronze temple statue. "Nothing short of resubmitting the paperwork and giving me time to process it."

Bertie channeled every Southern Belle that ever was; all she lacked was a parasol and hoop skirt. "These gentlemen were just trying to help me. There's so much to be done yet, you see, and I'm starting to fret."

His nostrils flared. "Badinage, Bertie?"

"And persiflage," she said. "Your idea, remember?"

"It was, wasn't it?" The anger leaked out of him, and his shoulders resumed their usual hunched position.

"One of your better ones," Bertie said. "Now, what can I do to set the situation to rights?"

Mr. Hastings sorted through the papers, muttering things like "I can fill this one out myself" and "I don't know why we still even use this form, it's clearly recapitulatory" every so often. In the end, Bertie had to initial the pink one and sign the green.

"I'll waive the one-week waiting period," he said as he straightened the pile. "But don't let anyone know, or they'll all want it waived."

Bertie nodded, not wanting to remind him that if the

new production failed to impress the audience, she wouldn't be around to let the secret slip. "Now, if you would be so kind as to rearm everyone? I can't have them pretending to stab each other with their fingers, can I?"

Mr. Hastings smiled, the first friendly expression he'd bestowed on her since the incident with Marie Antoinette's chaise. He even managed an eye twitch that might have been a wink. "Right away, Bertie."

"And Mr. Hastings?"

"Yes, my dear?"

"Mr. Tibbs is on the warpath about the necropolis."

Mr. Hastings held up a sheaf of papers. "The nerve! I have the paperwork right here for that!" He departed, muttering about signatures and inventory.

"Excuse me, dear," Mrs. Edith said. "I hate to trouble you with so much going on."

"No worries, it's your turn. What's wrong with Wardrobe?" Bertie waited to hear a complaint about the Chorus Girls wanting to wear high heels or the lack of beads and bracelets for Gertrude.

Instead, Mrs. Edith lowered her voice. "I wanted to speak with you in private for a moment."

"What about?"

"About how you arrived here."

The words jolted Bertie out of her caffeine-fueled stupor. "I thought you'd told me all you knew?"

"I gave my word to the Theater Manager that I wouldn't say more." Lines cut deep around Mrs. Edith's mouth, each word uttered as though it was a battle won. "It seemed like the right thing to do at the time."

"And now?" It hurt to breathe; with the hammering and shouting amongst the crew members, it even hurt to think.

Mrs. Edith's thin-rimmed glasses reflected the stage lights, and Bertie couldn't see her eyes. "I realize what a mistake that was." The Wardrobe Mistress leaned closer and lowered her voice. "That man is not as he appears. Please be careful. He—"

"Bertie?" The Theater Manager strode down the red-carpeted aisle. He'd loosened his tie, and the top button of his shirt was undone. "How's the repair of The Book going?"

Bertie cleared her throat and tried to look blasé. "We're making progress."

"Brilliant," he said. "I knew you could do it."

Bertie twitched, trying to reconcile the relief in his words with the idea that he was keeping secrets from her. "Mrs. Edith was just telling me—"

"That I'm having difficulty with Gertrude," Mrs. Edith interrupted. "She won't wear her new costume. In fact, she's refusing to go on in it, and I need our Director to speak with her."

Bertie nodded slowly. "Of course. Right away."

The Wardrobe Mistress pointed. "She's in the temporary

Wardrobe. The costume you're looking for is in the trunk in the corner."

Bertie made her escape, threading her way through sawdust and ladders to the silk-swathed changing area Mrs. Edith's minions had constructed in the back of the auditorium.

"Gertrude?" Bertie ducked inside the tent. "I've come to sort out the misunderstanding about your costume. Mrs. Edith says you don't approve?"

No one answered, though dozens of servitor costumes in various stages of completion swayed gently on a metal garment rack. Bertie slipped past a padded step stool and a full-length mirror. She peered up, impressed by the swagged draperies, the cream-papered Japanese lanterns that illuminated the various work stations, the dress form modeling a flowing robe of darkest blue, the hatboxes stacked at regular intervals.

But Gertrude wasn't there.

Whatever are you playing at, Mrs. Edith?

Bertie crossed to the trunk in the corner and pushed the lid back, expecting to find golden gauze or pleated silver tissue, light layers suited to the scorching hot Egyptian sun. Instead, her fingertips met the heaviest of silk: emerald and black, embroidered with golden moons. The dress rustled like the gown of a duchess or the kimono of a Japanese geisha, and underneath its folds glimmered a belt of shining disks.

All that was missing was the woman with hair and eyes like bits of the night sky. The woman who had brought Bertie to the Théâtre.

"I was right," she breathed. "There *was* a Mistress of Revels."

Bertie lifted the dress up, smelling only mothballs and the cedar lining of the trunk in place of perfume, Mrs. Edith's lavender water instead of campfire smoke. She checked inside the neckline, but there was no label of muslin tape, which the Wardrobe Mistress would have sewn into a costume before writing the Player's name upon it with permanent marker.

"Who do you belong to, then?" Bertie held the shimmering fall of fabric against her chest.

"What are you doing in here?" Peaseblossom said, appearing as though summoned. "You look as pale as . . . well, Hamlet's Father's sheet."

Bertie swayed her hips; the heavy skirts hit her legs in an uncomfortable reminder of the dream-dress summoned by the "Drink Me" bottle and the tango music. "Pease, does this look at all familiar to you?"

The fairy peered from the layers of silk to Bertie. "Is this a trick question?"

"Not at all. Just trying to make sure I haven't gone stark, raving mad, because it looks like Verena's dress. Only it's not a costume. It's the real thing."

Peaseblossom's wings paused mid-flutter, and she fell nearly a foot before recovering. "What does that mean?"

Bertie reluctantly replaced her discovery in the trunk and closed the lid with a bang. "I'm trying to puzzle that out myself, but I think it means I was right." She ducked out of the tent, searching for Mrs. Edith in the throng.

The fairy followed her, trying to catch up physically as well as mentally. "About what?"

"About the Mistress of Revels bringing me to the Théâtre."

Peaseblossom's eyes had gone huge and round. "Part of *How Bertie Came to the Theater* was true? But why would Mrs. Edith have her clothes?"

"Maybe," Bertie said, hardly daring to draw a breath, "Verena is still here."

"Bertie," Peaseblossom whispered, "she'd know who your mother is! And where to find her."

"Not just my mother, Pease."

Sedna couldn't touch me because I am "his child." But who is this mysterious father, and what's he got to do with my medallion? Was it uncanny luck that Nate chose it for me, of all the things in the Properties Department, or did he know more than he let on?

Bertie fell into one of the auditorium chairs and put her aching head between her knees. "I can't think about all this now!"

Peaseblossom patted her on the shoulder. "Do you

want me to gather the boys and look for your Mistress of Revels?"

"One thing at a time, Pease. We have to finish fixing The Book first."

"Oh!" The fairy straightened up and put her fingers to her mouth, letting loose an ear-piercing whistle. The group of Players onstage halted what they were doing. The lights on them cross-faded to a single golden spotlight that came up on The Book.

"What's happened?" Bertie asked.

"That's what I came to tell you! The last of the pages are back in, Bertie. Well, all except Nate's." Peaseblossom's voice faded, disheartened, then rebounded. "I have dozens of Players still saying his line."

Bertie paused, completely motionless for the first time since the retreating ocean had left her broken and sodden on the red-carpeted aisle. *Since Nate was taken from me.* "Keep it that way."

"Of course."

Guided by the spotlight, Bertie made her way to the front of the stage, up the side stairs, and to the pedestal that held The Book. Ariel sat with his back against the slim column, assigned to sentry duty but pretending to sleep.

Bertie had spent the last two days avoiding his pleading gaze and his angry silences, but now she nudged him with her foot. "Move, Ariel."

He affected a snore, cut short when she kicked him smartly in the thigh. He rubbed his new bruise and moved to one side. "Milady's clogs are verily pointy and sharp."

"They're Mary Janes, and you should have moved when I asked you to." Bertie ran a tentative hand over The Book's cover, tracing the edge with a fingertip. "How can we be certain all the pages are back inside?"

She'd addressed Peaseblossom, but Ariel answered. "They're all there, save one."

Bertie threatened him again with her foot. "How do you know?"

"You should trust me over anyone else in this accursed place. You have better cause." Ariel tapped a finger to the collar around his neck; the metal hummed when he touched it. "This got heavier with every Player who returned."

Bertie looked from the purple smudges under his eyes to the lackluster fall of his hair over his shoulders. Everyone was tired, dirty, and disoriented, but the droop of Ariel's shoulders was caused by more than fatigue. "You look awful."

"That's because your collar is killing me."

Bertie's stomach, already unsettled by her run-in with Mrs. Edith and the sudden confirmation of the Mistress of Revels story line, gave another lurch. "You're lying."

"I speak the truth. Please take it off."

The lump of guilt lodged just below her solar plexus shuddered and turned over. She could make out her reflection in the collar, twisted and distorted by the metal. "I can't take it off, but I can at least relieve you of sentry duty for a few hours. Peaseblossom?"

"Yes?"

"I need a few armed guards to stand watch over The Book."

"Right away." The fairy disappeared into the crowd.

Ariel got up, his movements stiff. "Why are we guarding it at all?"

"If you could destroy it, it means someone else could try the same thing. There are others not overjoyed to be back. It seems the taste of freedom is sweet on their tongues."

"I wouldn't know."

Bertie didn't have any answer for that, but when she turned around to leave, she smacked directly into the Stage Manager. A physically quicker man would have sidestepped her. A mentally quicker man would have skipped the glower.

"I need to know what you want done with these announcements," he said without precursor.

Bertie stared in horror at the sheaf of hand-addressed and gold-sealed envelopes in his arms. "Those should have been delivered days ago!" She snatched one off the top and examined it. "The Theater Manager said he would ask you!"

The Stage Manager made a startled noise, his mouth falling open in an unbecoming gape. "He didn't say anything to me."

Bertie clutched the scrimshaw, but there was no artifice to strip away from him this time, no foul trace of trickery to his words. "He must have forgotten."

"Of course," the Stage Manager said. "So many things going on, the commotion, the chaos . . . it must have slipped his mind."

"It couldn't have been sabotage." Bertie shook her head. "The Theater Manager wouldn't do that to me."

Just as he wouldn't have put live asps in the basket?

She looked at the half-finished sets, the open cans of paint, and the characters in various stages of costuming. "No one will come. No audience, no performance, no chance to stay."

"As much as it pains me to say this, fixing The Book might be considered an invaluable contribution." The words were tiny stones, caught in his throat and forced past his lips grudgingly.

Startled, Bertie could barely manage, "Thank you. But I didn't even do that right. There's still a page missing." She eyed the announcements with a fresh burst of incredulity. "I have been thwarted at every turn by bits of paper."

Ariel appeared and took the parchment-and-gold-ink burden from the Stage Manager. "I'll deliver them."

"Absolutely not. It's out of the question." Bertie tried to take the announcements away from him, but he only turned to the side and blocked her with his shoulder.

"Why?"

Bertie shook her head until she was dizzy. "You're the one who wanted freedom so badly that you nearly destroyed everything."

"You imprisoned me because you feared for The Book and the Théâtre," he countered. "You don't need my page to safeguard this place any longer."

Bertie turned her back on him and his insane suggestions. "It's over, Ariel. The Theater Manager got his way. I might as well start packing."

Ariel's voice reached around her; cool and seductive, it was just the sort of voice that would convince reluctant patrons of the arts to venture to her performance on so little notice. "Trust in me."

"I'd rather stick a hot poker somewhere vital."

"As delightful as that sounds, you know that I'm the only one who can travel on the wind, the only one who can reach every house in time."

"I don't question that you can do it, Ariel. I question that you'll come back." Bertie's real fear slipped out before she could stop it.

"Why would you worry about that?"

She turned around and searched his eyes for some hint he was lying, any excuse to deny him, but the scrimshaw showed her the truth: The collar had restrained his winds but not killed them. They uncoiled from behind the shadows, ready to surround her, to lift her up, to carry her away with only Ariel's silk-clad arms wrapped about her to keep her from falling.

Spirare, they whispered to her like an incantation. *Breathe us in.*

Bertie didn't mean to, but she inhaled, and everything inside her was a spring morning, a rose opening its petals to the sun, the light coming through the wavering glass of an old, diamond-paned window.

Tendrils of wind reached for Bertie with a coaxing hand. *Release him, and he will love you.*

"Bertie," he said.

If Ariel says he loves me, I might just die. Right here, right now . . .

"I told you it would come to this."

Her relief almost matched her disappointment, and she swallowed. "I know."

Ariel tilted his head. His hair, stirred by a hint of wind, fell to one side so she could see the collar, smooth and cold against his skin.

Bertie reached out before she could change her mind. She touched the circlet, and the two halves of the collar hit the stage with hollow, metallic pings that echoed in the silence. She stepped over them to reach The Book and turned to the page where Ariel made his first entrance. Looking at him as she did so, she ripped the page out.

Ariel's winds returned full force to gust around her, carrying the thousands of envelopes he'd promised to deliver. Caught in the eye of the storm, she thought for certain that he'd leave without so much as saying good-bye, but then Ariel's lips were on hers.

"Thank you," he said against her mouth.

She pulled back to look into his eyes, and there it was: the unspoken promise that he would be back.

"Thank you," Ariel said again before he leapt into the winds and rode the storm away from her. The two butterflies deserted Bertie's hair to give chase, the announcements swooping after them like so many fallen leaves.

When he returns, it will be for me.

Despite her misgivings, she felt a dark thrill that it was she who'd been his savior at last.

CHAPTER TWENTY-ONE

I Could a Tale Unfold

Exhausted, Bertie curled up in an auditorium chair only to have Ophelia appear like a genie, bearing a dome-covered silver platter big enough to hold a Christmas goose.

"What on earth do you have in there?" Bertie asked, startled.

"Food," Ophelia said. "The Green Room's repaired itself, and you haven't had a proper meal in days."

Bertie's stomach rumbled in anticipation.

"Proper?" Moth asked, appearing as though summoned.

"Meal?" Mustardseed joined them.

Ophelia took the cover off the tray. "Turkey, cranberries, mashed potatoes . . ."

"Gravy!" Cobweb said, swooning.

"Marshmallows!" Peaseblossom said with a happy squeak.

"What's the orange stuff underneath the marshmallows?" Moth asked. "It's not a vegetable, is it?"

"Yams are a starch, I think," Ophelia said.

The scent of it was intoxicating, so Bertie didn't even protest when the water-maiden tucked a napkin into her shirt like she was a child of three. Bertie started to eat as Ophelia fixed a stern gaze on the fairies.

"If you want food, go get your own. I won't have you running through Bertie's plate and eating all the pie."

"There's pie!" They disappeared with explosions of glitter, screams of excitement, and cries of "Dibs on the pecan!"

Bertie looked up from the mound of food. "You have to help me with all this."

Ophelia shook her head. "Oh, no, I never eat before a performance. Drowning is bad enough without doing it on a full stomach."

Bertie couldn't argue with that, so she ate instead. Within minutes, she'd practically licked the tray clean.

"I'll take the plates back to the Green Room and get you a cup of coffee," the water-maiden said. "You look as though you're about to fall asleep."

Bertie undid the top button on her jeans with a groan, thinking the food might as well have been laced with Juliet's sleeping draught. "I'm going to rest my eyes until you get back."

Ophelia laughed. "No one would begrudge you a cat-nap."

"A few minutes only," Bertie protested. "I still have to speak with Mrs. Edith about something very important." She yawned, jaw cracking.

"Pleasant dreams," Ophelia said with a smile.

But they weren't. The moment she closed her eyes, Bertie was caught in the tentacle-grip of a nightmare. The Sea Goddess sat upon a throne of obsidian with Nate at her feet. She laughed as he untangled her seaweed tresses with Ophelia's ivory comb.

"Look at me, Nate," Bertie begged him, but when he turned to face her, two mollusk shells had taken the place of his eyes. Bertie scrambled back, screaming, and then there was the sensation of falling from a great height, down, down, down, only to be saved at the very last second by the sound of his voice calling to her.

"Wake up, lass."

"Nate?" Bertie jerked awake with the scrimshaw humming against her skin.

The auditorium was empty, the house lights only at half, and someone had closed the heavy front curtains to obscure the stage. Bertie sat up, rubbing first at the crusty remnants of sleep that prickled at the corners of her eyes, then the mammoth crick in her neck. Her legs tingled as the blood flow returned to her extremities, denied nourishment for goodness knows how long while she slept wadded up like a ball of dirty laundry. Bertie staggered to her feet, praying the pirate lilt that had woken her had not been a dream.

"Nate?"

The room echoed with her query as Bertie made her way down the carpeted aisle and up the side staircase. The Book sat in front of the proscenium arch, exactly where it belonged and still guarded by two burly Chorus Members. She turned the pages, seeking only one.

But the thinnest filament of darkness served as Nate's placeholder in the binding, and disappointment stabbed at Bertie's middle like Juliet's dagger. With a sigh, she ducked behind the curtain. The stage was preset with all its Egyptian glory for the performance, turquoise light drifting over golden sand and carved stone.

"You're awake!" A tiny spark of light appeared from behind the central pyramid as Peaseblossom rushed to meet her.

"I thought I heard Nate."

The fairy shook her head. "He's still not back."

Bertie headed to the stage door. "I heard his voice."

"It was probably a dream." Peaseblossom alighted on her shoulder.

"Where is everyone?"

"Getting ready. There's only a few hours until the house opens."

"Why did you let me crash out in a chair like that?" Bertie demanded. "I have a million and one things to do!"

"You looked so pitiful!" the fairy wailed. "And you hadn't slept for ages."

"That's neither here nor there!" Bertie said.

"Don't worry, I saw to everything!" Peaseblossom puffed out her chest. "The stage is set, the props arranged backstage, crystal cleaned, brass polished, programmes folded, flowers arranged, the costume tent cleaned up—"

"Mrs. Edith." Bertie took off at a run, headed for the Wardrobe Department. "I have to ask her about Verena's skirt!"

A dozen mobcapped apprentice costumers looked up when the door flew open. "Yes?" the tallest inquired, setting aside an enormous steaming wand she was using to coax wrinkles from an emerald evening gown.

"I need to speak with Mrs. Edith," Bertie said.

"The Theater Manager sent her on a very important errand," the apprentice answered.

"Only a few hours before we open?" Bertie demanded, immediately suspicious. "What sort of errand was so important?"

"Flowers for the Players' Dressing Rooms," the apprentice answered, confirming Bertie's suspicions that he only wanted to keep the Wardrobe Mistress safely out of the way. "But Mrs. Edith did leave a message for you."

Bertie tried to not appear too eager. "Yes?"

"She said to remain here until she gets back."

"And?"

"In the meantime, we're to do something about your hair." The apprentice rolled her sleeves up, a determined glint in her eye.

"What's wrong with my hair?" Bertie demanded.

"You cannot attend an Opening Night with Cobalt Flame tresses. She believes the only color that will cover it properly is Raven's Wing Black." The apprentice signaled for reinforcements, and Mrs. Edith's minions surged forward.

"Hey!" Bertie yelled as they towed her to the dye vat. "Let go of me this instant!"

Not only did they not let go, they forcibly removed her clothes. Bertie screamed fit to do a banshee proud until she realized her destination was a small copper tub filled with hot water sitting just behind the dye bath. Still, it was disconcerting to have two girls apply thick black paste to her head while two more trimmed her fingernails. No doubt another pair would have grabbed her by the feet if she hadn't protested she was ticklish.

"It's rather like a spa," Peaseblossom said, trying to reassure her from the safety of the button box.

Bertie sputtered when they poured cold water over her hair to rinse the dye out. "This is nothing like a spa. I don't even have enough room to soak all of me at once. Either my chest is freezing or my feet are sticking out."

After that, there was a blur of vicious towel drying and hair brushing. The moment the apprentices turned their backs on her, Bertie nicked a bottle each of bleach and dye—labeled, appropriately enough, Egyptian Plum—and ran into the corridor. Still towel-clad, she ducked into the nearest dressing room.

By the time they had located her, gone for the key, unlocked the door, and managed to break in past the chair she'd wedged under the doorknob, Bertie had bleached the bottom three inches of her hair and colored it bright purple, much to her delight and their dismay.

Bertie put her hands on her hips, trying to ignore the drips of dye on her towel that uncomfortably reminded her of blood spatters. "What are you going to do about it, eh? It's my head."

The lead apprentice clucked her tongue against the roof of her mouth. "There's no time to correct that now."

"What time *is* it?" Bertie asked, disconcerted.

"Nearly seven," one of them answered. "A half an hour until the house opens."

"Mrs. Edith won't be pleased," another said.

"We'll just have to do our best on the rest of it," the first said.

Bertie's triumph faded. "The rest of what?"

The boys appeared sometime between the stern application of foundation garments and the hot tongs. They howled protests as they, too, were hustled into soap-filled teacups.

"I just had a Turkish bath!"

"This water smells like flowers!"

"I'm going to catch my death of cold!"

They appealed to Bertie, who was in no position to help them, dressed as she was in the emerald gown the apprentice had been ironing when she first arrived. Mrs. Edith's minions had coaxed her newly black-and-purple hair into dozens of ringlets, and the entire arrangement was so stiff with hair spray that Bertie knew she'd have to soak her head in a bucket to get it all out. "Sorry, guys. If I have to clean up, then so do you."

They balked again when they were introduced to their formal wear for the evening.

"I'm going to look like a monkey!" Cobweb protested.

"Dummy," Mustardseed said, "when's the last time you saw a monkey in a tuxedo?"

But Peaseblossom's appearance silenced them for a moment. The tiny sequins on her gown sparkled in the brilliant fluorescent light, and the boys stared at her.

"You look like a *girl!*" Mustardseed accused.

"I *am* a girl!" Peaseblossom managed to stamp her foot even while hovering.

"Good thing, too!" Moth said. "That dress would look really stupid on one of us."

"Shut up," said Cobweb. "I could wear that dress."

"You could not," said Mustardseed. "You don't have the—" he gestured to his chest, "for it."

Before there was a brawl over Cobweb's nonexistent chest, Bertie raised her voice to say, "That's fine. Either wear a dress like Pease's, or get in your monkey suit."

Mrs. Edith still hadn't returned from the Theater Manager's "errand" by the time Bertie exited the Wardrobe Department and walked down the deserted hall backstage. Everything smelled of sweat and taffeta and face powder. An expectant hush had fallen over the Dressing Rooms where the Players sat before mirrors framed with electric lights, coloring their lips crimson and smearing their skin with greasepaint.

Bertie tried to look competent and reassuring, which was difficult to do while hyperventilating. "Has anyone ever actually died of nerves?"

"Not that I can recall," said Moth. "But there's always a first time!"

"That's comforting!" Bertie moaned. "No one is going to come. I'll be homeless by midnight. I think I'm going to throw up."

"Put your head between your knees!" said Moth.

"Use a paper bag!" said Cobweb.

"Put your head between your knees while breathing into a paper bag," said Mustardseed.

"I don't think that's physically possible, even if I had a paper bag." Adrenaline poured into her system. "Someone do me a favor and go peek outside."

The fairies raced to a tiny, circular window set high into the wall, jockeying for space behind the glass.

"Get out of the way, you!"

"I was here first."

Moth crowed with laughter. "There are carriages lined up for miles!"

Bertie peered up at them, straining her neck and wishing she had wings and could fly, too. "There are?"

Peaseblossom clapped her tiny hands. "You need to get out front to glad-hand the ticket-holders."

"People are coming?" Bertie asked, hardly daring to believe it.

"People are *here*. And not just people, but People." Peaseblossom shook her head. "Kings and queens and a duke—"

Bertie smoothed a hand over her hips. "How do I look, really?"

"Not bad, even though it's a stupid evening dress," said Moth.

Cobweb sucker punched him. "Tell her she looks nice."

Moth rubbed the back of his head. "You look nice, Bertie."

"The diamonds in your hair show up really well against the purple!" Mustardseed said, not wanting to risk a blow to his noggin.

"Enough nattering on about clothes and hair," Cobweb said, massaging Bertie's shoulders as if she were a prize fighter. "We need to get you out there."

"You need to check the ticket sales," said Moth.

"Work the crowd!"

"Assure that standing ovation—"

"I got it!" Bertie took a deep, steadying breath, turned on her smile, and opened the door to the lobby.

The world she entered was one of silk gowns and diamond dog collars, old money and those rich in enthusiasm, if not cash. Nearly all the names engraved on the announcements were congregated before her: season subscribers, as well as titled patrons like the Baron Von Hedelburg, the Marquis and Marchioness of Glouglow, and the Viscount de Mewe. Bertie moved about the foyer, murmuring her greetings and checking every detail. Fresh flowers bloomed in the wall niches, the chandeliers glittered, and stacks of gilt-edged programmes sat on pedestals. Members of the Chorus were dressed in the theater's black-and-gold livery and stationed at the doors.

"And just who are you, young lady?" Baron Von Hedel-burg demanded.

Bertie curtsied, something she'd never practiced but managed to pull off with reasonable panache. "Beatrice Shakespeare Smith, my lord. I directed this evening's production."

"You don't say?" He adjusted his monocle to squint at her.

The scrutiny was disconcerting, but Bertie refused to squirm. The bodice of her dress was reinforced with steel boning that girded up her spine; although not quite a corset, it served the same purpose. "I do, and if I may be so bold, you have quite a presence."

"I do?"

"Yes, my lord. There is an air of authority and command about you." Bertie tucked her gloved hand under his elbow, the better to stroll the lobby. *Persiflage and badinage.* Perhaps a wealthy Benefactor would appease the Theater Manager if the performance didn't manage to achieve a standing ovation. "I was wondering . . ."

The Baron was pink around the edges from all the attention. "Yes, my dear?"

From "young lady" to "my dear" in less than sixty seconds.

Bertie leaned closer, until the emerald feather tucked in her ringlets tickled his ear. "We're always hoping to secure new patrons for the Théâtre. Have you ever considered financing the arts?"

A thoughtful expression wrinkled the Baron's high

forehead. "I might have entertained a notion or two along those lines."

"That's wonderful to hear." Bertie patted his arm. "We'll speak again at intermission."

"Is this the young lady responsible for this evening?" a general boomed through a bristling silver beard. When Bertie nodded, he pumped her hand up and down as though trying to draw water from her arm. "It's capital what you've done with the place."

"Thank you, sir!" Bertie only just stopped herself from snapping to attention and saluting him. "Beatrice Shakespeare Smith, at your service."

The carriages and limousines continued to arrive, their occupants streaming steadily into the foyer. The fairies sat in one of the chandeliers overhead and whispered encouragements every time she paused for breath.

"Keep going!"

"Yeah, the old guy thinks you're cute!"

"Quick, before you lose momentum!"

"Oh, Bertie, look who just came through the door!"

She turned in time to see the Countess of Tlön approach. The noblewoman gave Bertie's face a vicious pinch.

"Such rosy cheeks. You're certain you're not rouged? I can't abide girls that rouge."

"No, Madame, I assure you my coloring is entirely natural." Bertie did her best not to flinch as the Countess gave her another pinch for good measure. "I'm pleased you could make it on such short notice."

"I hear tell of great things happening in this place." The Countess tucked her arm in Bertie's and marched to the curving Grand Staircase. "Take me to my seat, there's a girl."

With a longing glance at the Box Office through the glass revolving door, Bertie turned and struggled to keep up with the spry dowager, getting a stitch in her side by the tenth step. "I hope you'll enjoy the changes we've made to the production."

The Countess's ivory walking stick marked her cadence like a drum major's baton. "Word spread so quickly about your ambitious project!"

"Really?"

"Oh, yes. After the announcement arrived by courier this afternoon—and such a charismatic courier at that!— people could speak of little else." The Countess paused at the top to allow Bertie to catch her breath, but strangely enough, air was in short supply.

Ariel. She's talking about Ariel.

Bertie opened the door to Box Five. "This is yours, I believe. If you'll excuse me, Madame, there are others I should greet."

"Of course." The Countess plonked herself down in her seat and reached for her opera glasses.

Escaping, Bertie headed for the Box Office door,

intending to check on ticket sales, but the lights in the foyer dimmed, then returned to normal. A voice crackled over the hidden loudspeakers.

"Ladies and Gentlemen, your attention, please. The performance will begin in fifteen minutes."

The fairies converged upon Bertie and herded her through the crowd.

"Come on! You need to get backstage!" Peaseblossom grabbed Bertie's earlobe and steered her through the nearest door.

"Are you going to be all right?" Moth asked.

"Ask me again after the show," Bertie said, leaning against the wall for support. "Is it hot in here, or is it just me?"

Even as she fanned her face with an extra programme, the temperature in the corridor dropped. Bertie's breath formed ice crystals in air that carried with it the perfume of the aurora borealis.

"You would do better to leave the stage fright to the Players, Beatrice." Ariel was dressed all in black silk again; even his familiars had wings of onyx and black pearl tonight. The butterflies, perched on his cuff links, moved with the winds that preceded him down the corridor.

Bertie's programme fluttered to the floor. "You came back."

Ariel laughed. "I did."

She took a step toward him. "But you had your freedom."

"I had something more important waiting for me here." His winds encircled Bertie and coaxed her into his arms. "You chose me, Milady, and I choose you in return."

"Chose you?"

"As your own," he specified, his smile as compelling as it was fierce. "Why else would you have given me the one thing I thought I wanted?"

"That big stack of announcements had quite a lot to do with it." Bertie tried to shove away her memories of the tango, of what had happened afterward.

That has nothing to do with anything, besides which I don't have time for my insides to melt into gooey puddles right now.

"In case you're curious," Ariel added, his beautiful mouth forming the magical words, "the performance is sold out."

The tattered remnants of Bertie's restraint drifted away. Before she could stop herself, she threw her arms around Ariel's neck and kissed him, hearing the fairies' protest only as distant mosquito buzzing until one of them bit her on the back of the neck. With a half-muffled yelp, she fell away from Ariel, giddy and stunned, but not the least bit sorry for her indiscretion.

"Pleased with the news?" he asked.

"As if you couldn't tell," she said, a flush creeping up her neck. "That leaves one flaming hoop left to jump through. I wish Mrs. Edith was here, so I could consult her bones about the chances for a standing ovation."

"Speaking of costuming…" Ariel looked from her gloved hand clasped in his to her ringlets, the diamond earrings, the satin column of her dress. "You look lovely this evening. I like what you've done with your hair."

"Thank you, kind sir." Bertie repeated the oft-practiced curtsy.

Down the hall, a door slammed. Gertrude had exited Dressing Room Ten and, even at this distance, Bertie could hear her muttering lines under her breath.

Gertrude spotted the group and bellowed, "The moment I put on this wretched headdress, I forgot the end of my speech in the first act."

"It's just nerves," Bertie tried to reassure her. "It will come back to you once you're onstage."

"This was a terrible idea." Gertrude shoved at the sleeves of her unfamiliar costume until Bertie heard the stitches pop. "Why are you even back here, making a nuisance of yourself?"

Distracted by the gentle pressure Ariel was applying to her hand, Bertie tried to remember exactly why she *was* backstage. "It's almost time for the curtain to go up, and I wanted to wish you good luck—"

"Good luck?!" Gertrude screeched. "You did not just say that to me! Oh! Oh!"

Bertie paled. "I'm sorry! I meant 'break a leg'! Really, I did!"

"Overture and beginners, please." The Call Boy shoved past them.

Gertrude chased after him. "Tell me to break a leg, this instant! Tell me!"

Bertie shook her head at Ariel and extricated herself from his grip. "Look what you made me do!"

"She'll be fine," he countered. "Perhaps she'll really break a leg, and we can send on the understudy in her place."

The fairies dissolved into snickers as the door to Dressing Room Four opened. Ophelia glided into the hallway and lifted a hand to touch Bertie's curls.

"You look lovely," she said. "I do like to see you wearing something other than jeans."

Bertie held very still and let Ophelia finish her ministrations. At such close proximity, Bertie was surprised to see tiny lines at the corners of the water-maiden's eyes, emphasized rather than obscured by the heavy application of eye shadow and mascara.

"Are you ready for the performance?" Bertie asked her.

Ophelia nodded. "I find the restaging invigorating."

"That's good to hear," Ariel said. "Gertrude just came through here, not the least bit invigorated."

"Most of the Players are ill-equipped to deal with change," Ophelia observed.

"You're not coming unglued," Moth said.

"This isn't the first time I've improvised." Even when

Ophelia didn't move, the ends of her hair and gown swirled about her, as though caught in the ebb and flow of an unseen river. "I've always walked the ragged edge."

"That's a good line." Ariel adjusted his cuff links, which seemed determined to flutter away.

"It is, isn't it? I'll have to remember to use it again." Ophelia smiled at him with such brilliance that a never-before-seen dimple appeared at the corner of her mouth. "I find my memory stirred by all the excitement tonight!"

With joyous steps, she started to walk, indicating that they should follow her. Her slippers skimmed the floor, and her robes billowed behind her in a silver stream, the flickering lining the same deep blue depths as the ocean.

The same deep blue of Cobalt Flame dye.

Bertie grasped the scrimshaw, wondering why she'd never before thought to use it to see into the heart of the water-maiden.

First Verena's skirts and now Ophelia's robes? What is Mrs. Edith hinting at?

Ophelia had all but disappeared into the red-lit gloom backstage, but she called from the darkness, "Normally I wear white carnations. Those are for innocence. But I like the pink ones you sent to the Dressing Room even better."

"I didn't send you the flowers," Bertie said. "Mrs. Edith went and fetched them."

"Every flower has a meaning," Ophelia sang out. "I just have to remember what pink carnations are for."

A dozen crew members shushed them, but Bertie chased the sound of the water-maiden's voice, which was the fading rush of water over stone. "What do pink carnations mean?"

For an answer, there was only laughter that turned into a lullaby.

Still clutching the scrimshaw, Bertie followed her into the darkness. "Ophelia! What do pink carnations mean?"

Pale blue light flared in the quick-change corner, illuminating Ophelia as she caught the silver fish of clarity. Her hands were unexpectedly warm, as was the kiss she pressed to Bertie's cheek. "Not what they are for, Bertie, but *who*."

"Who are pink carnations for, Ophelia?" Bertie asked a third time, her voice no more than the whisper of a lost child.

"Pink carnations," Ophelia answered, "are for mothers. *I remember.*"

CHAPTER TWENTY-TWO

Sweet and Bitter Fancy

"What do you remember?" Bertie whispered, fearing Ophelia's mind played tricks on them both.

The water-maiden held her close, as though afraid Bertie would slip away from her and be lost again to the memory currents. "What happened when I left the Théâtre. At least, I remember most of it. I remember . . ." She choked a bit before she finished. "I remember you."

It was too much for Bertie to hope that she'd finally found her mother after all this time, but the scrimshaw wouldn't let her doubt the truth. Ophelia slowly aged beyond her written years, until nothing was left of the bewildered, heartsick young girl betrothed to Hamlet. Even when Bertie let go of the medallion, time-passed remained etched on Ophelia's face, lines carved in ivory.

"Who's my father?" Bertie strained her eyes against the dark that would steal away the details of this most important moment. "Tell me, please. I want to know everything."

"I'll do better than tell you." Ophelia smoothed a hand over Bertie's cheek. "I'll show you."

"Show us what?" Ariel said, arriving with the fairies.

"Yeah, what's going on?" Mustardseed demanded.

Bertie turned to them, numb from the shock. "Ophelia's . . . she's my . . ."

But Ophelia didn't let her finish. "Don't spoil it for them."

"Spoil what?" Peaseblossom asked, looking as alarmed as anyone wearing that many sequins could.

"We have a show to put on," Ophelia said. "Ariel, take the fairies somewhere with a good view of the stage. You won't want to miss this."

"What don't they want to miss?" Bertie desperately wanted to drag Ophelia back to her Dressing Room, to ask her seventeen years of questions, but the orchestra was playing a vaguely familiar overture. Ophelia guided her through the pitch-black; Bertie knew every creak of the Théâtre's wooden floorboards, and so she panicked. "Why are we onstage? What about *Hamlet*?"

"Take your seat," Ophelia commanded instead of answering either question.

Bertie reached out her hands, locating the edge of a massive armchair. "But—"

"Do as you're told." Ophelia's tone was stern. "I'll be right back."

Bertie almost succumbed to a fit of hysterical laughter at Ophelia's first parenting attempt, but as quickly as could be managed in a ball gown, she obeyed.

Ophelia returned and put *The Complete Works of the Stage* into her hands. "Hold this."

Bertie recoiled from its soft glow. "Why are you giving me The Book?"

"You need to read from it." Ophelia gave Bertie's knee an encouraging pat. "That's how the story goes."

Bertie started to protest, started to slide down, but the whirring noise of the curtain opening pinned her to the worn brocade. A million watts of light hit her as the audience burst into applause. The overture faded in anticipation of the opening line; Bertie could hear the rustle of silk as ladies shifted in their seats, the staccato cough of a gentleman clearing his throat, then the expectant hush of the audience.

"Pssst," Ophelia signaled from the wings.

Bertie squinted at her, trying to suppress how ridiculous she felt with her high-heel-shod feet dangling over the edge of the enormous armchair.

"Open The Book," Ophelia prompted with an accompanying gesture.

Something black and oily slid through Bertie's veins.

She nearly choked as it crawled up her throat. "I'm . . . I'm afraid."

Four tiny lighting specials zigzagged across the stage and alighted beside her.

"Ready," said Peaseblossom.

"And I!" chorused the boys.

"We're right here," Ariel said in an undertone as he entered from Stage Left.

A spotlight tightened in on the group. The fairies watched her, Ariel watched her, the audience watched her.

"I don't know if I can do this," Bertie whispered.

"Yes, you can." That was Peaseblossom.

Moth nodded. "You've wanted to know the truth for a long time."

Ariel leaned forward until the strands of his windblown hair coiled over her arm. "Everyone is waiting, and they've paid to see a play."

"They came to see a dazzling new production, not the unremarkable story of some nobody!" But Bertie opened The Book, feeling as wooden as one of the mannequins in the Wardrobe Department. Her breath came in short little pants. She forced herself to focus, to turn the page. Even after so many surprises, it still chilled her to see her own handwriting in The Book.

"*How Bertie Came to the Theater*," she read with a quiver in her voice, "A Play in One Act."

Glorious illumination poured over Ophelia, who now wore a green dress. The flowers woven into the filmy overlay were embroidered with brilliants.

"My mother was an actress, and surely she was the star," Bertie said, her words a spirit returned to haunt her. "She was an ingénue on the rise, a society darling."

"Not really," said Ophelia, "but close enough. I didn't have as many lines as some of the other female Players, but I made every one of them count."

"Titled men filled her dressing room with roses and sent jewelry that sparkled like the night sky," Bertie continued. The spotlight expanded to include dozens of flower arrangements and heaps of diamonds. Glitter drifted from the rafters until the very air shimmered. Bertie stared at the scene, transfixed. "It's just like I imagined."

"That," said Ariel, "is not in the script. Keep going."

Ophelia sat down at her dressing table. "It got old, to tell you the truth, with Hamlet sulking all the time. I wanted to go dancing. I wanted to live, just a little, before I died. But every night was the same routine. 'Into the water with you, Ophelia. Suck the water into your lungs, Ophelia. Let them drag your limp carcass across the stage, Ophelia.' And those boys are rough with their hands, let me tell you."

She powdered her nose pale green and twined bracken in her hair.

"That is *not* how I pictured it," Bertie said.

"Shhh," said Peaseblossom.

Hamlet entered Stage Right and stalked into the spotlight. "God hath given you one face, and you make yourself another."

Ophelia turned to look daggers at him. "Are you calling me a harlot?"

"Maybe." He managed to slouch without leaning on anything. "Maybe not."

"Say what you mean for once!" Ophelia yelled at him. When she threw her silver-backed hairbrush at his head, he yelped and fled.

Bertie had a terrible thought. "Please tell me Hamlet's not my dad."

"Shhh," Ophelia admonished, along with half the audience.

"But—"

"Maybe," Ophelia said at the top of her lungs to discourage further interruption, "I looked elsewhere. Maybe I got sick of the accusations, sick of being Polonius's daughter, and Laertes's sister, and Hamlet's girlfriend. Maybe I wanted, for a short while, simply to be myself."

A stranger in black strode forward to meet Ophelia at Center Stage. She accepted his hand as the orchestra launched into a new song: a tango.

Goose bumps rippled down Bertie's arms. *She danced it with my father.*

Ariel's hand twitched involuntarily, tightening over hers. "The music's the same."

As was the choreography. Bertie could only hope she'd managed to perform it with half as much grace.

"Back to the titled gentlemen," Ophelia said over the bandoneón's song. "One of them must have captured my heart. Was it a young lord with a castle on the hill and a coach-and-four?"

A spotlight came up on an aristocrat with a greasy moustache and pallid complexion. He stood on a platform Stage Right and couldn't seem to get down.

"Oh, please," said Ophelia just as The Stranger dipped her low with a dexterous flourish. They reversed and slinked across the stage. "Was it the powerful businessman with a keen eye for finance and a generous nature?"

Another spotlight, this time on a florid gentleman stuffed into a too-tight three-piece suit.

"Not likely," said Ophelia. "Men like that always smell of bacon."

The Stranger whirled her back to Center Stage in a complicated series of turns that left Bertie dizzy all over again. With Ophelia cradled in one arm, he produced a single red rose from thin air. Bertie's breath caught and Ariel swore softly when The Stranger used the flower to trace the planes of Ophelia's face, the curve of her breast, the length of her body. The Stranger helped her to stand, and Ophelia gave him a smile that shot Bertie with equal parts wistful longing and jealousy.

To look at someone, anyone, like that! To be so very sure . . .

"It was another," Ophelia said. "Someone without name or coin, but who had instead a heart filled with love for me. I left the Théâtre to be with him." She left him standing Center Stage and approached the oversize prop version of The Book that rested atop a pedestal. "Nobody ever gave me credit for the way I was written: always drifting between the worlds of life and death, air and water." She opened The Book to the middle, took a deep breath, ripped out a page, and held it up for everyone to see. "But it was I who figured out how to walk the ragged edge."

Ariel let out a slow breath. "Well done."

Ophelia folded the large piece of parchment and slid it into the pocket of her dress. "I left the Théâtre and traveled to a small cottage by the sea."

The scenery started to change to the train station.

"No, wait. That's not right." Ophelia tilted her head to one side and thought for a moment. "Was there a train? I don't remember that bit." The train backed offstage. "I think it was a boat. No . . . perhaps a wooden cart?"

Both a boat and a cart tried to slide on Stage Right, colliding in an explosion of wood and dust.

"It doesn't matter how I left." Ophelia held out her hand to The Stranger. "Just that I left. I didn't take anything with me. Not my print Sunday dress, not my silver hair comb. Just my page from The Book."

The Dressing Room set disappeared as The Stranger lifted Ophelia off the stage with a puff of wind. They landed on the red-carpeted runner and ran, hand in hand, for the Exit door.

"Wait!" Bertie slid off the chair and nearly fell down a rabbit hole. One after another, more trapdoors opened around her, all over the stage, until nothing remained of the boat and cart crash save a few stray splinters. By the time they slammed back into place, Ophelia and The Stranger were gone.

Mrs. Edith entered. Or rather, Not-Mrs.-Edith: a Player wearing a mask of the Wardrobe Mistress's face that exaggerated her severe features.

Another Masked One, Bertie thought. *Another person who knew the truth.*

Not-Mrs.-Edith walked on stilts that towered over Bertie's chair. Every footstep echoed through the auditorium.

"Ophelia?" she called, scattering foot-long straight pins all over the floor. A massive staircase appeared Center Stage in an explosion of ribbons and lace. Not-Mrs.-Edith clomped up to a gigantic door inset with bubbled glass and lettered in black gobbledygook. She hammered on it with a pair of scissors as big as hedge clippers. "Sir, Ophelia's left the theater!"

"I'm sure she just chose a different bathtub tonight, Mrs. Edith." Not-the-Theater-Manager's great booming voice shook the room from floorboards to ceiling. "Inquire of the Company. No doubt she'll turn up." The amplified scritch-scratching of a fountain pen commenced.

"Sir, did you hear me?" said Not-Mrs.-Edith. "I don't know how it's possible, but one of Players has *left* the *building!*"

The pen fell silent. "Are you certain?"

"Yes, sir."

A very long pause, and then, "Yes. Well. The show must go on, obviously. We can't spare anyone to go search for her. Perhaps I should engage the gendarmerie."

"But, sir—"

"Ever so sorry, there's nothing more I can do!"

The stairs clacked over to become a slippery-smooth slope. Not-Mrs.-Edith slid all the way to the bottom, petticoats over her head and long stilt-and-striped-stockinged legs kicking, until she fell with a shriek through yet another trapdoor that opened at the bottom.

When the lights dimmed beyond the average blackout, Ariel's hand found Bertie's, but his winds were sucked into the void, along with the fairies' light.

"What's happening?" Peaseblossom whispered, reduced to a tiny, disembodied voice.

"I . . . I don't know." Bertie held her breath until a pin-prick appeared on the back wall. The spotlight flickered and swelled.

When it was large enough to hold her, Ophelia stepped into it, alone. She had changed into a gray velvet gown trimmed with shadows. In the shifting light, Bertie could hardly focus her eyes as the water-maiden flickered in and out of existence, disappearing time and time again into her lost recollections.

"Where did he go?" Bertie's words were thin silver strands that spiraled out like candy floss before breaking.

Ariel nudged her. "That's not the line."

Bertie had to strain to make out the words in The Book. "I like to imagine she was a simple person with an uncomplicated life."

"Oh, it was uncomplicated," Ophelia said, crossing down-stage. "I just don't remember much of it. I know there was water . . . there's *always* water, filling up my head and pouring into the holes in my memory." She brought the single red rose from behind her back, and the blotch of color made Bertie's eyes tear up. "Then he brought me back here and left me with only this rose to remember him by."

"Who was he?" Bertie whispered.

"He was supposed to be my handsome prince. He was

supposed to be my happily ever after." Ophelia tore a handful of petals from the flower and scattered them around her. They drifted to the stage, flecking the cobblestones like droplets of blood. "I don't remember how long I was gone, or where I went. But I remembered the drowning, so I returned to the theater to drown one last time."

An ivory gauze curtain skimmed across the stage, as graceful as any of the dancers. The lights faded up to reveal it was painted to look like the Théâtre's façade as it appeared on the scrimshaw. Bertie could see the extent of the detail work now that it was magnified a thousandfold: Previously hidden faces peered from the dome above the ticket booth, tiny renditions of the fairies scampered in wrought iron, and the statues of the Muses each wore a variation of Ophelia's face.

The lights shifted to the set behind the curtain, the curved lines and crosshatches fading as though erased. With the noise of rushing water, the scrim opened, and Ophelia stood in an enormous replica of the Théâtre's lobby. She curved her arms around a belly heavy with child.

Not-the-Stage-Manager appeared. "How did you get in? We don't want any riffraff here."

"I'm not riffraff. I'm the daughter of Polonius, the sister of Laertes, the betrothed of Hamlet, Prince of Denmark." Ophelia fell to her knees, burdened by the weight of her many names, weighted down by the many parts she played. Red rose petals began to fall from the flies.

Not-Mrs.-Edith strode out on her stilts to lift Ophelia in her arms as the lights faded to black.

An unseen clock tolled midnight.

There was a long, high cry.

Three wet smacks.

A baby's wail underscored by Ophelia's muted weeping.

"Hush now, my dears," Not-Mrs.-Edith said over the loudspeakers. "There's no need to cry. Everything will be right as rain, you'll see."

The music swelled.

"That's all I remember," Ophelia said from the dark. "So that's the end of the play."

"No, no, no!" Bertie jumped down before Ariel could stop her and charged Center Stage to catch hold of Ophelia. The lights faded back up slowly, as if with reluctance. "This can't be right. There are too many pieces missing. Who was my father?"

"I . . . I don't remember," Ophelia said, her face crumpling.

Hamlet poked his head in from Stage Left. "I told you she was a harlot!"

"Shut up!" Bertie and Ophelia said in unison. Bertie pointed her finger at the Conductor. "Stop playing the curtain call music! We aren't finished until I say we're finished."

The real Mrs. Edith entered, and Bertie ran to her.

"What about the Mistress of Revels? The prophecy and the caravan?"

The Theater Manager stormed onstage. "Bertie, you'd better have a good explanation for all of this."

"I could say the same to you!" Bertie shouted at him.

"This is neither the time nor the place—" the Theater Manager started to say.

"I'll have no more of your excuses and no more of your lies!"

Ariel grabbed Bertie around the waist as she lunged at the Theater Manager. "I don't think you want to do that," he said.

"Oh, yes, I do!" Bertie said, kicking at Ariel through the skirts of her ball gown. "There's more to the story, and he's hiding it!"

The Theater Manager recoiled as though she'd struck him. "I don't know what you are implying, young lady."

"Verena's skirt and belt! I found them! That part of my play is true, too!"

The Theater Manager turned to Mrs. Edith. The Wardrobe Mistress met his gaze, unflinching.

"I kept my promise," she said. "I *said* nothing."

Someone in the second balcony shouted, "Tell the rest of the story!" The suggestion was met with some laughter and a smattering of applause as the audience took up the chant. "Tell! Tell! Tell!"

"It's a command performance," Bertie said. "Those are your patrons and benefactors. Don't disappoint them."

The Theater Manager sagged as though something inside him had finally broken. "Go ahead. Tell her."

"Oh, Bertie! My dear, I'm so very sorry!" The words poured out of the Wardrobe Mistress as though a cork had been pulled from her mouth.

"Don't apologize!" Bertie said. "Just tell me where she is. Tell me why you have her skirt."

"The skirt and the belt are mine, my dear," Mrs. Edith said. "I was the Mistress of Revels."

CHAPTER TWENTY-THREE

Revels
Now Ended

Mrs. Edith's voice carried over the startled gasps of the audience.

The second revelation of the night slapped Bertie in the face. "It's like a bad comedy of manners, with mistaken identities set to rights and everything."

The fairies peered at Mrs. Edith with varying expressions of surprise and fascination.

"Can you really do jujitsu?" Cobweb asked.

Instead of answering, the Wardrobe Mistress put her dexterous fingers to her mouth to let loose an ear-piercing whistle. Seconds later, mechanical steeds entered, pulling a wooden caravan. The intervening years had left their mark: The horses' joints creaked a bit, and rust flecked their noses and ears. The red paint on the cart had faded, the curtains were moth-eaten, but otherwise it was all just as Bertie imagined it.

Except I didn't imagine it. I remembered it.

Thunder rolled through the rafters. The stage lighting shifted to Coming Storm, and Mrs. Edith was suddenly attired as the Mistress of Revels.

Bertie blinked at the quick-change, but all she said was, "I want to know the rest."

Mrs. Edith nodded, speaking her line. "Would you like a moonrise by which to hear your story?"

"No, thanks," Bertie said, "I'm good."

"It's a bit chilly, though." Another snap of Mrs. Edith's fingers brought the prop campfire up through a trapdoor.

My cue. Bertie couldn't suppress a shudder of anticipation as she crossed the stage. "It's my Past I want told, not a pretty bedtime story."

Mrs. Edith studied Bertie for a moment, her smile wistful. "You have stars in your eyes."

"It's a lighting special," said Bertie.

"Go along with it," Mrs. Edith said. "What do you think of your life here in the theater? Is it all roses and curtain calls and champagne?"

"Sometimes." Bertie thought of Nate, taken from her, and the Theater Manager's lies. "But sometimes it's ugliness and filth and greed."

"Yet you have been happy here. I have seen your smiles and heard your laughter."

"Yes," Bertie whispered. "But why did you take me? Where did we go?"

Mrs. Edith stood. "Everyone clear the stage so I can tell it properly."

The blackout didn't bother Bertie this time, nor did the rustling noises of hundreds of people shifting in their seats with anticipation. She waited for Mrs. Edith to speak again, but it was the Theater Manager, playing himself, who entered and broke the silence.

"Mrs. Edith, would you be so kind as to come speak with me for a moment?"

Lights up on the Theater Manager's Office.

"This matter with Ophelia is very serious indeed." The Theater Manager poured himself a drink from the brandy decanter and held it up. "Will you take some, as a stimulant?"

"No, thank you," Mrs. Edith said, sitting across from him.

The Theater Manager took a large swallow, coughed a bit, then continued. "I think it would be best for everyone if you took the child away from the Théâtre."

"Why me, sir?" Mrs. Edith asked.

"You're not bound to this place as the Players are," he

said, shifting uncomfortably in his chair. "And you seem like the maternal sort."

"I seem like a woman, is what you mean to say." Mrs. Edith sniffed with barely concealed disdain.

"I seem to recall that you told me you wanted children of your own, once—"

"Don't you dare use my longings-past as a weapon against me," the Wardrobe Mistress flared. "Don't you ever dare. My life before I came to the Théâtre is just that: my own."

"Yes. Well." The Theater Manager twitched and fell into an uneasy silence.

Mrs. Edith let him stew a while longer before she inquired, "What does Ophelia think of your plan?"

"Not a thing," he said. "She remembers nothing of the outside world, nothing about the child."

"As I came back to the Théâtre, my memories drifted away on a salt-laden wind," whispered Ophelia's small voice from the shadows.

Bertie's hands curled into fists; she would not cry here, now, in front of all these people. "Then why did he send me away?"

The Theater Manager rose to look out the window, though there was nothing to see beyond the leaded glass. "I don't understand how Ophelia's memory was broken, but I fear she might recall everything during one of her more lucid moments. Take the infant away and return when the child is older, less recognizable. If we keep her identity hidden, perhaps it will be all right."

"Why bring her back at all?" Mrs. Edith asked.

"She's our responsibility, isn't she?" The Theater Manager turned around to pour himself another drink. "No different from a foundling child left on our doorstep."

Mrs. Edith sat, her perfect posture evident in the line of her back, stiff and straight as an exclamation point. "It's a mistake to keep the child's past a secret. The truth will out."

A knock at the door, and the real Stage Manager entered carrying a bundle in his arms.

"What are you doing here?" Bertie asked.

The Stage Manager glowered at her as he passed. "It wasn't by my choice. You wanted your story told."

"Hush, both of you. You'll wake the baby." The Wardrobe Mistress took the blanket-wrapped bundle from him. "What would you have me do, sir? Take her to a cottage somewhere in the forest until she turns sixteen? Keep her safe from spinning wheels?" There was a cutting edge to Mrs. Edith's voice that forced the Theater and Stage Managers to take a step back.

The Theater Manager shook his head. "Don't be ridiculous. Take the caravan. You will be able to move about as needed and earn your living as wandering performers."

"If you will not be persuaded otherwise."

"I will not."

Mrs. Edith nodded. "We will leave within the hour."

"And both of you will swear," the Theater Manager said. "Not a word to anyone about this child's mother or how she came to be."

"We promise," the Stage Manager and Wardrobe Mistress said together.

There was a noise, like a large, hollow door slamming shut. The Office set disappeared overhead, and light painted the cyclorama backdrop in shades of blue and green.

Mrs. Edith stood before it with the blanket-wrapped bundle in her arms. "You'll need a name, poor child. I think I shall call you Beatrice. Of all Shakespeare's heroines, she best speaks her mind and is put upon by no one. Perhaps the name will gift that strength of spirit upon you. Yes. Beatrice. Shakespeare will do for a middle name."

"And the Smith?" Bertie stage-whispered, just outside the pool of light. "Where did the Smith come from?"

"It was my name, once upon a time." The Wardrobe Mistress climbed atop the caravan. "So it was mine to give you."

The wagon lurched, "traveling" on a moving belt so that the horses plodded and the wheels rolled while the cart remained Center Stage.

"For a time, we two roamed just as you imagined," Mrs. Edith said. "You learned to dance and make merry and speak in rhyme."

Infant Bertie gurgled and cooed.

"I spoke in rhyme when I was six months old?" said Bertie.

"Who's the skeptic now?" Peaseblossom sniffled. "You sound just like Nate."

Nate. Bertie couldn't help but wish he stood on her left side just as Ariel stood to her right. *I wish you could have seen this.*

"The years passed." Holding the edge of the baby blanket, Mrs. Edith let the bundle unroll toward the floor. Everyone gasped, but Young Bertie somersaulted from the folds and landed on her feet with palms upraised. The Player had fat, dimpled knees and an infectious laugh.

"At least I was a cute kid," Bertie said. "I look happy."

"Happiness is subjective," said Mrs. Edith, because that was the line. "But I truly believe you were a happy child."

As the caravan rolled forever Center Stage, Young Bertie scattered rose petals and turned cartwheels. She scrambled over boulders and up trees, leaping down with a fearlessness that took Bertie-the-elder's breath away.

"Get down from there," Mrs. Edith called to Young Bertie when the child stood on the roof of the caravan, her arms thrown out wide.

"But I like to see everything!" Young Bertie protested before she jumped off.

"It's a miracle I didn't break my neck!" Bertie exclaimed,

both fascinated and horrified. She suddenly recalled her maneuver on the chandelier, hanging upside down by her knees and reaching for Nate. . . .

"Our journey was fraught with danger," Young Bertie said. "We hit potholes—"

The caravan hit a pothole with a bump and a shudder.

"See!" yelled Moth. "I told you there were potholes!"

"The horses stampeded," continued Young Bertie, "although they did *not* run over us with their big metal-shod hooves."

"Aw, nuts," said Mustardseed. But he was cheered by the mad dash, which included sparking horseshoes and a small brushfire.

"We were set upon by brigands," Young Bertie said as she sat upon the stage with a fat stack of paper and a box of crayons.

The Brigands charged in with weapons drawn.

"Who are you?" Young Bertie asked.

"We're the bad guys!" their leader announced.

"What are you going to do?"

"Plunder and pillage!" one of them yelled.

The others immediately shoved him. "Not in front of the kid. Ralph! Fer cryin' out loud . . ."

"Oh, yeah. Sorry! We're here to take your candy!"

Young Bertie considered this idea as she drew a bright red jelly bean on the paper. "That's not very nice."

"Well, no, I suppose not," said the Lead Brigand, scratching the end of his nose with a dagger.

"Do you steal candy from a lot of people?" she asked next, adding peppermint canes and chocolate humbugs to the drawing.

"Everyone we meet," said another Brigand.

Young Bertie looked up from her paper. "I don't think I believe you. You don't look very trustworthy."

"Brigands aren't supposed to be trustworthy," said their leader. "It ain't in the job description."

Young Bertie looked up from her paper. "See this word? C-A-N-D-Y spells 'candy.' Maybe now you want to turn out your pockets?"

"Er, well," the Lead Brigand said, caught in his lie.

"Go ahead," she urged. "I double-dare you."

The Brigands weren't about to ignore a double dare, and they turned out their pockets. Approximately seventy-nine pounds of jelly beans, peppermint canes, and chocolate humbugs hit the stage in a rain of cellophane-wrapped sugar.

"Whoa, wait just a second," their leader started to protest. "Where did all this come from?"

"It's there because I wanted it to be there," Young Bertie explained. She held up her drawing. "See? I put the word on paper, so it's true. Would you like to see me spell 'avalanche'?"

The Brigands stormed out Stage Left, crawling over one another in their eagerness to flee.

"You always had a way with words," Mrs. Edith said. "Anywhere you thought to go, we went: the mountains, the valleys, the mystical places, and the mundane. But over and over again, you were drawn to the sea."

The shifting kaleidoscope of gray returned, but this time, Bertie could make out the call of gulls and waves smashing against the rocks. Chalk-white cliffs rumbled into place.

"This is where I went with your father." Ophelia peered at the set with luminous eyes.

Bertie's heart thudded. "You remember this place?"

Ophelia twisted her hands together in a knot. "I . . . I think so!"

"But that's good!" Bertie's heart leapt at the thought that something had triggered Ophelia's memory. "I wonder—"

"Bertie!" Ariel spun her around in time for her to see her younger self climb to the top of the towering wooden cliffs and stand facing the audience.

Young Bertie looked over the edge, down into the orchestra pit. "I wonder."

"What do you wonder, dear heart?" Mrs. Edith asked her, trying to catch up.

"I wonder if I can fly."

Mrs. Edith held out her hand. "Come back, dear. You're making me very nervous."

Bertie started to shout that it was making her nervous, too, but she couldn't manage it. The scrimshaw hummed, and Bertie stood in two places at once: next to Ariel on the stage, and atop the cliff, looking down, not at the musicians, but at the frothing churn of a restless ocean. She'd never before been afraid of heights, but vertigo seized her. "Step back!"

Young Bertie only grinned. "Why?"

Mrs. Edith answered the question. "Birds fly, my darling, not little girls."

Instead of obeying, Young Bertie put her bare toes over the edge. "Maybe I'm not a little girl. Maybe I'm a bird, too."

Mrs. Edith shook her head, a desperate note creeping into her clipped tones. "You're not. Come away from the edge."

"Come away from the edge," Bertie echoed.

Bertie's younger self looked directly at her older incarnation, smiled sweetly, spread her arms . . .

And jumped.

Everyone in the audience screamed as the stage plunged into a blackout. When the lights faded up to half, Mrs. Edith sat upon the caravan once more, holding a sodden and limp child-Bertie in her arms.

"What happened?" Bertie whispered. "After I jumped?"

The Wardrobe Mistress's expression was both grim and determined. "By some miracle, you survived, and I took you straight back to the theater."

The curtain painted with the Théâtre's façade skimmed into place. Mrs. Edith climbed down from the caravan as the child sat up and rubbed her eyes.

"What is this place?"

Mrs. Edith beckoned to her. "Your new home, my dear."

Young Bertie hopped down and frowned. "I don't want to stay here."

"You'll have your own room," said Mrs. Edith.

"I don't want my own room."

"Of course you do," said Mrs. Edith. "Every little girl wants her own room that she can paint any color of the rainbow. And you'll have friends—"

"I don't want friends," said Young Bertie.

"Of course you do," said the Wardrobe Mistress. "Fairy friends who will sing you to sleep and tell you bedtime stories and weave ribbons into your hair."

"She's not talking about us, is she?" asked Moth. "Because I've never put a ribbon anywhere on your person."

"Shut up," Bertie said without taking her eyes off the scene.

"You'll be able to play in Paris and London," Mrs. Edith said. "Visit Neverland whenever you want. There are pirates and peasants and clowns."

"No clowns," said Young Bertie. "Clowns creep me out."

"All right," Mrs. Edith conceded. "No clowns."

"And no one will boss me around or tell me what to do," Young Bertie continued.

"All right," said Mrs. Edith. "You'll answer to yourself and no one else. It will be lonely that way, I fear."

"I like being lonely," said Young Bertie with her fists balled at her side. "I don't need anyone, do you hear me? I don't need you."

The Theater Manager appeared in the doorway. "You're back. And this is—"

"Beatrice," Mrs. Edith answered. "Beatrice Shakespeare Smith."

The Theater Manager nodded to Young Bertie. "How do you do?"

"Much better than you think," the child said, crossing her arms.

"Has her mother returned to us?" Mrs. Edith said, wording the question so carefully that Young Bertie almost missed it.

"My mother?" the child asked. "Is she here? Can I meet her?"

"I'm sorry, Beatrice," the Theater Manager said, "but that woman has never returned."

To fill the silence, the Wardrobe Mistress said brightly, "I think you will find Bertie has a talent for writing that is quite extraordinary. She has power over words."

The Theater Manager looked down at Young Bertie, the polite mask her older counterpart knew so well settling into place. "Ah. I shall have to watch her carefully, then. Such a skill might prove useful to her someday." He knelt next to the child. "You can stay, on the condition that you forget how you came here."

Young Bertie looked as though she might make a run for it, but under the combined, stern gazes of the Theater Manager and Mrs. Edith, she deflated. "All right. Fine. I'll forget, and I'll stay. But only until I'm ready to remember all this." She held her hands up to her head and squeezed her eyes shut.

"What are you doing, child?" Mrs. Edith asked with a quaver in her voice.

"I'm squeezing all my memories out."

"My dear—"

"Leave me alone!"

Ghostly figures danced across the back wall: fleeting tricks of lighting specials that suggested a small child's adventures with her guardian. The amber wash on the scene began to fade as the mechanical horses pulled the caravan offstage.

"What is this place?" Young Bertie whispered into the growing darkness.

"Your new home, my dear," said Mrs. Edith, no longer wearing her brightly colored gown but costumed once again as the Wardrobe Mistress.

"How did I get here?" Young Bertie asked, her forehead puckered in a frown.

"We'll talk about that later." Mrs. Edith patted her on the shoulder and exited.

Young Bertie stood alone, Center Stage. For a moment, Bertie thought that was the end of the story, the end of the play. Tears gathered in her eyes for that lost little girl.

But as the child went through the glass revolving door, violins and flutes started to play a merry tune, softly at first, then with growing insistence and speed as new memories streamed in to replace those she'd lost. The Mistress of Revels was gone, but her good work continued behind the scenes, for there was the Harlequin in his brilliant diamond-patched jerkin juggling flaming billets of wood and tiny stuffed animals. The Fairy Court in shades of moss and rose, surrounded by a thousand gold-and-silver flickering fireflies. The pirates swinging on ropes, hanging by wrists and ankles while brandishing swords and flinging gold coins. The tap-dancing starfish, triple-time-stepping.

Young Bertie slowly yielded to the enchantment of the Théâtre, her smile growing ever wider as she frolicked amongst the Players.

Mrs. Edith was right. I was *happy here.*

The music built to a crescendo as the Players rushed to the side of the stage to surround the elder Bertie.

"Come," they insisted, "you're part of this!"

"Are you insane?" she protested.

"You must! It's the finale!"

When Ariel laughed, Bertie grabbed him by the elbow. "You're coming, too!"

But he didn't protest, and though it wasn't the tango, he knew every bit of the choreography. Young Bertie disappeared through a trapdoor with a wink and a wave. The four fairies rushed in to surround Bertie's head like a halo. The Gentlemen of the Chorus twirled her about, one right after the other, as pirates and starfish and fae rushed to take their places for the final pose: Bertie, sitting on Ariel's shoulders, her arms outstretched, surrounded by the Players.

The cannon fired with an almighty *boom!* and a shower of golden confetti sifted down from the flies. Panting from exertion, Bertie smiled when someone clapped once, twice. She'd almost forgotten the second part to her bargain with the Theater Manager, and so she held her breath until the applause rolled toward the stage in waves, just as the water had. Flowers hit the floorboards alongside cries of "Brava!"

Bertie lifted a hand to cut out the glare of the lights; the audience had found its collective feet.

I can stay.

"I suppose we ought to bow," she whispered to Ariel with barely contained triumph. "You can put me down now, and get your hand off my butt!"

He grinned and pointed at the Stage Manager. "Curtain call!"

Mrs. Edith and Ophelia entered to take their places on one side of Bertie, and Ariel stood on the other. The fairies fluttered forward to cling to her hair as the lights tightened on Center Stage, blinding Bertie as she bowed. Beyond the cheering crowd, the Exit sign beckoned.

The curtains crashed into each other, signaling the end to *How Bertie Came to the Theater*. Heavy red velvet muffled the sounds of the audience filing out, though Bertie caught snippets of "How unusual!" and "Delightful! We should renew our subscription."

When the low murmur of conversation finally faded, the Theater Manager spoke, almost to himself. "You'd remembered almost all of it."

"That's why you wanted me to leave, isn't it?" Bertie said. "It didn't have anything to do with the cannon—"

"It had everything to do with the cannon!" he fired back. "Everything to do with the changes you wrought here. It's only by chance that the Théâtre yet stands. . . ."

"The pages are back in The Book," Bertie said. *All but two.* "I repaired it and saved the Théâtre when you couldn't. I fulfilled the obligations of my contract: a sold-out show concluded with a standing ovation. And I discovered that I am more than a foundling child, or even a Director." Bertie reached for Ophelia's hand. "I am her daughter."

"My ward," Mrs. Edith said.

"Our friend," said the fairies.

"My benefactress," Ariel said with a wry quirk to his lips.

"And the Writer of Words," Bertie finished. "I have a place here, whether you like it or not. Mrs. Edith named me for the other Beatrice, and I will be put upon by no one, not even you."

"Have your way, then," the Theater Manager said, his voice hoarse. "Next time, you might not be so lucky. Next time, the building may well crumble about our ears."

Bertie shook her head. "The audience might have been content with the play, but it's only a draft. A work in progress. A character's still missing from my story."

"Pluck from the memory a rooted sorrow." Ophelia's hand trembled in hers. "Would that I could remember his name for you!"

Bertie turned and kissed her mother on the cheek, vowing to remember the delicate scent of her: pink carnations and water-blooming flowers, ice-fed streams and the iron-tang of strength under her wistful vulnerability. Bertie whispered, so that only Ophelia might hear. "I will find him, for the both of us, and bring him back."

There was more than one man to find, though. *This damsel will rescue the pirate in distress.*

Peaseblossom yanked hard upon one of Bertie's diamond earrings. "You can't be serious! You're not going to leave!"

"Yes, I am. I have to." Bertie turned to the Theater Manager. "I will go the way I came: with the caravan, with companionship. You will not gainsay me these things."

"Not if you actually agree to go," he said. "It's a meager price to pay for the safety of the Théâtre."

"Spoken by someone who doesn't understand the value of loyalty, or friendship." Bertie turned to Ariel. "The Bard's words should remain in the Théâtre. Give me your page from *The Tempest*." Ariel hesitated, but Bertie didn't flinch under the intense scrutiny that could have burned a hole right through her. "This way, no one shall be able to call you back. Trust in me."

His promise and hers; now they'd both said it, and together the words were like the wind. He slid his hand inside his silk shirt and pulled out his page, grimacing as though its removal tore his flesh.

She took it from him with steady fingers and turned to the Theater Manager. "A pen, sir?"

Without saying a word, he took a fountain pen from his pocket and handed it to her.

Bertie spared only a glance for the man who had worn the thickest mask of all, before she called out, "Open the curtains."

Red velvet parted to reveal the empty auditorium. Bertie crossed to The Book, held Ariel's page up to the light, and whispered his opening speech.

Ariel's body spasmed as he was recaptured.

"Just a moment. It will only take a few words, I promise." With a shaking hand, Bertie turned to the back of The Book. At the top of a blank sheet, she wrote:

Following Her Stars: In Which Beatrice (& Company) Take Their Act On The Road

She paused, long enough for a blot of ink to appear.

Enter BERTIE, ARIEL, PEASEBLOSSOM, COBWEB, MOTH, and MUSTARDSEED.

"It's my turn to walk the ragged edge." Holding her breath because she couldn't cross her fingers, Bertie ripped the page out.

The Exit sign in the back of the auditorium flickered, died, then blazed brighter than ever before.

"I think The Book will be safer in my Office." The Theater Manager pushed past Bertie to remove it from the pedestal.

"I think you might be right about that," she said with a sidelong look at Ariel.

The Theater Manager made his exit without a backward glance. Ophelia and Mrs. Edith rushed to embrace Bertie one last time.

"Promise you'll be careful," Ophelia said, touching a gentle finger to Bertie's cheek.

"That's like asking the tide never to come in," Mrs. Edith said with a suspicious hitch in her voice.

"You two will have each other while I'm gone," Bertie said, joining their hands together.

"I will watch you go, though each step pains me," Ophelia said. "I will hold your memory close to my heart every second you are gone."

For a moment, all three women stood with their heads inclined toward one another. Were it not for the medallion hanging about her neck, Bertie might have permitted a few hasty tears to fall. Pulling away, she tilted her head at Ariel.

"Shall we?"

His smile was one of the most beautiful things Bertie had ever seen. He offered her his arm. "Let your indulgence set me free."

"Never say I didn't give you anything." Bertie tucked her hand under his elbow, and a great burst of wind lifted them from the stage to the red-carpeted runner. The fairies flew ahead, all pushes and shoves and exclamations of excitement.

When they reached the end of the aisle, Ariel opened the auditorium door. Bertie looked back long enough to see

Ophelia and Mrs. Edith, standing Center Stage, arm in arm. Bertie lifted her hand in farewell before the door slammed shut between them.

"This is it." Peaseblossom's voice quavered a bit as they crossed the lobby.

"Last chance to change your mind, Bertie," Ariel said with a raffish smile.

"What's past is prologue, and the world awaits." She placed one hand over the scrimshaw and the other flat against the glass of the revolving door. It turned slowly, whispering the Théâtre's farewell, and Bertie lifted her eyes to gaze upon the night sky.

CURTAIN

Acknowledgments

The author's grateful thanks to everyone who rode the roller coaster from start to finish:

My agents, Ashley and Carolyn Grayson, and my publisher, Jean Feiwel, for seeing the magic in this novel's earliest incarnation and giving the curtain at the Théâtre Illuminata the chance to go up.

My editor, Rebecca Davis, for asking the right questions until I found the right answers. The book is immeasurably better for your Mrs. Edith–like attention to detail.

My husband, Angel, for dealing with the frothing and flailing in person, laughing in all the right places, and listening to me puzzle through the plot twists while nodding like it all made sense. When I stand in the spotlight, I know the best of the warmth and brilliance is your love for me.

My daughter, Amélie, who learned so quickly to say, "Shhh! Mommy's writing!" and "Is your chapter done yet?" for her sweet kisses after a long day at the computer, and for not unplugging my laptop more than strictly necessary.

My mother, Gladys Burton, for always having a stack of books on her nightstand, letting me sit on the floor of Mendocino Book Company and the Ukiah Library until my backside went to sleep, and providing a constant stream of child care, dessert delivery, and support.

My sister, Lori Hunt, for enduring a thousand games of make-believe in our youth in which she was bossed around and tied to trees, and for holding up a certain fantasy anthology in the middle of Barnes & Noble and yelling, "My sister has a story in this book and YOU SHOULD BUY IT."

My family by marriage, Nick, Gisele, and Rita, for their unfailing support and love.

My father, Ronald Hunt, for the advice that I shouldn't wait to chase my dream.

Sunil Sebastian, Sidekick Extraordinaire, for his friendship, his many hours of careful reading and thoughtful critiquing, his ninja technical skills, innumerable telephone conversations in which I was informed "it still doesn't suck," and the loan of his precious girls.

Michelle Joseph, who loved Ariel, and Cheryl Joseph, who thought (perhaps rightly) that he's a very bad boy, for their fresh eyes, energy, and e-mails.

Kari Armstrong, for her uncanny ability to draw things that exist only inside my head, her swift, headlong dive into watercolors, and her boundless enthusiasm for my descriptive work.

Jenna Waterford, for introducing me to stealth clothing and reassuring me that Women Of Any Age were allowed, nay, encouraged! to wear skirts covered in buckles. I will always give thanks that I sat down at your table.

Stephanie Burgis, for trading ribbon-bound chapters, cupcakes, and dark chocolate over the virtual back fence, and loving the fairies right away.

Tiffany Trent, for reassuring me that there will indeed be a LisaCon someday aboard a cruise ship, including fruity drinks topped with paper umbrellas served by men in kilts.

Glenn Dallas, for apologizing every time he pointed out a mistake and his constant gifts of great vocabulary words.

Elissa Malcohn, for her grammar expertise and good-natured tutelage.

Stephen Segal, for knowing that first chapter was going to need some work, providing my daughter with wench clothing, and that quiet pause he takes before answering any of my questions.

Phillip Boynton, for rejoicing with me during all my proudest moments.

Dr. Douglas Scott-Goheen, for letting me play Queen of Show and Tell at the University of California, Irvine Research

Symposium, which reminded me of all the reasons I fell in love with the theater in the first place.

Heather Ortiz, for reading the funny bits over the shower curtain.

Christy Flynn, for all the cheering and applause.

Rafe Brox, for the reminders that he's not my target audience and that fairies are actually a plague upon all our houses. Also, the line about the tarantella.

Joshua Palmatier, for dancing when he didn't want to and being the first to offer a blurb.

Daniel Erickson and Xcentricities corsetry, for the fabulous costume changes and pin-striped inspiration.

To those who read the various incarnations of the manuscript and offered their support and feedback: Amanda Mitchell, Kate Amirault, Rebecca Way, Brian and Katie Hill, Erin Cashier, and my friends on LiveJournal. The theater thanks you for your patronage.

Discussion Questions

1. The novel describes the art nouveau style of the theater, Mrs. Edith's Victorian clothing, patrons arriving by both carriage and limousine, and Bertie's clothing choices (which include jeans and black nail polish). What are possible explanations for the multiple time periods referenced?

2. Several non-Shakespearean stage productions are referenced in *Eyes Like Stars*, including *Peter Pan, Man of La Mancha,* and *Les Misérables*. Discuss how the various themes of these plays (the refusal to grow up, going on a quest, revolution) tie into Bertie's own story.

3. Nate is a superstitious member of the cast, stepping into his ship right foot first, never uttering the word "drowned," and always referring to *Macbeth* as "the Scottish play." These are all classic theater superstitions. Are there other superstitions in the theater? Why might people who work in the theater develop such beliefs? How does the idea of being superstitious particularly affect the Théâtre Illuminata and Bertie?

4. Mrs. Edith warned Bertie to keep her distance from Ariel. What might Mrs. Edith's reasons be for forbidding this relationship?

5. Bertie's two love interests—Ariel and Nate—couldn't be more different from one another. How can Bertie be so attracted to both of them? Could Ariel and Nate each help Bertie compensate for a certain side of her personality? How?

6. Bertie knows nothing—and can remember nothing—about her life before the Théâtre Illuminata. How does Bertie use her play, *How Bertie Came to the Theater*, to discover herself? Why is it important for Bertie to see herself as the daughter of a young, famous, beautiful actress who left the theater? In what ways was Bertie correct about her own unknown story?

7. Are there any hints in the book that help to identify who might be Bertie's mother? Does Bertie share any characteristics with her mother?

8. Bertie's father is known only as The Stranger. Who could this mysterious stranger be? Is he more likely to be a character from this book, or one not yet introduced?

9. By the end of the book, it is revealed that Bertie is, in fact, *not* a foundling or an orphan. Why was it so important to the Theater Manager to convince Bertie that she was?

10. Bertie proves to have a special kind of "word magic" which makes her unique at the Théâtre. What could be the reason for Bertie's special ability?

11. Why was Bertie so reluctant to see the outside world when she had the opportunity to leave the Théâtre? What events help her to change her mind about the outside world by the end of the book?

SQUARE FISH

For more information about Square Fish books, authors, and illustrators visit
www.squarefishbooks.com.

GOFISH

LISA MANTCHEV

What did you want to be when you grew up?
From the time I was about five years old, I wanted to be an actress or a movie star. I wrote a short story about winning an Academy Award in the third grade (and should have realized then that writing was my true calling!).

When did you realize you wanted to be a writer?
I've written short stories since I could form a sentence, but I realized I wanted to be a professional author sometime after college when I returned to creative writing and started selling my short stories for publication.

What's your first childhood memory?
I remember, in a hazy sort of way, playing with a set of alphabet magnets, which is something I received for my second birthday. They were on a board next to a Weebles circus in the living room of my parents' first home.

As a young person, who did you look up to most?
My mother. She worked, took me to play rehearsals and ballet class, chaperoned field trips, and made cupcakes for class

parties. She also let me spray paint and glitter scenic pieces against our back fence when I was in high school, which left sand dune-shaped outlines on the wood.

How did you celebrate publishing your first book?
My family went out for breakfast (I am a big fan of breakfast!) with coffee, pastry, flowers, and little gifts. It was like my birthday, only better, and in July.

Where do you write your books?
Wherever I can set up my laptop. I've worked on our dining room table, at my husband's office, in coffee shops, in the car on a road trip, and now I have a little writing nook set up next to the wood-burning stove in our front living room.

Where do you find inspiration for your writing?
Absolutely everywhere, but mostly in the arts: theater performances, photography, art, crafts, movies. I attended my first Cirque du Soleil performance in 2008 and it had a profound effect upon me.

Which of your characters is most like you?
Bertie certainly has my love of coffee. Also, my smart mouth and my love of bright hair dye.

What's your idea of the best meal ever?
Anything on a (real) Parisian baguette. I've had them buttered, a tiny bit stale with a cup of mint tea, and used to construct ham and cheese sandwiches with little sour pickles . . . all delicious!

Which do you like better: cats or dogs?
We have a large horde of hairy dogs and two outside cats; the cats are far more useful, but the dogs are our babies. We lost

our eldest, a Chow Chow princess named Teddy Bear, this year, and on my more insane days, I entertain notions of puppies.

Who is your favorite fictional character?
Probably Anne Shirley from L.M. Montgomery's *Anne of Green Gables*. She's such a winsome creature, it's impossible not to love her.

What time of year do you like best?
I'd have to say autumn . . . I'm a huge fan of cool weather, apple cider, and Halloween.

What's your favorite TV show?
Right now, it's *So You Think You Can Dance*. I am beyond thrilled that the performing arts are getting increased exposure on television.

If you were stranded on a desert island, who would you want for company?
I'd totally take my husband. Not only is he handsome and charming, but he could build us a raft out of coconuts. And a coconut GPS and radio. And probably some kind of blender to make coconut milkshakes.

If you could travel in time, where would you go?
Turn of the century Paris or London.

What's the best advice you have ever received about writing?
Paraphrasing Stephen King's book *On Writing:* You have two hats, an editorial hat and a writer hat, and you should only wear one of those hats at a time.

What do you like best about yourself?
My dogged determination to make things happen.

What is your worst habit?
See above. The sword cuts both ways!

What would your readers be most surprised to learn about you?
I actually have a shy streak! For all that I'm pretty outgoing online and in person, I really do love crawling into my hermit cave.

Will Bertie learn the true identity of her father?

Is her magic strong enough to battle the Sea Witch?

Will she *ever* decide between Ariel and Nate?

Keep reading for an excerpt from

Perchance to Dream

by LISA MANTCHEV

CHAPTER ONE

Beginning in the Middle; Starting Thence Away

"It is a truth universally acknowledged," Mustard-seed said, flying in lazy loops like an intoxicated bumblebee, "that a fairy in possession of a good appetite must be in want of pie."

"Yes, indeed," Cobweb said over the rattle of the caravan, "though I awoke one morning from uneasy dreams, I found myself transformed in my bed into a gigantic pie."

"It was the best of pie, it was the worst of pie," was Moth's contribution as he hovered near the gently swaying lanterns.

In the following lull, the mechanical horses snorted tiny silver-scented clouds and the wagon wheels creaked like an old woman's stays. There was no way of knowing how much time had passed since they'd departed the

Théâtre Illuminata. A thin sliver of a moon had risen, recalling the gleam of the Cheshire Cat's smile, while the hours had slipped by them as steadily as the sullen, secretive landscape. Exhausted to her toes, Beatrice Shakespeare Smith leaned against Ariel's tuxedo-clad shoulder, barely marking the continued whinging of the fairies. Drifting along the hemline of sleep, she heard a voice call to her, like the fading remnant of color at the edge of darkness.

Lass.

Bertie jolted as though Mrs. Edith had jabbed her backside with a pin, knowing that it was only a cruel trick her mind played upon her but unable to stop her eyes from scanning the edges of the lanterns' light for Nate.

"We should have had a prologue," Peaseblossom fretted. "Not all this nattering about pie." She paused, but no one offered up any introductory words, so the fairy took a ponderous breath.

PEASEBLOSSOM
A gloaming peace this evening with it brings
In the countryside where we lay our scene.
Toad-ballad accompan'd, crickets sing,
and cupcake crumbs make fairy hands unclean.

An indignant Moth squeaked, "There were cupcakes?!"

Mustardseed, however, was most impressed. "You just pulled iambic pentameter out of your—"

PEASEBLOSSOM
(hastening to add)
Lights up: a caravan incredible.
Nature's moonlit mirror reflects these six:
Four fae, depriv'd of chocolate edibles;
Ariel, winds attending and transfix'd;
And the playwright, named for the Beatrice fair,
Hair purpl'd where it had been Cobalt Flame,
Her many-hued hopes tinged with sad despair
O'er the stolen pirate she would reclaim—

"THAT," Bertie announced loudly, before the fairy could discourse further upon their Sea-Goddess-kidnapped comrade, "will be enough of that, thank you kindly."

Under the pretense of driving, Ariel kept his gaze on the horses. Like a maladjusted shopping trolley, they had a tendency to veer slightly to the left toward the open field. On the right, unidentifiable but towering trees kept their own counsel, secrets bark-wrapped and leaf-shuttered.

"This is the first moment we've had alone since I returned from your delivery errand." Ariel's voice coaxed tendrils of enchanted quicksilver from the air.

With one ear trained upon the renewed demands for pie, Bertie tried to brush off his words as easily as she would a wayward firefly. "We are no more alone than Titania was in her bower."

And I refuse to act the part of the ass.

The moon passed behind a cloud, and the swinging lanterns on the Mistress of Revels's caravan flickered; in the ensuing darkness, the world spread out before Bertie in every direction at once. Accustomed as she was to only being able to go as far as the theater's walls, the limitless possibilities should have terrified her.

Instead, she held out her hands in welcome. Their exit page, torn from *The Complete Works of the Stage*, crinkled inside her bodice, just over her thudding heart.

"Perhaps I can appeal, then, to the romantic nature of our situation." Without moving, everything about Ariel reached for her. "The open road, the veil of night drawn over the world, us living as vagabonds."

Usually Peaseblossom played the part of Bertie's tiny little conscience, but this time, she issued the requisite Dire Warning to herself:

Don't think about how close he is, or the fact that all you'd have to do to kiss him is tilt your head. Think of Nate. . . .

"If you're done with whatever fierce internal argument is creasing your forehead—" Ariel's low laugh undid the knot she had tied on her resolve. A bit of his wind pushed her nearly into his lap, and their lips met.

Bertie's brain fogged over until the fairies' collective noises of disgust recalled her to her senses. Pulling away, she muttered, "Vagabonds don't wear crinolines."

"No doubt you would feel more at home in a pair of men's trousers." Every word was a caress. "Something with rips at the knees and a splash of paint across the seat."

"I will have you know that despite the layers in this skirt, I'm freezing and likely to catch my death of cold." She tried to look as though she might perish at any second.

"You're as sturdy as a pony and too stubborn to die of something as minor as a cold." Nevertheless, Ariel let her go long enough to shrug out of his jacket and drape it over her shoulders.

"A pony?" Bertie tried not to revel in either the gesture or the vestiges of warmth and failed miserably. Turning her nose against the ivory lining, she breathed in the scents of wind-ruffled water and moonlight on pearls. Never one to let an opportunity pass him by, Ariel devoted his attention to the cascade of disheveled black-and-purple curls that tumbled alongside her neck. Though Bertie did her best to ignore the gentle tickling, she couldn't help the resultant goose bumps. "Pay attention to the road, please. You're going to drive us into a ditch."

"I won't let that happen."

"You think so?" Bertie wasn't thinking of his role as chauffeur when she added, "Not all of our history is good. Why should I trust you?"

"If anyone should hold a grudge, milady, it's me." The muscles in his throat clenched in protest. "When I swallow, I can still feel that damn iron circlet around my neck."

The chill of his winds seeped into Bertie's bones, and she fought the cold with hot temper. "Then I suggest you behave yourself."

"Misbehavior is part of my charm."

"Tearing nearly every page from The Book was hardly what I'd call charming—"

"I paid my debt to the theater, didn't I?" Catching her by the coat sleeve, Ariel pushed the fabric up to kiss her knuckles. "And though you freed me, I am verily still trapped in a prison, for what else is love?"

"Don't be ridiculous." Bertie flapped her hands until they were protected again.

"There is nothing wrong," he said, "with a little romance."

"Sure there is. Look where 'a little romance' got Ophelia." The discovery that waterlogged, oftentimes cryptic Ophelia of *Hamlet* fame was her mother still hovered on the surface of Bertie's skin, beads of moisture yet to sink in.

"You have to respect her nerve, do you not?"

"I do!" Moth said with a tilt of his little head. "The respect inside me is so big there's no room for my guts." He made horrible groaning noises and doubled over. "I respect her so much, I burst. Oh, help! I'm dying!"

The others looked at one another and dropped to their knees with rousing cries of "oh, my innards" and "my spleen!" which led to "my gizzard!" and "no, spleen was funnier."

"What about the man she ran away with?" Cobweb paused to ask.

"The Mysterious Stranger!" Mustardseed frowned and picked his nose, which made it difficult to tell if he was confounded by the matter at hand or the contents of his right nostril.

"As soon as we rescue Nate, we'll find my father and bring him back to Ophelia." But Bertie knew her promise would be difficult if not impossible to fulfill, with no clues to his identity and only the knowledge that he and Ophelia had run away to the seaside.

The sea, Bertie realized, the direction in which they'd already turned their noses to search for Nate.

But stage directions are better than happenstance.

"We need a script," she said without preamble.

"I beg your pardon?" The moment Ariel took his eyes off the road, the caravan hit a pothole.

Wincing at the jolt, Bertie pulled out their exit page.

"Be careful with that," Peaseblossom fretted.

"I am!" Bertie smoothed the softly glowing sheet from *The Complete Works of the Stage.* Back at the Théâtre, before tearing it free, she'd inscribed the page with

Following Her Stars: In Which Beatrice (& Company) Take Their Act on the Road

and paused, long enough for a blot of ink to appear before adding

Enter BERTIE, ARIEL, PEASEBLOSSOM, COBWEB, MOTH, and MUSTARDSEED.

Bertie splayed her fingers over the words and took a deep breath. "If I want to rescue Nate and find my father, I really will have to become the Mistress of Revels, especially the Teller of Tales bit of the job description." She turned to Ariel. "Do you have a pen?"

Catching sight of the page, every line of Ariel's body shifted, resettling into something distinctly uneasy. "Why, yes. I carry a lovely quill and inkpot in my trouser pocket."

"I'll take that as a no then."

With a bit of arguing that topped off the lemon pie discussion with meringue, Peaseblossom turned to tug at

Bertie's elaborate coiffure. "The Theater Manager's fountain pen, remember? You purloined it."

Reaching up, Bertie found that she had indeed tucked it into her curls.

"You can use blood for ink!" Cobweb suggested. "By the pricking of your thumbs and all that rubbish."

Bertie tapped the tip of the pen against the page. "Thankfully, there's still ink in it, and I won't have to open a vein."

"Pity," Moth said. "There's magic in blood."

Her hand sought out the scrimshaw medallion hanging about her neck. Thinking of its bone-magic, Bertie scowled. "I'd like to get away from using magic that requires body parts." She spread the paper across her jacket-clad knees.

Ariel leaned over, his breath tickling her ear. "What are you going to do?"

"I . . . I'm not quite sure." She stared at the paper, willing it to whisper some hint as to what she should write.

"Aren't we going to stop for the night?" Cobweb wanted to know. "I fancy a nice campfire—"

"And a meal or three!" added Mustardseed.

Bertie shook her head. "Absolutely not! We have to keep going."

"In the dark?" Moth said, each word more incredulous than the last.

"In the cold?" Cobweb continued to climb the scale.

"Without supper?" Mustardseed tried valiantly to continue the ascent, but his little voice cracked on "supper" and so did the pane of glass in the caravan window.

"Nice going." Peaseblossom applied her knuckle to the back of his head.

"What do you mean, 'without supper?'" Bertie asked. "Isn't there any food in this thing?"

"Afraid not," Peaseblossom said, scuffing her little toe against the air. "I checked every cupboard and drawer when the boys were lighting the lamps."

Bertie suffered a swift pang of regret that she'd not properly appreciated the Green Room's continuous and bountiful offerings back at the theater. "I suppose we'll have to buy some tomorrow."

"Did you bring any money?" came the cheerful query from Ariel.

Mouth falling open, Bertie sputtered a bit. "I . . . I . . . didn't think about it. I guess I assumed the Theater Manager would . . . er . . . provide us with ways and means."

Peaseblossom was quick to point out, "But you're the Mistress—"

"I know I'm supposed to be the new Mistress of Revels!" Bertie interrupted her, feeling a myriad of fresh obligations piled about her, like invisible baggage atop the caravan. "But that doesn't mean I have pockets full of muffins!"

"With the title comes great responsibility," Moth said.

"The responsibility of meals at regular intervals!" Mustardseed added.

"We could sing for our suppers, I suppose," Peaseblossom ventured. "Come on, Bertie, let's hear your singing voice."

"Yes, Bertie," Ariel said. "A rousing chorus of 'What Will Become of You?' feels particularly appropriate at this juncture."

"You shut your mouth," Bertie told him. "No singing, no jazz flourishes, and especially no lifts. You keep your hands away from my backside."

He leaned back on one elbow, his laughter low and teasing. "Then cue the pirouetting angel food cakes."

Bertie heard the voice echo again.

Lass.

"Not cake." Though the fairies immediately protested, Bertie barely heard them over the crackling in her ears. "I'm going to save Nate." Possibilities put down roots, each idea a bloom on an unexpected but welcome vine. "I'm such an idiot! All that time wasted, having the Players say his line, hoping his page would be acted back into the book . . . I never thought to *write* him back."

"You did have other things on your mind, at the time."
If Ariel was striving to sound nonchalant, he almost
managed it. "You might try something small and manage-
able before attempting to drag the man out of the clutches
of the Sea Goddess."

"Careful there, you almost sound concerned." Slanting
a look at him, Bertie added, "Two seconds ago you didn't
lodge a protest over the idea of dancing cake. In fact, you
were the one to suggest it."

"I've changed my mind."

"I hate to side with Ariel," Peaseblossom said, her face
a study in fretful agitation, "but if you write Nate back,
what's to keep Sedna from following? You could put us a
thousand leagues underwater in seconds."

Bertie shoved the unwelcome idea away before it could
grasp her with tentacle-arms. "That won't happen."

"You don't know that," Ariel said.

"No more than I am certain of anything," she retorted
as she penned the stage direction,

Enter NATE

For my mother, who left a
half-crimped pie crust on the kitchen counter
to take me to my first audition

Eyes Like Stars

CAST LIST

Beatrice Shakespeare Smith, a seventeen-year-old girl

Peaseblossom
Cobweb
Moth
Mustardseed

} the fairies from *A Midsummer Night's Dream*

The Stage Manager
The Theater Manager

Nate, a pirate from *The Little Mermaid*
Ariel, an airy spirit from *The Tempest*
Ophelia, daughter of Polonius in *Hamlet*

Sedna, the Sea Goddess (also the Sea
Witch from *The Little Mermaid*)

Mrs. Edith, the Wardrobe Mistress
Mr. Hastings, the Properties Manager
Mr. Tibbs, the Scenic Manager